Tannion
Stepping Out

Book Two in the Tannion Series

Wayne Elsner

ISBN-13: 9781502566867
ISBN-10: 1502566869

Edited by Michelle Heumann
Cover Design by SelfPubBookCovers.com/yvonrz

Visit the author's website: www.wayneelsner.com

Printed in the United States of America

To my mother, Gladys Elsner, with love.

1

When Tannion walked into the room, there were six people already there. He only knew two of them. One of them was Watson, a guard he had gotten to know a little over the years. He was standing over next to the door doing his duty.

The other five were sitting behind a long table leaving the other side with a solitary chair. It was obvious which chair was his. Tannion had never been in this room before, but he knew what he had to do. He took the seat. At least he got to sit down.

The second person in the room Tannion recognized was the warden. He was sitting at the left end of the table, a little away from the other four. Tannion and the warden had gotten to know each other quite well over the last five years. He had turned out to be a strict but fair man. Although Tannion respected him and almost liked him, he didn't owe him anything.

The other four were strangers, but they held his future in their hands. It was up to them to determine if Tannion would get out or not. Tannion had been there for five years; they could set him free, or they could make him stay for as many as fifteen more years. They were his parole board. His sentence had been twenty years, with possible parole after five. The charge was manslaughter.

Tannion found it hard to believe that five years had passed already. It wasn't that the days sped by, but only that when the end of a long period of time was reached, it was easy to forget the daily drudgery. He remembered the day he got there five years earlier, and it seemed like only yesterday.

It had been an interesting five years, to which the warden would attest. Tannion had wanted to be there to find the men who he knew were in there, and to do what needed to be done. These men were difficult to find in the outside world, but in prison, they were a captive audience. It was a place where Tannion was happy to spend some time, but five years sounded like enough.

In the five years since his incarceration, more than a hundred men had been taken out of the warden's prison in body bags. That sounded like a lot, but with a prison of that size and the type of hard cases it contained, it really wasn't that large of a percentage. It might not have been that many more than the prison's average for that time period.

Some died from an act of violence, some from illness, and a few from unknown causes. Tannion had a hand in almost all of them. Or maybe that might be a little too much to say. He at least had his hand in a large number of them. More than the warden would ever know.

It had started only about a week into his sentence when the local toughs thought they needed to soften him up and take what they wanted. They saw him as a potential threat and had decided to ensure that Tannion knew his place. He thought it best to become the head tough guy instead, and they gave him the opportunity. The boss's name was Gus Balkin, but he went by the name of Big Gus. From his appearance it was immediately obvious why he got the nickname.

Big Gus came at Tannion with three of his men. Men who didn't get to live much longer. The warden never did find out if Tannion had anything to do with their deaths. He didn't need to know. Big Gus belonged to Tannion from that point on, as much as he didn't like it.

Because of hits put on Tannion from his time in Los Angeles, there had been at least a dozen attempts on his life, and they all took place within the first year or so. Either the perpetrators gave up after the failures, or all his enemies were dead. All of them failed. Tannion was still standing. The warden knew about most of them and they had come to an understanding. Tannion was prepared to protect himself, and the warden was prepared to consider self-defense as a means of getting rid of a few inmates he didn't like either. The warden was a very pragmatic man, and could occasionally see a good thing when it hit him on the head.

The rest of them died from various illnesses or an occasional busted head, but each was based on their situation. Tannion didn't feel any remorse for ridding the place of guys the world didn't need. The world was a better place when these guys couldn't get out and repeat what had put them in prison in the first place.

Tannion's parole board consisted of three men and one woman. They all looked to be in their late forties or maybe early fifties. The older looking man in the middle was obviously in charge, and he started the session.

"Mr. Jim Tannion. My name is Merle Adams. I will be chairing this session. On my left is Mr. Janson, and to my right are Ms. Williams and Mr. Chance, and of course you know Warden Saunders. Before we begin, do you have any questions?"

Tannion told him he didn't and Adams went on. It took only a couple of minutes to explain the process, and it was pretty simple. They had reviewed Tannion's file and had talked to the warden. As Tannion had waived council and refused to have anyone talk on his behalf, Tannion would either get out on his own merit or spend more time inside. It would be their decision to make.

As it got closer to the date of Tannion's parole hearing he had decided that he wanted out, especially since knowing that this day was scheduled. He still felt there was a lot of work for him to do inside. It left him with mixed emotions. The decision he made was to go ahead with the parole hearing by himself, and if that wasn't good enough then he would stay. If it were good enough then they would let him out.

If Louisa had still been in the picture then maybe it would have been different. They were supposed to get married, and it had been the application for the marriage license that had gotten him caught. Tannion needed to use his real name and somehow they had found them. Despite all she had told him about how much she loved him, after a year and a few months she had stopped visiting. It was almost impossible to keep that kind of long-distance relationship going for long.

The parole session lasted just over an hour. There were questions from all four of the panel members, and they asked the warden a few as well. He had submitted his written report and the questions were for clarification only. When there were no more questions, Tannion was told that they would take a few minutes for discussion and he was taken out into the hall. Watson went with him, and even though they were still well inside the prison walls, he kept an eye on Tannion.

When the time came, the warden stuck his head out of the door and motioned to Watson. Tannion saw the nod and stood up, ready to meet whatever they had decided. His chair was still waiting across the desk from the panel. Without asking, he sat down.

The chairman was the only person who spoke. He told Tannion that they had come to a decision, and that based on his record over the five years of incarceration, and with the input from the warden, they were granting his parole. They were well aware of what Tannion had done in Los Angeles and had taken that into account along with his behavior inside. The warden must have filled them in on the attempts on his life and the results, and they obviously had decided that they were self-defense and not to be held against him.

The warden had a very slight smile on his face, and Tannion wasn't sure if it was because he was happy that Tannion was going to get out, or if the warden was happy that he was getting rid of him.

Other than the results of the attempted hits on Tannion, he was probably what the warden would call a model prisoner. Occasionally a few hard cases would end up dead in some corner, but the prison was relatively quiet once Tannion arrived, with one notable exception.

The warden might not know that Tannion had a big hand in that exception, but Tannion would not have been surprised if he had his suspicions. The warden had his people on the inside and they would have kept him informed. Tannion wondered what it might be like inside over the next few months.

Tannion was told the processing would take a couple of days, and by Friday he would be a free man. They also told him that he needed to decide where he would live. They needed to set up his parole officer, and although he would be out of jail, his life was still not completely his own, but they were letting him go. He was getting out.

2

During his five years in prison, Jim Tannion had only three regular visitors, and after the first year that number had dropped to only one. Tannion's mother had visited a couple of times, but found it too difficult based on the distance. After the first year, she resorted to phone calls only. Louisa Francia Fluentes had visited regularly once a month for almost a year, and then again only once almost a year and a half later. The other regular visitor was an FBI agent by the name of Mike Rallin.

Rallin and his partner Bill Pansloski got a lot of attention in the FBI world when they caught Tannion. The FBI saw Rallin as the obvious leader. Even more attention came as a result of the number of criminals Tannion helped to put away in Los Angeles. Rallin's stature rose from an insignificant agent in small-town middle America to a true FBI hero.

As a reward for what had gone down, and to use what the FBI saw as Rallin's skill set, Rallin was asked to head a special task force stationed in New York. This was a new group and was to be made up of a small number of agents handpicked by Rallin.

Of course his partner for several years, Bill Pansloski, was first on the list. Pansloski and Rallin went way back in the FBI, and the two were an obvious set. The second guy on the list surprised the FBI top brass. Rallin wanted to get a New York detective to come on board. Jeff Martin had been a key figure in finding Tannion in New York. Rallin had gotten to know him as a good cop, and liked him and wanted him on the team.

The group that Rallin headed had a lot of autonomy. They were allowed to decide upon most of their own cases, with only a few cases officially handed down to them. The team reported to the Director of the FBI, but rarely saw or had any contact with him. As long as file reports were submitted and cases were solved, no one questioned what the team was working on, and no one complained.

The group's success rate had been very good since it was established, solving several gang-related and organized crime cases, as that was their specialty. With the work they had completed on the Tannion case, and the experience that Martin had in New York, it was an obvious fit.

The Director also saw the work on organized crime as a very good fit. He would have demanded it if Rallin hadn't made the decision on his own, which made keeping the group intact that much easier. There also was no end of need.

An additional three members on the team came from the elite of those FBI agents already in New York, as that was where Rallin was stationed, plus one bright kid fresh out of the academy.

Both Rallin and Pansloski didn't like the idea of moving out of the quiet, almost rural life of Kansas, but they had waited all their careers for a break and they couldn't turn it down, even if their wives might be a little pissed off.

Rallin's wife reacted just as he knew she would. This was a great thing for him and she was on side immediately. She was still often as not Rallin's best source of wisdom, and provided a much-needed grounding and an off-time sounding board. The brass still didn't know how much he passed down to her and depended on her, and they never would.

Pansloski didn't like the idea of moving either, but there was no question in his mind. Wherever Rallin was going to set up shop was where Pansloski would be found. He knew that Rallin would need him to look over his shoulder and keep him out of trouble.

Martin resisted a little, as he enjoyed working for the NYPD, but in the end the possibilities in the new team far exceeded what he could do with the locals in New York, and he joined on. The rest of the group was happy to belong to a high-ranking task force. The team worked well together and it showed.

The prison that Tannion was in was not far from New York, which made it easy for Rallin to stop in and see him from time to time, but Rallin knew that no matter how far away Tannion was, he would have gone to visit him.

There was something about the man that seemed to pull Rallin towards him. Tannion had done considerable good providing evidence and testimony in Los Angeles, which decimated the organized crime families, but that wasn't it. There was just something that Rallin couldn't put his finger on, and he had to find out what it was. He needed to know what Tannion had.

It wasn't that way at first. At first, he wanted Tannion to pay for the murder of an FBI agent and he wanted him bad.

After he caught Tannion, it looked like Rallin was going to have to let him go as a result of Tannion providing evidence and testimony against so many of the major organized crime families in Los Angeles. Rallin knew that Tannion was going to get a free pass on any wrongdoings in Los Angeles, both as a result of the information he provided, and as the cops had very little on him. Rallin also thought that for the same reason, Tannion might get off on the murder charge pending in New York.

When Rallin heard that Tannion was going to stand trial for manslaughter and then go to prison, he was very surprised. He was even further surprised that Tannion wasn't going into a witness protection program or anything remotely close to it. When Tannion ended up in a maximum security prison under his own name, Rallin thought he wouldn't last long, but Tannion had, and that made him even more of an enigma to Rallin. He just needed to know whatever there was to know.

Each visit Rallin made to the prison to see Tannion seemed only to make Rallin want to see him more. It was also evident that they were slowly becoming friends. The animosity that Rallin held for Tannion ended early, even before Tannion was sent to prison.

Tannion saw Rallin only as an inevitable end to what he had in Los Angeles. If it hadn't been Rallin, it would have been someone else.

Maybe they were friends. If anyone asked if that were the right word to use, both of them would have said it was unlikely, but they were getting closer.

3

When Tannion stepped outside the prison gates, the only friendly face he saw in the small crowd was that of FBI Agent Mike Rallin. He hadn't called anyone he knew to tell them that he was up for parole or that he had gotten his release, and therefore he wasn't expecting anyone to be there for him. He was only a little surprised to see Rallin.

"Hi, Mike. Fancy meeting you here."

"Yeah, right," Rallin said. "You knew I'd be here."

"Yeah, I guess if I had thought about it I would've known you'd be here," Tannion replied.

Tannion and Rallin had spent many hours talking over the years, and Tannion still didn't know how to take Rallin. Would Rallin be spending the next five years of Tannion's parole trying to catch him slipping so he could put Tannion back in prison, or was he becoming more like a friend who was there to help?

Rallin opened the door to his car, which for the first time that Tannion had seen, did not say 'cop' as soon as he saw it. It looked like Rallin had chosen a midsize non-gas-guzzler to be a more responsible driver, or maybe he just liked the smaller American-made cars. After all, he was at least fifty, and a midlife crisis car might still be next.

Tannion had been booked into a halfway house on the south side of New York, and Rallin was well aware of it. Without much discussion, he stopped to drop Tannion off in front of the door. Tannion had decided to stay in New York, and he had a meeting the next day with his parole officer. The first thing on his list would be to look for a job.

He only needed to stay in the halfway house for as long as it took to get a job and some cash so he could get a decent place of his own. That might be a month or two, or if it became difficult for an ex-con to get a job, then it might be longer. Supposedly his parole officer would have a list of possible jobs where ex-cons were tolerated, usually because the employer could get a government break for hiring them.

Just before Tannion opened the door to get out of the car at his new home, Rallin started talking. Tannion had been waiting the entire trip for him to say something other than just chitchat, and to this point he had said almost nothing at all. There had to be a reason for Rallin to be there to pick him up. Tannion didn't think they'd become that close.

"I talked to your parole officer. He's a pretty good guy and he can be quite tolerant, unless you fall off the rails, and then he won't hesitate to throw you back."

"Okay, here it comes," thought Tannion. "Rallin trying to play big brother, or at least trying to act as a friend and pass out some advice."

"I don't plan on going back," Tannion replied.

"I know, but I also know you. If something were to happen, I believe you could do a very good job of disappearing. You've done it before."

Rallin remembered the time they had seen each other in New York, just before FBI Agent Leed was killed. As

Tannion was running out the back door of the bar he was in at the time, he had hit Leed. Leed was working undercover. His job was to keep an eye on Tannion and call in the troops if necessary. He called them in, but they didn't get there in time to save one member of a motorcycle gang, who was dead on the floor, and Leed died when Tannion ran.

Just before Tannion hit Leed, it appeared as if Leed had shot Tannion twice in the chest. Tannion was still able to get away, including getting across town and cleaning out his bank account. He was able to catch a bus while the cops were still searching a few blocks around the bar. They were looking for a guy with multiple gunshot wounds, probably dying of blood loss, or from his injuries. Rallin obviously didn't want to go through any of that again.

"I plan on going straight and getting my life back together, Mike, and maybe eventually I'll go home. I'm going to need some time and I'll need a job."

"That's good to hear," Rallin said. "I'd like to help. I would like you to come and work for me."

"I'm done being a snitch, Mike," noted Tannion, but with a slight lift of an eyebrow, and Rallin could see he had piqued Tannion's interest. No matter what, Tannion was going to need a job.

"No, it wouldn't be like that. With your record, you wouldn't be allowed to be an FBI agent, but I can get you on staff in a capacity that would allow you to work alongside us. You just wouldn't have a gun or a badge. The money would be lousy, but the work could be exciting."

Tannion knew all about Rallin's new task force. He knew they were mostly organized crime hunters, and he certainly had learned a lot about organized crime in LA. Rallin had filled him in on his new job after they started meeting in prison. It sounded like a new life for Rallin. Tannion didn't feel as if Rallin owed him anything, but he wasn't sure that Rallin didn't feel at least a little obligated to him.

Tannion knew that Rallin got the job as the head of the task force because Rallin had caught him, but he also thought it was very likely that if he hadn't turned snitch and given the LAPD and the FBI the information in Los Angeles, Rallin's new job wouldn't have happened. Tannion didn't like to think the job offer was just to pay off a debt. The job did sound interesting though. Especially if it got him close to the people he wanted to find.

He told Rallin he would sleep on it and let him know in the morning, but Tannion had already made up his mind. He would keep his friends close and his enemies closer. He just wasn't sure into which of those categories Rallin fell.

4

"Have you gone nuts, Mike? I don't think it's a good idea at all. I can't see how the hell it would work out. How about you, Jeff? Don't you agree with me?"

Bill Pansloski had just found out that Mike Rallin had offered Jim Tannion a job on their task force, and that he would be making his way into the office in the morning. Pansloski wasn't too keen on the idea, and he was letting Rallin know how he felt. Rallin had waited until they were both in the office near the end of the day to tell them.

Jeff Martin looked over at his two partners and couldn't help but smile. The three of them had been working together for almost four years now, not including their time chasing Tannion, but it still made Martin smile when Pansloski and Rallin had a disagreement.

Rallin was the obvious leader, but Pansloski wasn't just anyone's yes man. He might follow Rallin to the ends of the earth, and certainly he would take a bullet for him, but that didn't stop him from ragging Rallin's ass anytime he didn't think Rallin was right. Pansloski might not like it, but never once had Martin seen Rallin lose this type of argument, and he didn't expect to see it now.

"Hold on, Bill," Martin said. "What Tannion did in Los Angeles was amazing, and we could always use a little of that here. He might be a lot of help to us."

"He's a cop killer, Jeff," Pansloski continued. "I don't care how much good he did out west. This is New York, and he killed a cop here. That's not easy for any of us to forget."

"Just a minute, Bill," Rallin jumped in. "He paid his dues and he's done his time. I have to admit it wasn't the easy time that he could have done as a result of what he did in LA. After all, he went to prison for five years under his own name and according to the warden, there were at least a dozen tries on his life while he was in there. I think we need to give him the benefit of the doubt."

"I don't know, Mike," Pansloski said, and Martin couldn't help but smile again. Pansloski was already backing off and Martin could tell that Pansloski might not be happy at first, but he was willing to go along with Rallin, as long as Rallin stated his case, and Rallin always stated his case.

"I understand what you're saying," Rallin said. "I was there too, but I've gotten to know Tannion since he was sent to prison, and he's actually a nice guy. He's intelligent, and he cares about his fellow man. In New York he was running, and he didn't mean to kill or even hurt anyone. Besides, he has some skills that could do us some good, and I don't think he can hurt us at all."

Rallin couldn't bring himself to tell the other two about the extra thoughts he had regarding Tannion. If there were something there, he was sure that the other two hadn't had enough contact with Tannion to suspect anything, and in reality Rallin didn't have anything more to go on than a gut feeling.

"If it will help you feel any better, we'll keep him on a short leash and keep our eyes on him. If he doesn't work out in the first couple months, we can let him go," Rallin added.

"I'm okay with it, Mike," Martin said. "As a matter of fact I'd like to see this guy in action again, but this time on our side."

"Okay. I'll play along," Pansloski said. "As long as he plays along too."

"Thanks, Bill. He'll start tomorrow and we'll give him a day or two before he meets with the group. Randy and Kamal are out of town until the day after tomorrow, so that will be the best time for a meeting. I'll set him up tomorrow and he can have the office at the back. Do you have any more questions?"

"Sure," said Martin. "What's he going to do? How do you expect him to be of any help? Whose files will he be working on? Will he partner up? There are lots of questions."

"I understand Jeff, but I can't answer them all just yet. I think we'll have to see how it goes. First, I plan to give him a few files of mine just to see if he sees anything that I might have missed. He might just see things with a different eye than we do, and see things that we didn't even know were there. Then he might go on some calls, or maybe sit back and watch us work. He won't be an actual FBI agent, so he won't be anyone's partner. Does that answer most of them?"

"Shit Mike." Pansloski threw out. "It sounds like we're going to be babysitting this guy. It's possible that he might be of help, and I hope he does something worthwhile, but we can't operate while we have to watch out for him."

"Okay, okay. I get you," Rallin conceded. "I hope he'll be of some help too, but with what the FBI will be paying him, it really won't cost anything to just call it an experiment. For the first while, I'll be directly responsible for him and you guys can just watch. Anything else?"

As there were no more questions, they said their good-nights and headed home. Rallin wanted to get home to his wife. Arlene would have a thought about what was happening, that was for sure. She always did and it never surprised Rallin anymore how close she would be to the mark. Very astute that woman.

Arlene met Rallin at the door. Rallin knew she wouldn't have a drink or anything like that in her hand to give to him to welcome him home. That wasn't her way. She was okay with him drinking the occasional beer in the house, but only if he bought them, and he knew that she would never just bring him one. She did have a smile on her face as she usually did when she met him.

Arlene wasn't that interested in moving to New York at first, but she knew it was the break that Mike had been working towards for years. Breaks like that didn't come along in everyone's career, especially in small town Kansas.

She was only a little surprised when she found she actually liked New York, especially Manhattan. They had managed to find a place in the Upper West Side that wasn't costing Mike everything he made. The promotion had come with a nice pay raise, including a living allowance.

The living allowance might have been large in Kansas, but in New York, it didn't quite pay the rent, but they were in, and she was finding it better than she expected. She had made a few friends in four years and had found a part-time job, which was all she really wanted. Mostly she wanted to be there for Mike. She knew what the job had taken out of him over the past twenty-plus years, and thought it had to be her job to put some of it back.

Rallin filled her in on what was said about adding Tannion to the roster. He'd told her about asking Tannion to join the team several days before he had told the rest of the team. She felt a little along the same line as Bill Pansloski had. She wasn't sure Tannion was going to be much help, and, after all, just as Pansloski had said, he was a cop killer.

Rallin told her that at least they should give Tannion a chance and repeated the idea that it might be a good experiment. She thought at least approaching it that way made it seem a lot less permanent, making it easier to live with.

"Okay," she said. "I'm not at all surprised by what Jeff and Bill said. I would have the same concerns if I were in their shoes, but I guess you'll have to give it a shot."

As usual, she knew what Rallin was thinking and cut to the chase.

5

Tannion spent much of the night thinking about the offer that Rallin had made him. He wasn't trying to decide if he wanted the job, as he had already made that decision. He was thinking about how he could use his special abilities to his advantage, without arousing any suspicions. Rallin had seen some of what he could do, and was aware of how physically strong he was, but as far as Tannion knew, Rallin had no idea of what he was really capable of.

It had been more than eight years since he had been struck by lightning back home when he was living in Kansas. For eight years he had lived with the knowledge of what he could do, and he had spent much of that time using and improving his skills. Somehow that lightning strike had stirred something inside him that might have allowed Tannion to use a much larger percentage of his brain than would have been expected in the average man.

He could control his body to the point of what Ponce de Leon would have called the Fountain of Youth. He could control his body functions and every cell in his body. He could strengthen muscles and joints, becoming much stronger and much faster. He vastly improved his hearing and eyesight. He had made himself into the next best thing to Superman.

He had almost completely eliminated personal aging and illness, but there was more than that. He found that by touching someone else he could feel what their body was like and what it needed. He could tell what was wrong with a person's health in the brief time it took to shake their hand or to touch their shoulder.

He then found that he could control their body just as easily as he could his own. This was perfect as he could heal his mother's illnesses, and help people who needed help, but it placed fear in his mind. If he were caught, they would want to find out what made him tick, and he would lose his freedom as much as an alien would if he crashed on Earth.

Along with the fear, however, came the feeling of power. When he found that he could cure, he also found that he could tell a body to die. He could kill. He could stop a person's heart and make it look like a heart attack, and then over the next few years he found he could cure and cause almost every disease in the book, and cause people to die from these diseases more or less on command, and people had died.

Tannion found that he felt good about the type of people he made die. He didn't think of himself as a vigilante, but just that he had a job or a purpose in life and that was to make the streets safer for everyone else. He only had a few regrets.

Tannion knew he could not give up his skill any more than he could give up breathing. He also was sure that he was the only one who knew about his skill, and it had to stay that way.

One thing that he did need was a job and Rallin had offered him one, so what could it hurt. As long as he could ensure that anything he did looked like something a strong man could do, there should never be a problem.

In addition, working with Rallin would potentially bring him into contact with exactly the same types of guys he knew in prison. That was the key ingredient. Only these guys would be out in society, and maybe they shouldn't be. If Rallin could help him find them, and if Tannion could do his job on the side without Rallin or any of his team suspecting anything, then he would be fulfilling what Tannion saw as his destiny. If he helped Rallin put them away using the law, then that was good as well. It was a win-win situation.

Tannion had been very involved in the organized crime scene in Los Angeles before Rallin caught him. He had worked for a man by the name of Jackson T. Philips, and with the big Russian, Vladimir Potenlikov. He had spent well over a year in Philips' employ and had learned the business.

Tannion had also spent a large part of his own time learning everything he could about a group of people whose names appeared on a list Philips was given. This was a list of the forty heads of organized crime in Los Angeles. Tannion learned a very large amount about these people as he watched and followed them. When he was finally caught, he turned over all his information in order to keep Louisa Fluentes in the country.

This resulted in the largest organized crime bust in US history. It also gave Tannion a formidable education in organized crime. Rallin's task force couldn't have found a better partner.

There were many things Tannion could do with his body. He could stay awake for days, if necessary, by a simple adjustment of certain chemicals in his system. He couldn't stay awake indefinitely though, as eventually he had to sleep, but he could stretch it out for far longer than anyone thought possible, and still function well above normal standards. Tannion could also put his body to sleep on command, and after he had spent some time thinking about the job that Rallin had offered, and after he had decided what he was going to do, he called sleep to him and slept a deep sleep without dreams. The morning would be a new day, and a job was waiting.

6

Rallin was at the halfway house early the next morning. Tannion was ready for him. He had met a couple of the guys in the house the night before, and then met the other three that morning over breakfast. In all there were just the six of them, and as all of them had been in jail recently, they had things in common. Why else would they be there?

Peter Davis was the "house mom", or at least that's what the others called him, even after he told them to shut up. His job was to run the house. That, he told Tannion, did not include being his maid, picking up after him, or doing the cooking and cleaning. Then he proceeded to make Tannion an omelet and pour his coffee. "This place might be fine after all," Tannion thought. "At least for a while."

Tannion left the kitchen, and headed out the front door to where Rallin waited in the car. He said his morning greetings to Rallin and proceeded to get into the passenger seat. Rallin didn't wait a second; he asked Tannion for his decision as soon as he sat down.

"Hold on Mike. Not so fast. I'd like some more information. I haven't made up my mind yet."

"What more do you need? You need a job and I'm offering you one," Rallin said.

24

"I do have a few questions first," Tannion told him.

"Okay. Ask away."

"What is my role with you guys? What do you want me for?"

"First," Rallin answered, "you'll get an office in our headquarters on the south end. You'll have your own desk, phone, computer, and access to support staff. In that way you will look like any other agent. You are, however, a civilian, and you will stay a civilian."

"You won't have a gun or a badge." Rallin continued. "You will have FBI identification, but if closely scrutinized it'll be easy to spot that it says civilian support. You will be given access to all the non-confidential files, and initially you will find a number of files on your desk when we get to your office.

For now you'll be working on files that are mine, or possibly ones that haven't been assigned yet. We'll see on that one as they come. You might do some calls, mostly with me or Bill Pansloski, and you might be asked to take a look at crime scenes if we think you can tell us something based on your experience."

Rallin pulled out into traffic and kept talking as they wound their way towards the office. "Of course all the files on your desk are to do with organized crime. I was able to sell your entry to the team by giving heavy weight to your time with organized crime in LA, and what you did five years ago. That's what we deal with, and you should fit right in."

Rallin continued talking as he kept up with the flow of traffic. "The team is aware that you're coming. You'll know two of them from your past. My partner from Wichita, Bill

Pansloski, who I just mentioned, and Jeff Martin. Jeff was an NYPD cop back when you were in New York. The rest are new to you, but they all know what you did in LA. The director is onside with you working for us. In fact, he was quite interested in having you join."

"Will that be a problem?" Tannion asked.

"I don't think so. As I said, he was quite receptive when I brought it up, and you wouldn't be here now if he hadn't agreed to it. I'm sure he thinks you have something to add, but who knows with him. He often has different agendas. We don't usually see that much of him, and I don't expect that to change."

"What do you expect me to do with your files?" Tannion asked. Rallin had said a lot, but hadn't really answered his questions.

"What we want is for you to review the files and see if anything twigs. Maybe something we've missed. You might go as a passenger on some trips, and you might be asked to review crime scenes on occasion for the same reasons. We think as a result of your experience in LA you might see things slightly different than we do. We're cops and we've always been cops, and usually cops look through cop's eyes. We need a different set of eyes."

"I'm not going to say that it will be the most glamorous job in the world and it might be very boring at times," admitted Rallin. "But we can use your knowledge and your expertise and you might find it rewarding. Now, what do you say?"

Tannion hesitated for a few seconds before he answered. He wondered if he was just trying to make it look like he was thinking about it, or only trying to increase the tension he thought Rallin could be feeling. It never hurt to keep Rallin on his toes. Tannion had known what his answer was going to be long before he sat down in the car.

"Okay, I'm in."

"Good," answered Rallin, looking genuinely relieved.

7

The rest of the trip went quietly. Tannion noted that it was more than a half an hour by car from the halfway house to the office, which meant he would have to find a new place to live sooner than he thought. It would be nice to be within walking distance, that way there would be no need to get a car.

Rallin noted that never once did Tannion ask how much he was going to be paid, or what kind of hours he would be working. They weren't a concern of his, obviously. Rallin knew that the pay wasn't great, but it would allow Tannion to live and even save a little. The hours wouldn't be excessive, and how much extra time Tannion spent on the job would be up to him.

Rallin pulled into the parking garage and stopped in front of a reserved parking sign, which must have meant it was reserved for him. The elevator opened on the sixth floor where Rallin showed Tannion to a small office in the back. Tannion was relieved to see that it had a window and a door. He wasn't in the broom closet.

The floor consisted of eight offices, and wasn't a big area for the FBI to use. There wasn't a receptionist. This was not a building anyone went to without an invitation, and not many people wanted that invite.

There was a large meeting room beside the open area that Tannion thought would be used for official meetings. Over against the wall was a small coffee station, and Tannion could smell coffee when he walked in.

Rallin left Tannion in his office with instructions to start on the files that were on his desk, and to have coffee if he wanted. Rallin would drive him back to the halfway house at five. Tannion knew that Rallin wasn't going to be his chauffeur for long. As he had thought in the car, he would have to find that new place, or he would have to get a car. Either that, or get very used to riding the bus again.

Tannion had used the buses a lot when he was in New York a few years back, as it was his usual mode of transportation. They worked well then, so they would work well this time. At least they would for a little while.

Rallin told him that the rest of the team would drop by and introduce themselves as they saw fit. There wasn't a meeting planned for the day, so there wouldn't be an official introduction until the next day when all the staff would be in. Two of the team were out of town at the time, but Rallin expected them back the next day.

Tannion looked around for support staff on the way in, and not seeing any, he asked Rallin about typing and filing. Rallin told him that was all on the floor below, and for now if he needed anything he was to go through him. "Most of us do our own typing. You have the software on your computer." With that, Rallin left him alone with the files on his desk.

"So this is what it's come to," mused Tannion. "Here I am, sitting in a cop shop, looking through cop files, and I might even get paid for working with cops. Not where I expected to be, especially not in New York. All I really need is to get back in the game. This might just be the way."

The first file was a murder. The victim was a white John Doe, about forty years old. The team had the file as the style of the murder indicated it was organized crime related. The John Doe had been found in a field with his hands tied behind his back, and one thirty-eight caliber round in the back of his head. That usually meant an organized crime assassination. Tannion couldn't disagree. There wasn't a lot of information, and probably there would be no leads until the body was identified.

The second file was a dossier on what Rallin's team must have believed was an organized crime group. It included pictures of a number of the members, taken from concealed locations. There was a rap sheet for each of the people named, and a few pages of police reports and comments from the team; a very large file.

It looked like a group that were known to be in the business, but as of yet there wasn't even enough to go for a wiretap or anything other than long distance surveillance. Probably the type of file that Rallin had built on his own, and not one that would have come from higher up. Just the type of file that Tannion thought he should be working on, officially or unofficially.

The rest of the files were similar. Each one had a presumed connection to organized crime, and anyone not knowing what the team were working on before would have known as soon as they read a few of the files. A number of the files contained specific crimes that made it look like those files might have been given to the team. There were others similar to the one that Tannion thought he might want to work on. They didn't have specific crimes, but talked about criminal activities that a group was involved in.

Tannion picked up the first file again and studied the picture. It showed the John Doe in a field facing up at the camera. His eyes were open, and there was blood on his face that had run down from the wound in the back of his head. The bullet had not gone all the way through, and the picture was taken after he had been rolled over.

The small amount of blood on his face made Tannion think that the body must have been turned over almost immediately after he was shot, and not several hours later. Probably by whoever found him, or maybe by the police.

Tannion read the documentation and wondered what he could do in a case like this. He was unknown in the New York underworld, and even if he were in LA, he might not be much good.

Rallin stuck his head into Tannion's office. He had Bill Pansloski with him and they talked for a minute working out the introductions. Pansloski had never really talked to Tannion one-on-one, and had only been around the edges in Los Angeles and in New York, when Tannion was on trial. Tannion had seen him with Rallin on several occasions, and he recognized him immediately. He remembered the handful Louisa had been for Pansloski when Tannion had first been arrested. Pansloski's ears were probably still burning from the tongue-lashing she had given him.

Tannion shook Pansloski's hand and took a look inside. Pansloski had some minor aches and pains, but other than being a little overweight and having slightly elevated blood sugar, he was pretty healthy. The thought crossed Tannion's mind that a few years ago Rallin and Pansloski were his only real enemies in Los Angeles, and here he was work-ing with them. He might even say that Rallin was almost a friend. Pansloski, however, might never get to that level.

After Pansloski left, Tannion took another look at the John Doe murder file. He knew there wasn't much he could do in a case like that, but he thought he knew who might be able to help, as long as he could find him.

He had left his former boss in Los Angeles in a situa-tion where he would probably become the largest organized crime head in Los Angeles, and possibly the biggest any-where in the United States. With all the big heads and most of their close family behind bars, Jackson T. Philips was able to walk in and take over, or, in many cases, he was asked to take over until the family got out of jail. Either way, he had grown.

Philips had never gone to see Tannion in prison and nei-ther had the big Russian, Vladimir Potenlikov. Potenlikov was Philips' right hand man. Potenlikov was a very large and dominant individual who provided Philips with muscle and sometimes a little brain. He often acted more as a lis-tener. Tannion had worked alongside Potenlikov, and the two of them had become the combination of muscle and brain that Philips needed.

Neither one of them had come to see Tannion in prison, as they needed to show the break that had taken place. They had no idea what Tannion was doing and had put as much distance as they could between them. They needed to look as clean as possible to whomever was left behind, and dis-avowing Tannion was a requirement.

They did, however, also know how much they owed Tannion for what had come their way after he had left. They both knew that Tannion had more dirt on them than on any-one else in Los Angeles, but he had left them completely alone.

Tannion dialed operator assistance and asked for a Vladimir Potenlikov in Los Angeles, thinking there was a good chance there wouldn't be too many people with that name. To his surprise, three names came up on the search, and Tannion wrote down all three numbers.

The first number resulted in an older gentleman with faltering English. Not the Russian that Tannion knew. The second number was answered by a woman. Tannion asked to speak with Vladimir Potenlikov, and the voice indicated that he was not in at that time.

Tannion felt an odd tug, and thought that the voice sounded familiar. The woman asked him if he wanted to leave a message, and he told her to tell Vladimir Potenlikov that Jim Tannion would like to talk to him, and was about to give her the phone number when she interrupted him.

"Jim, is that you? This is Louisa."

Tannion instantly recognized the voice that he thought was familiar. "Louisa," he said, and then had the realization that she was answering the Russian's home phone.

"What are you doing there?" he asked.

Louisa hesitated for a moment, and then went on to tell Tannion what had happened over the past few years since the last time they had seen each other. At that time Louisa was being well looked after by Philips and Potenlikov, and her citizenship was working through the system. This was information that Tannion was aware of from the times Louisa had visited him in prison. He wasn't surprised that she still wasn't a citizen after all these years.

What he hadn't known was that eventually she had gotten to know Potenlikov very well, and had finally moved in with him, and they had been married for almost three years now. The last visit that Louisa had made to see Tannion in prison was to say goodbye, but she hadn't told him about her relationship with Potenlikov at that time, and now Tannion was stunned. It caught him completely by surprise.

Tannion came out of it quite quickly. He knew that he had lost her a long time ago, and he was happy that she was happy. He gave her his phone numbers at the office and at the halfway house and asked her to have Potenlikov give him a call.

After he put the phone down he took some time to think back. He had found Louisa and a number of illegal Mexicans being trucked in from Nogales, Mexico. Somehow they had made it across the border with help from another Los Angeles-based group who intended to sell them off when they got back to LA. It was Potenlikov's and Tannion's job to get them to Los Angeles, and they had picked up the truck in Houston, Texas.

There were an equal number of men and women, or in reality, girls, in the truck. The girls were going into the sex trade, and the men were going to work off their debt in the fields picking vegetables. Tannion had dropped the truck off at a warehouse, but he had a feeling that he needed to help. When he went back to the warehouse, he found the girls being raped. After disposing of the men, he took the girls and hid them. He eventually fell in love with Louisa and asked her to marry him. The cops got to him only a few days before their wedding date.

Tannion realized that he had forgotten to ask Louisa about the other girls. When he had last talked to her she was still in contact with four of them, and they were all doing well, but that had been over three years ago. He had always felt some responsibility for them, and time and distance had not overly diminished that feeling.

He would have to ask her the next time they talked, and he hoped there would be a next time. He also hoped that Potenlikov would call and be able to lend a hand. Contacts were probably one of the reasons that Rallin thought Tannion could be helpful.

8

Tannion left work for lunch a little early. He was scheduled to have his first visit with his parole officer. His parole officer knew about Tannion's position with Rallin already, and when he phoned, he suggested lunch at a place very close to Tannion's office.

Tannion didn't have a clue what this guy looked like, but obviously he had a picture of Tannion. As he walked into the restaurant, a man in the closest booth stood up and walked over to him.

"Jim Tannion. My name is Frank Sarvo," the man said, introducing himself with a quick handshake and then turning Tannion towards the booth he had come from. Tannion took a deep look when they shook hands, and wasn't surprised to learn that Sarvo was a smoker with damage already done that was irreversible by the usual means, but not yet cancer. Tannion thought it best to just leave well enough alone and keep an eye on the guy.

As they both sat down, Tannion looked around the restaurant. They had come in a little early, and only a small number of customers had made it in before them. The place was a family restaurant with booths along the walls and tables in the middle. A waitress moved over to ask them to order drinks, and they both asked for coffee.

Sarvo looked to be just over fifty with a noticeably receding hairline of graying dark hair that no longer matched his eyebrows. Ladies probably weren't beating down his door, but Tannion did notice a ring on his finger.

Sarvo started the conversation. "I've known Mike Rallin pretty much from the time he moved to New York almost four years ago. He's filled me in on your situation before and after your release, so I really don't have any questions and as you have a job, there's not much to talk about except to reiterate the rules that I'm sure you're already aware of."

"I know a few of them," answered Tannion. "I can't be caught in anything illegal and I can't be found with known felons. No guns or weapons, and I need to check in with you on a regular basis."

"Yeah, there are a few more, but those are the big ones."

The waitress placed the coffee on the table and took their meal order, and the conversation started again when she left.

Tannion jumped in. "With this job that Rallin has given me, there's a good likelihood that I will run into people that would violate my parole. I might not be issued a gun, but everyone else in the office has one. Are there any concerns?"

"As long as you're working for Rallin and are in an official capacity at the time, there won't be problem. I know Rallin well enough to trust his judgment and he's vouched for you, so I hope you don't let him or me down."

Sarvo continued, "I usually meet bi-weekly with most of my clients, but with you working for Rallin, I expect to talk to him on a regular basis anyway, so I think, unless there are any problems that he points out, we only need to meet once a month. Today is the first Wednesday of the month, so let's meet in this restaurant at the same time, every first Wednesday."

"How long do you expect to stay at the halfway house?" Sarvo asked.

"I don't think it'll be too long. I'd like to find something closer to the office so I can walk to work, but the house is good for now."

"Peter does a good job with the house. You'll be comfortable there for a while, or for as long as you stay there. I'll need you to let me know when you decide to move, and get me the address."

Sarvo pulled a business card out of his pocket, and passed it to Tannion, telling him to call at any time if there were any problems. Tannion took the card and thanked Sarvo, but assured him that he would be okay. Things were looking good from this end, too. As long as he could keep his wanderings official, then he might be able to get away with almost anything.

They ate their meal amidst small talk that was mostly coming from Sarvo. He asked a few more questions regarding the halfway house, and then talked about his wife and kids and the job he had. Tannion got the impression that this was not the way most of his meetings went. Sarvo seemed to look at Tannion as more of a peer than a crook with a grade four education; someone he could actually talk to.

They finished their meals and Sarvo picked up the tab, which Tannion hadn't expected. They then shook hands at the door of the restaurant and went in opposite directions. Tannion headed back to his little office in what had become an FBI outbuilding and Sarvo headed for his car to go and meet another client.

Tannion took one last look at Sarvo when he shook his hand and cured a couple of minor ailments, but left the near-cancer that was starting in his left lung. He might have to fix that later he thought, but in reality, it was always scary to heal something big that the person might be aware of. He had started to like Sarvo in the short time he had known him, and he might have to heal it to ensure that Sarvo didn't die on his shift. Then Tannion might be stuck with someone he didn't like. Time would tell.

The rest of the day sailed by with nothing to do but read the files, and he left work on time. Rallin gave him a ride home. The house was quiet when he got in and after a quick bite to eat, he decided to do a little reading and then get some sleep as the next day was going to be interesting.

The next day the entire unit was scheduled to be in the office, and Rallin had set up a meeting for ten o'clock when Tannion was to meet those he hadn't already met. Rallin had told him a little about the team members, but had saved most of it for the meeting. At nine forty-five, Rallin knocked on Tannion's door and stuck his head around the corner. "Ready for this?" he asked.

"Sure, why not." Tannion said as he put down the file he was looking at and stood up. The two men walked down the short hall, and opened the door to the meeting room. The room had a large table in the middle that more or less filled the room. There was a white board at the far end, which had a few scraps of writing still not completely erased, and there were eight chairs around the table. A small table in the far corner had a phone on it, sitting on a New York phonebook, and that was all there was for furniture. A working man's meeting room. Nothing fancy, but there was a standard issue picture on the wall.

Rallin and Tannion sat down on the chairs farthest from the door and made small talk while they waited for the others to show up. Rallin was interested to know how Tannion's meeting with his parole officer had gone and Tannion filled him in. Rallin reiterated what Sarvo had told him before he had met with Tannion and was happy to hear that it had gone the way he had asked.

At almost ten o'clock on the dot, the team arrived. Tannion looked them up and down as they came in and sat. They had obviously planned this out before, as they seemed to know what to do. They nodded at Rallin and Tannion, but sat down without a word exchanged and only when they were all seated did Rallin start the meeting.

"Good morning, gentlemen," Rallin started as there were now eight men in the room and no women. Apparently there had never been a woman considered for the group. Organized crime investigation was predominately a male-dominated bunch and Rallin had not found a woman qualified or willing to join the team.

"As you know, this meeting is for you to meet our newest member." Rallin went on to introduce Tannion by giving only a little information on what his job was to entail and even less on his past. The team had this information and there was no need to reiterate it.

As each man was introduced, he got up and walked over to Tannion or reached across the table and shook his hand. It started with Pansloski and Martin and Tannion looked inside as they shook his hand. Each was relatively healthy and Tannion left everything as it was.

The third man was Geoff Ramsay. He was a heavy-set man in his late forties who Tannion thought had a very engaging smile and a very bad case of diabetes. Following him were two African-Americans. Both Brandon Milbourne and Kamal Jenkins were native New Yorkers who had been working in the area in some capacity or another with the FBI for close to twenty years. Both were healthy, and Tannion had the feeling that they were very committed to their jobs. The determined set in their jaws also seemed to mean they weren't overly pleased with working with an ex-con, and especially an ex-con who had killed an agent in New York. Tannion couldn't help wonder if either or both of them had known Agent Leed.

The last agent looked to be the youngest. Randy Silton looked to be just out of the academy, but as he was on the team and had been for a couple of years, Tannion had to assume he was skilled. He had the look of youth, both inside and out, as Tannion shook his hand.

Rallin used the meeting to go over the files they were actively working on, and each of the men gave a short state-ment or report depending on what they had been doing. It looked to Tannion that they might work well as a team, but for the most part a lot of the initial work was done either in two-man units or independently.

When the meeting was over, it was almost noon and time for lunch. Rallin told Tannion that these meetings were generally held once every two weeks or as required, but as members of the team might be anywhere at any time, it was subject to change and never seemed to happen at the same time. The team was usually given a day's notice for each meeting. Tannion was sure that wasn't normal FBI procedure, but Rallin didn't tell him anything different.

Finally all the talking was over and lunch was called. The team broke up and went their separate ways, leaving Rallin and Tannion alone for lunch. Over lunch, Rallin spent a few minutes going over the strengths of each of the team members to give Tannion a feel for who he would work with most. In the end it was pretty obvious that he would be working with Rallin and Pansloski almost exclusively, and based on the looks he got from at least two of the men, Tannion thought that would be for the best. There was no need to start a confrontation this early and not in his own back yard. He would save that for a different time and place, and only if they started it.

9

Tannion walked into Rallin's office first thing after lunch. He had the John Doe file in his hand and an 'I have a question' look on his face. Rallin called him over and had him sit down in the chair across the desk.

"Can you tell me who turned the body over?" asked Tannion, showing Rallin the picture he was talking about. Rallin took it from him and examined it before looking up.

"We weren't the first on the scene, but the patrols told us that the body hadn't been touched, so I have to assume that the picture shows the body in the exact position we found it. Why?"

"I had the bad luck to witness a couple of gang-style executions in LA. I saw them from a fair ways away, but in both cases, when the victim was put to their knees and then shot in the back of the head, the killer just walked away. The job was done and there was no reason to inspect the body. He knew the victim was dead, and there was never a reason to check."

"So what you're saying is the fact that it looks like the killer turned the body over to see if our John Doe was dead isn't consistent with what you saw in LA, so maybe this isn't a gang hit," Rallin recounted to Tannion, obviously quickly catching on to his meaning.

"Maybe," answered Tannion. "Maybe it was just a hit that was made to look like a mob hit. Maybe we're looking in the wrong files for this guy. Maybe he isn't a crook who got what was coming to him and you don't have a file on him. Maybe he's just some ordinary run-of-the-mill guy who's gone missing."

"Shit. If you're right, then we have been looking in the wrong places. I saw the blood on his face, but I hadn't put two and two together. This is exactly why I asked you to be here. Thanks, but that's the kind of thing we shouldn't miss. I'll take the file and see if we can get anything from a different direction. Maybe the locals can give us a hand," Rallin told him.

Rallin took the file with the thought that there was some real work to do, and Tannion went back to his office where maybe he could get lucky on another file. Maybe this cop work would be better than he had first thought, and maybe he could be of some help. He also knew that he would be asking Rallin about the John Doe file later.

The rest of the week went by without incident. Tannion became familiar with most of the files on his desk and a few more that Rallin had added. He hadn't come up with anything else for Rallin, but he had an idea of where he was going to spend much of his weekend. Rallin had more or less left him alone, and hadn't asked him to comment on any of the other cases he or the rest of the group were working on. Tannion hoped that John Doe was keeping them busy, but thought Rallin was probably just letting him get settled and not putting any pressure on him.

When he had met with Sarvo, Tannion was happy to learn that he wasn't banned from bars and that sort of place, as that was where he did his best business. One of the files pointed out a bar where one of the guys in the file was known to hang out, and that was where Tannion was going on Friday night.

He knew he could do some damage when he got to the bar, either physical or more subtle, but he had decided it was best to get into Rallin's good books early, and maybe the rest of the team's. What he hoped to do was find something that would help solve one of the files on his desk. He might have gotten lucky with the John Doe file, but that case was small potatoes, even if it were a murder. It was probably big to the homicide unit, but it was insignificant to the organized crime team. That, and it wasn't solved yet. He hadn't heard anything from Rallin.

Instead he was looking at a file about a known drug dealer who they hoped to pin something on, and with luck, move up the food chain. At this point they knew he was dirty, but there was no real proof. To Tannion, this looked like organized crime had its hand in it big time.

The file, however, didn't necessarily agree. It indicated that the FBI were not one hundred percent sure that this was truly an organized crime case at all, except that almost all drug-related crime had some organized crime involved somewhere.

Rallin had mentioned that it was a file that had been dropped on the team, and not one they had chosen, which in Tannion's mind, made it a better file for him to work on. It would be good to get something on this guy and get the case off the books so they could work on something big that the team wanted to work on.

Tannion read through the file and suddenly had a thought, and let out a chuckle. The guy's name was Clive Bankhead, not a name you would expect to see in a file like this. As a white guy he didn't sound Italian, and it wasn't like he'd be with the Russian mob. He didn't fit any of the stereotypes. If he were organized crime, his name just didn't fit. Tannion hadn't heard of any upscale English mob.

What Tannion had found funny wasn't just the last name, but the additional data on the Bankhead family. Bankhead was known to have two brothers and a sister who didn't appear to be in the family business with him. Tannion thought it was funny that Bankhead's parents had named the four kids alphabetically.

The four Bankheads were Anthony, Benjamin, Clive, and Denise, in that order. Coincidence maybe, but Tannion didn't put a lot of faith in coincidences. It had nothing to do with the case, but Tannion found it funny. If the rest of the family wasn't involved, then it was even less likely that there was an organization behind it.

The file was light and there wasn't much to go on, with the exception of a suspected drug dealer. The last note was to watch for leads and to locate Bankhead's supplier. It was always the supplier, or even higher up the food chain, that the FBI wanted. The dealers were a dime a dozen.

At the end of the day on Friday, Tannion went back to the halfway house and changed clothes. He never wore a suit at the office, but he was overdressed for the bars he would be going to. He changed into well-faded blue jeans and a tee shirt with something written on it.

The bar looked like a lot of other bars in town, but with the no smoking policy in effect, it no longer had that smoky haze that it would have had a few years back. He could still smell the faint smoke clinging to the paint on the walls as if waiting for its time to come back.

Tannion took a seat next to the bar, trying to look at ease, and yet scanning the crowd for the face he had seen in the file. The room was less than half-full, which made it easy to spot the guy. He was sitting over in the opposite corner and had set up camp, or at least, that was what it looked like.

Tannion had seen a similar thing a number of times in LA and knew the setting. Move into a spot where he could see most of the room, and especially the front door, ensure that he had a couple of his guys around him to block off any unwanted guests, and then run his operation.

By the way he acted, it looked like Bankhead probably owned the bar. He appeared to be a guy sitting in a bar feeling comfortable with his life, knowing that the bartender couldn't have a bouncer come over and kick him out, or give him grief for not ordering the nachos. He might not be big time overall, but in this bar he looked to be the real thing. The fact that he might own the bar was not in the file, so it was obviously not in his name, but he sure acted like he owned it.

"That might be of interest to Rallin," Tannion thought.

The first thing to do was to get close and see what he could see, or maybe hear, and as a table was open near the mark, he pulled up a chair and sat down. A couple of guys got up off their chairs immediately and moved Tannion's way.

"Find yourself another table. This one's taken," the first one said, as he got within a step of Tannion's table.

"Doesn't look that way to me," Tannion replied.

"I don't care what it looks like. Now, get off your ass and find another table."

"Or what?" asked Tannion, but then quickly added, "Alright, it's yours."

The last thing Tannion wanted at this stage was a fight. He wanted to remain within earshot, and he knew as he moved to the next table that his enhanced hearing would make the conversation a couple of tables away seem like they were talking into his ear even over the usual noise.

Tannion had done similar things in Los Angeles. He had watched, listened, and learned, and that was what he wanted to do in this case. He ordered a beer and settled in for a long wait. He knew that eventually the dealer would get up from his table and walk out, and his entourage would follow. When he did, Tannion intended to follow as well.

The fact that they had all seen Tannion didn't worry him. His advanced eyesight and hearing made it possible for him to stay well back and track them if they stayed on foot, and if they got in a car, a taxi was always handy. After all, it was New York.

Tannion spent the better part of the night watching and listening. A number of times men would come in off the street and hand over cash, and be handed an envelope. Tannion noted at least five different street dealers working for Clive Bankhead. All the real dealing would be done on the streets, or at least not in the bar that Tannion believed Bankhead owned.

Bankhead finally shut it down, but just before he headed out with one of his men, he handed off the cash. The money man took the cash, and took one of the men with him. Tannion decided to follow the money. The two of them didn't have far to go, and they walked the two blocks. Another reason Tannion was sure they were pretty small time. Nobody walks anywhere in New York.

The two men turned into an old hotel. The hotel was only three stories, and as he watched the men go inside he hoped he could find what room they were in. Tannion had to do a little jumping and climbing on the outside fire escape across the alley to get in a spot where he could see what he needed to see inside. The lights went on in one of the second story windows and Tannion could see that he had gotten lucky.

The place wasn't the factory or even the warehouse, but it sure looked to be the bank. The bank was almost as important as the goods. If Tannion knew how they were making the money look legit, it would be a big step. Then there would be legal ways to get to the bottom line. Tax evasion had been a way to catch some of the best of them every since Al Capone.

Tannion could see a set of file cabinets and knew that the books were in the room, and who knew how good the books were. After about an hour, a third guy showed up and they all left the hotel. They had walked to the hotel, but the three men piled into a car as soon as they stepped outside. "That's more like it," thought Tannion.

Tannion had to hustle to get down from where he had found a perch so he could follow. A taxi was handy and Tannion was still able to see the car, as it had stopped at the next light.

A few minutes later and the car in front stopped. Tannion got out of the cab a couple of blocks back. The taxi driver had taken one look at the FBI identification that Rallin had supplied Tannion with that morning, and did as Tannion asked. He was sure that the cabbie hadn't seen the fact that it said 'civilian' on it. Once people saw the big FBI marking on it that was often all it took.

Tannion didn't know exactly where he was, but the area had what looked to be old office buildings. A quick look in the nearest window didn't tell him anything, but he was able to pry a door open and make his way in the back. The door didn't stand a chance, and once inside he found the room to be empty, but he could hear voices and noise coming from outside the room. A quick look and he saw what appeared to be a warehouse and factory combined. There were probably ten men working inside and it looked like crystal meth was the main product.

It wasn't the lab, but it appeared to be the assembly and distribution hub. The remains of what were once a number of office cubicles had been cleared away, and a large working area had been created in the middle, surrounded by offices that blocked anyone from seeing anything from outside the building.

Tannion wasn't able to get any closer and thought there were probably guards around who would eventually find the door he had pried open. He took one last look and went out the way he had come. Tannion finally called it a night almost in time for breakfast the next morning.

10

The next morning Tannion should have looked a little worse for wear than he did, but sleep wasn't something he required much of. By the time he got back to the halfway house, everything was closed down for the night, and he let himself in just as Peter was opening up. Peter didn't say a word other than "good morning". None of his business, Peter thought. Tannion showered, shaved, ate the breakfast Peter made, and then went to work.

Even though it was Saturday, Tannion thought he would head into the office. Having to find his own way made him fairly sure he would have to look for a place of his own to live in that was closer to the office before too long. It had been a good night, though.

Tannion spent an hour in his office typing out all that he had seen and heard. He knew that much, if not all of it, would be inadmissible in a court of law, but he made sure to locate as much of the operation as he could. All he had to do was pass it on to Rallin and let the rest of the team look after the operation. With that done, Tannion had the rest of the weekend to relax and wait for Monday morning.

As soon as Tannion got into the building on Monday morning, he stopped off at Rallin's office and passed him a five-page report on what he had seen. Rallin told Tannion to take a seat and took the few required minutes to read over each page, and took more time to read a couple of the paragraphs for a second time.

"Good work, Jim. I knew having you on the team was going to pay off. It says here that you got all this by following the dealer and his people around for a night. How did you get close enough to see all this?"

"Good eyesight for one thing, and there were enough hiding places close by that I was able to find, including some close enough to hear what they were saying."

"Great. I think we can take it from here. We should be able to get enough on them to make a lot stick. The channels will take a little time, but I think you gave us a start that we can use. By the way, nothing new has come up on our John Doe."

Tannion knew that with what he had given Rallin in his report there was a very good likelihood that the rest of the team would be able to find the major parts of the operation that Tannion hadn't seen. He had noted the main distribution house, the main warehouse, and where the money went after it left the bank. Maybe even the lab. It was all in his report, but he knew they had to get subpoenas and the like and couldn't just waltz in. Still, that should put a small time operation out of business. Nothing in the file pointed beyond it being anything but small time, and Tannion made a point of telling Rallin exactly that.

Tannion had also noted that it didn't appear as if any of the rest of the family were involved in the business. If it wasn't a family business, then in Tannion's mind it was not that organized, just a guy out on his own trying to make a buck. The family would probably be embarrassed. Not exactly the American dream.

Tannion went back to his desk and picked up the John Doe file. It was starting to bug him and Rallin's lack of news didn't help. Without contacts in New York there was no way he could get inside far enough to hear what might have happened. If this had happened more than five years ago in Los Angeles, he would have known who had done it. He might even have been the guilty party, but in New York, he was at a loss. That is, if it were really a mob hit, and the one fact seemed to be against that. Still, Tannion wanted to know who the guy was.

Tannion knew a little about the man, as he was not well dressed, and about forty years old. Ballistics indicated a thirty-eight was used, and the coroner identified the cause of death to be trauma caused by the gunshot to the back of the head. Nothing like a shot in the back of the head to make sure the guy had a bad day.

John Doe had his hands tied behind his back and there was nothing interesting about the rope. His picture had been given some airtime, and was now a couple of months old and gathering dust. Not much to go on, but the file had Tannion intrigued.

As Tannion put the file down the phone rang.

"Tannion here," he said. It was his first phone call at the office, and he didn't know whether he should announce that it was the FBI or not, and decided that it wasn't necessary.

Tannion recognized the voice on the other end as soon as the first word came out of his mouth, even if he hadn't heard from him in years. Definitely a voice from the past.

"French. Is that you?"

"Vladimir Potenlikov. It's good to hear your voice. I go by Jim Tannion now."

"Yeah, I know, but somehow French is easier," Potenlikov told him. "And you know that's all Mr. Philips knows you by. I doubt he would ever call you Tannion. Maybe I'll get used to it, but he never will."

"Sure, okay. We can keep it French between the two of us for now. How is Mr. Philips?"

Potenlikov wasn't a big talker and it was quite possible that Tannion got more words out of him in one phone call than he might have heard from him in a year back in Los Angeles. Potenlikov brought him up to speed on what was happening with Philips, making sure not to say anything that might be considered incriminating. He knew he was talking to the FBI, even if it were French.

Potenlikov went on to tell Tannion a little about Louisa and their son. Vlad Junior was one and a half and a walking terror, as his father put it. Tannion had made a point of not bringing it up, but he was glad when Potenlikov had.

"I'm happy for you and Louisa. Couldn't have happened to two nicer people, and I hope to call you both my friends."

After their small talk and catching up, Tannion explained to Potenlikov the situation with the John Doe. Potenlikov told him that he would do some checking, but as the murder happened in New York and not Los Angeles, there wasn't much he thought he could do. Some of the families range a long ways and many have connections in New York, so he told Tannion, "You never know."

Tannion mentioned the position of the body and Potenlikov agreed that it was unusual for the body to be touched after the shot. Shoot and walk away was the routine, unless they were in an area where they were going to bury the body or dump it somewhere else. If they were going to just leave it then standing around and checking to see if he were dead was a good way to get caught. A shot to the back of the head and the guy was dead, no need to check.

Tannion thanked Potenlikov, asked him to say hello to Louisa, and said goodbye. Maybe Potenlikov would find something on John Doe, but for now Tannion would have to keep his eyes open and look into other files.

Having talked to Potenlikov brought back a flood of memories. Mostly good memories of working with him and Philips, but there were some not-so-good memories as well. Memories of seeing Rallin and Pansloski sitting one on either side of Louisa, and each of them having their gun on her, was one of them.

Still, he couldn't hold that against either of them, as they were just doing their jobs. After all, he had killed an agent in New York, and had made the FBI's most wanted list. He thought that his life as Victor French had been a good life for the most part, even if it felt like more than a lifetime ago. His life was in New York now, and he might as well get on with it.

11

Tannion hadn't seen much of the team during the first week, other than the first meeting when they were all introduced. Now he was into week two on the job and he was still waiting for his first payday.

When Rallin knocked on his door and stuck his head around the corner, Tannion was glad to see him. Most of the team would leave Tannion alone and he knew it, but it was nice to have some company. Tannion had spent too much alone time in prison to want much more of it now that he was out.

Not that the guys resented him being there, or at least not openly; they just didn't have a reason to interact with him, and somehow they hadn't been able to get too friendly just yet. Maybe in a while they would come around, but probably only if Tannion proved his worth.

Rallin walked over and sat down in the only other chair in the office, across the desk from Tannion.

"I thought you might want some follow up. We took what you gave us and got a warrant to search a couple of places. Didn't think the judge was going to give us anything at first, but then I thought to tell him that you had done the initial legwork. He remembered reading about what you did in LA and it did the trick."

"I'm surprised," answered Tannion. "That's a bit of ancient history, but glad that I was able to help."

"I agree, but when it comes to lawyers and judges, there's no such thing as ancient history if a precedent can be served. Anyway, we found enough stuff in the two locations we searched to put them away for a while, but more importantly, the first places allowed us to get more warrants and then we were able to seize it all."

"Good to hear, but you know there'll only be someone that will step in and take their place."

"I know," answered Rallin. "But for now we got someone off the streets and we'll just have to go after the next guy. I thought you might find this part interesting. The rest of the Bankhead family was embarrassed, just as you thought they might be. They knew their brother was into something that he shouldn't be, but they had no idea how deep. I don't know how he kept them as clueless as they were. They knew enough that charges could be laid, but for now, no charges are pending against the rest of the family. Their embarrassment might be enough."

"That's good to hear. I didn't think they were really involved, They might have enough to have gone to the police, but sometimes people only see what they want to see. By the way, did the press make anything of the kid's initials?"

"You mean the A, B, C thing, right?"

"Yeah, I thought that was especially funny."

"No. Looks like the press fell short on your little inside joke. They must never have put the kid's names together the way you did. You've got to wonder what the parents were thinking, don't you."

"You never know what parents will do with kid's names. Remember that rock and roll guy?"

"Yeah, I do. You're not kidding there. Another thing," Rallin said, as he changed the subject. "We still have nothing on the John Doe, but I think we might be on the right track. I talked to Homicide and they tend to agree that it might not be an organized hit and are tracking down a few leads from missing persons that they had discounted before."

"Good," Tannion said. "It looks to me like some-one wants you to think it was a gangland style murder to either get away with the murder, or to put some pressure on someone in organized crime. It might be someone who has something to gain, and the only one I see gaining from this type of hit would be other mob groups. That would make it an organized hit and therefore it doesn't fit with him being turned over."

"Not sure I quite followed that, Jim," Rallin countered, "but I think you mean that it might have been more personal than just an organized hit."

"Exactly. The motive had to have been personal gain, or even a jealous lover. Whoever killed him wanted to be sure he was dead, and yet wasn't sure that a shot to the back of the head from close range was going to do the job. This guy probably doesn't know much about guns, or at least he doesn't know what kind of damage they can do close up. Then again, maybe whoever did it had been watching too many old gangster movies."

Rallin had to chuckle at that last one, but went on. "So far nothing has shown up in our searches through missing persons, but the file's a few months old already and that just makes it harder,"

"Somebody should be looking for him."

"You're right. Missing people usually don't just disappear as there's almost always someone out there who wants this guy to be found. Now we just have to find that someone and show them John Doe's picture."

"If he hasn't shown up anywhere it's possible that he's from out of town. Possibly from a long way out of town," Tannion said.

"The homicide detective brought that up and you might both be right. When we were sure it was a mob-style hit, we didn't look any further than our own backyard. They're going to look further afield, so we'll have to wait. For now it's out of our hands, thanks to you."

Rallin stood up and went back to his office. Tannion was left with a world of thoughts, as well as the files in front of him. The technique he used on the drug dealer had worked, so why wouldn't it work again? With the FBI on his side, all he had to do was dig up enough dirt to allow them to get the warrants they needed to grab whoever Tannion wanted them to grab.

The thought went through his mind as soon as he looked at the next file. He knew he would be able to do what Rallin wanted him to do, but was that enough? Was Tannion doing what he needed to do, and was he having fun doing it? Was fun important, or was it more important to get some of these guys off the streets?

Tannion had enjoyed what he had done in the past, but the enjoyment part was mostly in getting scum off the street. Maybe the FBI way was just as good.

He opened the file and took a look, with his decision already made. For now it would be just fine to use his skills to find a few of these guys and then let Rallin step in. Sooner or later, however, he was going to have to go out on his own as well.

There would be times when the FBI way wouldn't work and then he would have to resort to the Tannion way. Then the only concern would be to see if Rallin suspected him. That would probably depend on exactly what Tannion did.

Unleashing some form of cancer or some other disease should be safe, but using force might not be. It was a disease he created that almost got him caught in the first place, which wasn't a good idea then and probably wouldn't be now. Time would tell on that one.

12

The night was especially dark as a thick fog had rolled in. Tannion sat outside a bar in the South Bronx waiting for just the right guy to come out. The guy had been in the bar earlier when Tannion had stepped in to take a look, and Tannion thought it best to wait outside. He really didn't need to get too close to get what he wanted, and felt it best that the guy didn't see him.

"Not the best neighborhood," Tannion thought, as he sat back on a park bench that happened to be across the street from the bar, a place where there was only limited light. Tannion's eyesight, even in the poor light, was good enough to see the entrance to the bar as if it were broad daylight. He could easily hear the music and laughter that emanated from beyond the door.

When the guy Tannion was looking for finally came out of the bar, he wasn't alone. These kinds of guys rarely were. He had two of his men with him, and a girl; two tough bodyguard types, and a good-looking blond, who was more likely to be a hooker than his girlfriend, based on the file on Tannion's desk. She probably worked for him and might be working off a little bad debt, but more likely she was new and he hadn't hooked her on whatever shit he would hook her on and then put her to work. She didn't have that hard-used look yet.

She was young and good looking, and she dressed the part of a hooker, especially with the short skirt and boots. Tannion didn't give her a second thought. It was not his job to save somebody's daughter tonight. If he could get some idea of where this guy ran his business and get enough information to allow Rallin to take him off the street, it might save other girls down the road.

Tannion had learned early in this type of life that it wasn't his job to save the world. If he could touch everyone and cure them of their ills, then he could actually cure the world, but with billions of people and a few seconds each, well, he could do the math. If he saved a hooker from one pimp, she would only go to the next.

Tannion followed the group like he had done previously with different people, but this time, as they hadn't seen him in the bar, he decided to get a little closer. Not so close as to be noticed, since the streets weren't full, but they weren't deserted either. There were a few people out, including a few homeless people.

Tannion didn't like the way the two toughs had treated a couple of street people as they walked past them. One of the homeless drunks made the mistake of asking for a handout and got a kick in the ribs for it. The guy next to him said something, and he took a punch to the head for his troubles.

Tannion didn't have a lot of love for his fellow man if they were nothing but societal leeches, but he was one to always side with the underdog. From across the street he saw what happened to the two homeless men. Tannion had occasionally had run ins with homeless people himself. The bums were usually harmless and not worth bothering about, but the toughs didn't seem to see it that way.

After the second bum took a punch to the face, Tannion decided to step in. "Hey. That's not nice," Tannion called out from across the street.

As one, all four in the party looked at Tannion, and he could tell that at least three of them thought he must be nuts. The two toughs stepped off the sidewalk in the general direction of Tannion, who was crossing the street in their direction.

"Maybe you should shut your fucking mouth and keep walking, asshole," the one closest to Tannion said. The second guy uttered something that Tannion heard, but realized that it was pretty much garbled swearing. He didn't seem to be the talker in the bunch.

At that moment, the leader of the group called to his men. The leader was a man of about forty with an average build, just starting to get soft. He wasn't dressed in a flashy pimp like outfit like in the movies, but he was well-dressed in slacks and a sweater. The girl hadn't left his arm.

"You had better just walk the other way, if you know what's good for you," he said. Tannion noticed not only what he said, but the fact that he said it almost in a nice, conversational way. He obviously sounded like he had a lot of faith in his guys.

Tannion wanted to see if that faith was warranted. "That's okay. I think they might want to try someone a little more their size after kicking a couple of garbage bags."

"Suit yourself," said the leader, and he made a small motion to his men to give them the go ahead just to let Tannion know who was calling the shots. "Tony and Rick here will teach you to keep your nose out of where it doesn't belong."

Tannion had no intention of letting them even get a shot in. As much as he had made the decision to work on Rallin's files and leave his own work until later, he was going to do this for himself. He wasn't even doing it for the two bums.

Tony only had to take a couple of steps before he was directly in front of Tannion, while Rick went to Tannion's right. Tony swung his right hand at Tannion's head, knowing that even if Tannion was able to duck or get away from the first attack that Rick would be able to close in from his left. They had done this before.

Tannion decided to let the punch just slip by his chin on his right side as he stepped to the left. This put him to Tony's right side and away from the Rick. With his left hand he hit Tony in the kidney with enough force to throw him into Rick. It wasn't enough to stop Tony, but he would be pissing blood for days even if that was all Tannion did to him.

Tannion now had the two men together and he waded in first with a left and then a right. Tony took a punch to the side of his head, and Rick took one on the chin. He hit both of them hard enough that the fight was over, but not enough to kill them. Both were still semi-conscious as they lay on the pavement.

"Okay. That's enough," came the voice from behind Tannion. The leader had come up from behind, and he had drawn his gun. He held it pointed at Tannion's back from only a few feet away.

His men weren't getting up and a look at them told Tannion that they wouldn't be up for quite a while. The girl had backed off and was standing on the sidewalk with an almost panicked look on her face. To her credit, she hadn't screamed.

"You sure you want to do that?" asked Tannion.

"What the hell do you think? I've got the gun, not you."

Tannion didn't hesitate. He moved before the guy had a chance to think, let alone pull the trigger. If anyone would have asked him later, he would have told them that he hadn't even seen Tannion move. Tannion had a lot of practice at that sort of thing in prison. Moving quickly in a tight spot had saved him on more than one occasion. This time was no exception.

Tannion had the gun in his left hand, and he grabbed the guy with his right hand around his throat. "Now, tell me why I shouldn't just keep squeezing?" Tannion asked him.

It was all the man could do to talk with Tannion's hand almost crushing his windpipe, but he managed to rasp out. "I can pay you."

Tannion didn't really care what he had to say as long as he said something. Tannion let him go as quickly as he had grabbed him, and although Tannion had only lifted him up to his tiptoes, he fell to the ground in a heap.

"Pick up your guys and get out of here," Tannion told him.

The leader looked over to where his two guys lay on the pavement, and he knew he wasn't going to get them off the ground without help. He also had already regained some of his composure, and Tannion thought that at least the guy had some guts. The girl had come back to his arm, trying to help him up, which he didn't appreciate. It looked like only his pride was hurt, especially with the girl as a witness. The street was surprisingly empty and quiet.

"Wait. Please wait," he rasped out, as he pushed the girl off him.

"Why?" asked Tannion.

"I can't just grab my guys and get out of here. It looks like you might have hurt them bad," he said, pointing over to the two men still lying on the street.

Tannion had gone this route before. When he wanted to get inside the group in Los Angeles he had roughed up some goons, and their boss had decided that he wanted Tannion on his side. With Tannion's skills and intelligence, he was able to get deep into the group, and able to learn the things he needed in order to put many of the rival groups out of business. Maybe it would work here too.

"Where's your car?" asked Tannion.

"It's just around the corner where we're headed."

He had pulled the keys out of his pocket and had them in his hand. Tannion reached over, grabbed the keys from his hand, and walked to the end of the block. He pressed the key fob and the lights came on in the typical late-model sedan that he knew would be sitting there.

After all, there were four of them, and they would need the room. Tannion got in and drove around the block to come up behind the three men and the woman. By this time the leader had managed to get one of the two toughs to his feet, with the other still lying in a heap. The one standing was holding his face and not moving very quickly. He had only taken one hard shot to his chin. The other guy was still down, but he wasn't sure where he hurt the most.

Tannion stopped beside the one who was still down, and got out of the car. He opened up the back door and with one hand he picked the guy up and threw him in the back seat.

The second tough got in the back and the leader and his girl got in the front.

It was obvious to Tannion that they no longer had a driver, as they both got in the passenger side, with the girl in the middle. It looked as if they expected him to do the driving.

He had no idea where they would be going and how many of the rest of their group they would find when they got there. Tannion felt it was wiser to just walk away, but he didn't think wise was necessary today. He was pumped up.

Tannion got back in the car and took directions from the girl, who guided them to a house in the Bronx. Maybe she was his girlfriend after all. The house was nothing out of the ordinary, but it had a driveway to park the car and the lights were on. Tannion got out of the driver's door, and wasn't sure what was up next, but the leader made it very clear that he was to go inside with them. Tannion was willing to oblige.

Once inside Tannion took a quick look around. It appeared there was only an older woman in the house, and she was probably the leader's mother. She looked to be in her sixties, based on Tannion's guess, and she was apparently alone.

Tannion helped the tough who could at least walk carry the other into a bedroom and dump him on a bed. The first guy stopped at a second bedroom and lay on the bed. Tannion thought they would probably be okay with a little time off and he went back to the living room.

"Have a seat," the leader told Tannion, and he used a tone that made it sound as if he were in control again. Tannion had stuffed the gun in his pocket, but he knew he wouldn't need it. Tannion sat down on a slightly overstuffed sofa. He wanted to see what this guy had to say for himself. He had decided it would be best to just wait it out and see where things went.

He wasn't sure what Rallin would have to say, but getting inside was basically the way Tannion had gotten the goods on so many in Los Angeles. "Probably breaking my parole orders this time, though," he thought. That is, if Sarvo ever found out.

It didn't matter now anyway. It was already too late. Assuming Tannion got out with everyone still intact, Rallin could make the decision about where to go with this later, unless of course Tannion had to get rough with them again. That probably wouldn't leave too many standing.

"My name is Steve Franklin. This is my mother, Grace, and you've already met Tony and Rick. Oh, yeah," he said pointing at the blonde, "She's Sal."

Sal nodded in Tannion's direction.

"I don't like what you did to my guys, but I have to admit I like how you did it. No one has taken them on and walked away without a mark in a long time, and I appreciate you being good enough to drive us home."

Tannion was starting to feel like this might turn out better than he thought.

Then things took a turn for the worse. "As much as I like how you did it, that isn't something that I can let go," he continued.

Tannion thought it was time to take back a little of the control he had. He pulled the gun out of his pocket and stood up. "You forgot that I still have this, haven't you?" Tannion said, showing him the gun.

"You might as well put that down. I never keep it loaded. That would be in violation of my permit."

Tannion looked, and sure enough, there were no shells in the magazine. "So that was why he hadn't looked that worried, and he had used what appeared to be weakness to get me to drive him to a place where he could get back in control," thought Tannion. "Not bad."

Tannion wasn't worried as he knew what his abilities were, but he was pretty sure that Steve Franklin thought that he now had the upper hand. His bodyguards might not be effective, but it looked to Tannion that Franklin had enough firepower around to make him feel comfortable.

Tannion thought it would be best to take an aggressive stance, and started talking. "Nice play with the gun. I thought you went too easy, and now I see why. You guys are pros. My name is Jim Small." Tannion had to come up with a name that was unknown.

Tannion didn't carry any identification with him so he knew they couldn't catch him in a lie, at least not right away. He had decided that this guy was small time, and therefore the alias, but the guy he caught on with in Los Angeles was small at the time too. Small time could always become bigger, or at least lead to bigger people, and Tannion wanted in.

"Would you have need for another pair of hands now that at least one of your guys is going to take a few days off?" Tannion asked.

"Why would I do that?" Franklin asked. "I could just have you put down like a dog and be done with this."

"You saw what I did to your guys. Do you think I'll go down easy?" Tannion countered. He still wasn't worried about his health, but he was worried about where this was heading.

Franklin took a couple of steps over to a small table beside the window, and reached in the drawer. Tannion assumed that the gun he pulled out was loaded this time. As he walked back towards Tannion he didn't bother to raise and point the gun. The fact that he had it in his hand was enough for him.

Tannion weighed his options and once again went for the more aggressive, or at least assertive, approach.

"You saw me take the last gun away from you. What makes you think I won't do it again?"

"Not this time. This time I'm ready for you. Show him, Ma."

Franklin looked over towards his mother, and both he and Tannion watched as she pulled a sawed-off shotgun out from beneath her apron. Tannion was surprised that he hadn't seen it before, as it had to have made a lump under her clothes. Tannion suddenly realized what an older lady, someone you just don't suspect, in her own house, with an apron on, can hide right in front of his eyes.

"Okay," Tannion said. "It's your show. What do you want?"

"First I think I want a beer. Ma, how about one for me and another for my friend over there."

Tannion didn't particularly like the way Franklin said 'friend', but he sat back down on the sofa as he was directed. He looked over towards Franklin's mother to see that she had set the shotgun down on the side table and had gone off into the kitchen. That made him feel a little better.

"Okay. Let's talk turkey. Who the hell are you, and what do you want?" Franklin asked.

"As I told you," Tannion started, "my name is Jim Small. I just happened to be walking by when your goons started to rough up those homeless guys and I didn't like what I saw. Call me a good samaritan or whatever you want, but that's all there is."

"You handled my guys like a pro."

"That was easy. I'm a black belt in Karate and I've competed in kickboxing, and what you saw was me holding back on your guys. I didn't feel the need to hurt them too badly, but just teach them some manners."

"You a cop?" asked Franklin.

"No, just a guy out looking for a job." Tannion thought it might help to put that on the table and see what happened.

Franklin looked at him for what must have been close to a minute. Finally he said, "I think you're a cop. That might be the only thing that's keeping you alive right now, but I like your style. This is what I'm going to do. I'm going to have one of the guys take you home, and the two of you are going to hang out for the next couple of days and we'll see what comes of it. If he reports the right things back, then we might just have an opening. I'm giving you a chance here against my better judgment."

Tannion wasn't so sure it was a good idea either, as he couldn't go into work, but then the guy thought he didn't have a job, so maybe it would work. He'd have to get hold of Rallin and see where he wanted him to go.

Franklin made a call, and a few minutes later a car pulled up outside. He walked Tannion out to the car and gave the driver his orders. Tannion gave him the address of the halfway house and the driver drove Tannion home, just as Franklin had said he would. As soon as they stopped outside the house, the guy looked over at Tannion and grinned.

"You just got out of the joint, didn't you?" he asked.

"Yeah, and I need a job. So what now?" Tannion wasn't sure why this guy knew what he knew, except that he must have recognized the house.

"This'll look good on the boss's table, so you go ahead and I'll meet you here at seven tomorrow morning. Then we'll drive around and see if the boss has a job for me, and if he does you get to come along. Easy as that."

Suddenly Tannion seemed to be in this guy's good book. Just the fact that he was an ex-con was enough to make the guy like him. He introduced himself as Mickey. They shook hands before they parted and Tannion took a look to see if he was healthy, and to decide if he wanted to unleash anything. He decided against it this time. Next time Mickey might not be so lucky.

Tannion knew that Rallin would be home, as it was getting late, but he also knew that he had better make the call. Rallin answered on the second ring. Tannion filled him in on what happened and he had to hold the receiver away from his ear for a minute to allow Rallin to vent.

Rallin didn't exactly see it the way Tannion did. He didn't think that Tannion had been lucky. He thought he had been stupid and ended up getting caught. After Tannion filled him in on how he got things going in Los Angeles, Rallin came around a little. At least he came around enough to tell Tannion to go ahead and meet the guy the next day and to see what happened, but also to get the hell out of there if anything went even the least bit sideways. With the guy knowing where he lived, for now it didn't seem to leave a lot of options.

Rallin knew that Tannion was strong and tough and he had seen him shot, and shot badly, but he was able to run away from it. Rallin had no idea what Tannion was really like. Tannion knew that he could have taken the gun away from Franklin's mother and killed them all, but he also knew he would have had trouble killing the girl or the mother. Until he knew the amount they were involved, he would have to consider them to be innocents. For now, he would just do as Rallin ordered and hope he could get something that Rallin could work with. That would have to wait until tomorrow.

13

It was Jeff Martin who spoke up first. Mike Rallin had been filling Pansloski and Martin in on what Tannion had told him over the phone the night before. It was a team operation most of the time, and Rallin liked to keep his team informed as much as possible, especially Martin and Pansloski.

"I think it's a really shitty idea, Mike," Martin said. "What the hell was he thinking?"

Bill Pansloski didn't waste any time either, and jumped right in. "I have to agree. We can't just let a civilian take over an operation by going undercover, no matter who he is, and I don't trust the guy."

"Come on, Bill. With what Tannion did in Los Angeles, how could you not trust him?"

"What he did in LA he did because we had a gun to his girlfriend's head, remember, and not because he was a pillar of society. We don't have a gun to her head this time. Why should we trust him, or better yet, why do you seem to trust him so much?" Pansloski asked.

"I know what you're saying, but I got to know Tannion while he was in prison, and I believe he has a deep-seated desire to do things right. Most of what we know he did, or think he might have done here in New York, or back in

Kansas, looks to be the work of a vigilante and not a crook. He worked for us even then. I trust him because I know him."

"Still doesn't make him an undercover agent does it, Mike?" Martin added.

"No, and I can't say that I like it much better than either of you two do, but I trust him and I need to give him some rope and hope he doesn't hang himself, or hang any of us with him. In this case I'm not sure he's given us much choice, either."

"It looks like the only way out would be to have him move out of the halfway house. Shit. He actually told them where he lives," Pansloski said. Pansloski hadn't done any real undercover work in his life, but he knew a mistake when he saw it.

"It gets worse, Bill. He had one of Franklin's men drop him off at the halfway house. They know exactly where he lives. He either goes in deep or he gets out fast. If he has to get out, then we'll have to move in. All they would have to do is talk to anyone at the house and they would have his real name and they might even be able to trace him to us. We would lose any edge that he might be able to give us."

"This does get worse and worse," Pansloski moaned.

"I trust Tannion to be on our side and I've seen him in action a little. I think he can take care of himself and work his way through this. Remember, he was in the thick of it back in Los Angeles. So are we good for now?"

Both Martin and Pansloski said they were good, but they also added that they were in a wait and see mode. Rallin hoped that Tannion wouldn't let him or the team down. When the day ended, Rallin went home and met Arlene just as she was coming home with groceries in her hands. After helping her carry the groceries into the kitchen, he started to tell her about his day, and especially about what Tannion was doing.

Arlene usually had something to say and she didn't disappoint him. "If he can do the same thing with this case as he did with the last one, then I say you have to let him try. I still remember what he did in Los Angeles, too."

Rallin smiled. He knew where Arlene would stand. She was always a practical, say it as it is type of person. If there were a chance that some good could come out of this, Arlene would have seen it, and she had. She was always the optimist, and she would see an opportunity when it came along.

"I guess you're right. I don't want to sound like Jeff or Bill, but as much as I trust Tannion, and as much as I think I know him, how easy would it be for him to suddenly turn to that side of his life again and leave us holding the bag. He did just get out of prison. Boy, would I ever hear a big 'I told you so' if that happened."

"Well, not much for you to do now but sit back and watch. If you get involved and get too close, it's quite likely you or your men would be noticed and then that might be the end of Tannion. Sounds like you need to let him do his thing and see what happens."

"I hadn't actually thought of putting a tail on him, and I agree that it wouldn't be a good idea. We aren't in the spy business, and following people, let alone our own people, isn't our style. We might put in bugs and other surveillance systems just like the spies, but we usually deal from behind curtains, not out in the open."

"And I like it that way," Arlene told him. "A lot less chance of any of you getting hurt when you're in the next room listening to someone's conversation rather than if you're sitting across from them in the same room. Those guys always have guns."

"True, but no matter what, no one's going to get hurt if I can help it. I just hope Tannion is careful. For both our sakes."

14

Mickey parked outside the halfway house at seven the next morning as promised. As soon as Tannion got in the car the guy began to talk, and he pretty much didn't shut up the entire day. He saw Tannion as another ex-con and that made him all right in his book.

When Mickey had introduced himself to Tannion the night before, he hadn't told him his last name. Tannion knew from his experience in Los Angeles that names were not given out easily, and last names even less often.

However, Mickey didn't have any qualms about telling Tannion all about Bill Franklin. According to Mickey, Franklin was still pretty small, but he was smart and he was on his way up. Mostly drugs and prostitution, but there was good money in those two. There was a little protection as well, but that was a small part of the business.

Franklin also owned a small bar in the Bronx that allowed him to look legit even when the cops were pretty sure it was used for money laundering. They couldn't catch him with anything and they had tried. He had been audited a couple of times by the IRS and they hadn't found anything.

Mickey told Tannion that they had an excellent accountant and that was the reason Franklin looked as good as he did. The cops had raided a couple of his places, but they were just empty houses that the girls were using. They couldn't trace anything back to Franklin. The girls were just living there, so again the cops had nothing.

Mickey seemed to have the idea that him and Tannion could work together and maybe even hang out. He was a few years younger, and Tannion thought that he might look up to an older ex-con. Mickey had heard about what Tannion had done to Franklin's guards, and to him that meant that Tannion was for real.

Rallin had told Tannion to take it easy and to see what happened without putting himself in any danger. As Tannion wasn't sure what would put him in danger, he knew he could just ride along with Mickey and see what happened. Rallin couldn't have any problems with that.

Early that afternoon Mickey dropped Tannion off at the halfway house, and told Tannion that he would be there to pick him up at the same time the next day. It had been a rather uneventful day, with only a few errands to run and not much else to do. Tannion was surprised when he found he was glad to be home.

Mickey picked Tannion up again the next morning exactly when he said he would. They drove around for the better part of the day doing odd errands and nothing much more. It was a repeat of the day before. Tannion's second day with Mickey gave him even more information on Franklin, as the guy never shut up. If Franklin knew what Mickey had told Tannion, he would probably have killed them both.

On the third day Mickey picked Tannion up, the same as before, but this day was different. When the day was done, instead of heading for the halfway house, it looked like they were heading for the South Bronx. It was time to see the boss again. Mickey had gotten all his instructions by phone and Tannion hadn't even seen Franklin in three days. Tannion knew that was probably for his sake and not the normal procedure.

Mickey told Tannion that he had put in a good word, and the boss was ready to take him on. It didn't really sound like Tannion was going to have any say in the decision making at all. Either Franklin let him in or he didn't, and Tannion was pretty sure whatever it was that Franklin did to those he didn't let in, it wouldn't be very nice.

They pulled up in front of the house that Tannion had been in a couple of days before. He took his usual look around to see what defenses might be up and to see what his escape route would be. He had what Rallin needed just from talking to Mickey and the little he had seen. He knew he was going to turn down any offer Franklin had and get the hell out of there if he could. If it looked like he couldn't get out, then he might accept the offer and go from there.

Tannion assumed it might get a little rough and he was prepared. Once inside he kept his back to the front door and his eye on the window. He wanted this to go down easy and let Rallin do all the heavy lifting, as long as Franklin would let him go.

Franklin met Tannion and Mickey at the door. Mickey started to say something, but Franklin quickly raised his hand to shut him up and told him to go into the kitchen. Tannion was alone with Franklin.

"Mickey tells me you're living at a halfway house," Franklin started.

"I need to move real soon," Tannion thought, but then said out loud, "That's right."

"Where did you spend your time?"

Tannion told him, and it was obvious that Franklin knew the place, but he wasn't too impressed. It wasn't known as the roughest hellhole, but it wasn't a country club either. There were places much tougher.

"So, do you want to go to work?"

Tannion had his story all worked out. "Mr. Franklin, I just got out of jail and I don't want to go back. Working for you would probably violate my parole."

"Hey, I'm legitimate. There isn't anything on me that anyone can dig up. Your parole officer would be glad you were able to get a job."

"I understand that based on what Mickey told me, but I don't think I can take that chance. I know the business you're in, and if my parole officer found out, he'd send me back."

"It's too bad you think that way. I could have used someone like you. Rick. Tony." He hollered into the kitchen, keeping an eye on Tannion.

The two goons came out of the kitchen, along with Mickey and Franklin's mother. Tannion wasn't happy to see her there and hoped she had left the sawed-off shotgun somewhere out of reach. Rick and Tony looked to be mostly healed from the little roughing up that Tannion had given them, and were probably hoping to get a second shot at him. This time they would know a little more of what they were up against and wouldn't make the same mistakes. They wouldn't rush in the next time.

"Small here says he doesn't want to work with us. What do you think of that?"

Mickey started to say something, but Franklin shut him off before he got started. Mickey wasn't smart enough to know that it was a rhetorical question. The other two weren't that bright either, but they stayed quiet.

"Mr. Franklin," Tannion started. "I would rather just walk out the door and look the other way. There's no need for anything else."

"Well, Small. You said it yourself. You know what my business is, and I can't afford to have someone knowing all about me and not working for me. I know Mickey. That, and I still haven't thanked you for what you did to my guys a few days ago, and if you've decided not to help me then I'm going to help myself." With a quick motion he waved at the two guys and Mickey to take Tannion.

Mickey was the first to speak up. He addressed Tannion, and not his boss. "What the hell, Small? I thought you wanted this job." The two toughs were in an obvious quandary. They didn't want to disobey their boss, but they had already had one outing with Tannion. They had come out on the losing end the last time they met and they were wary.

They wanted at him badly, but weren't sure exactly how to go about it. The frontal assault had only gotten them beat on the last time, and they knew that Mickey wasn't going to be a lot of help. Mickey was more of a talker than a fighter.

None of the three of them had a gun out, but Tannion was pretty sure they had guns on them. He knew Franklin had one, and quite possibly his mother still had the sawed-off shotgun close by. He knew their hesitation was his advantage, and having already made his choice, he took it.

Two quick strides had him to the window, and with another he was through the glass and onto the ground outside. He landed on his right shoulder, rolled, and was up on his feet in an instant.

This happened quicker than anyone in the room could react. By the time they got to the window, Tannion had taken a few steps towards the sidewalk. Franklin grabbed the guy beside him just before he took a shot at Tannion's back. The tough might not have known what a shot in the neighborhood would lose for them, but Franklin did. The last thing he needed was for the cops to show up after someone heard shots fired.

Franklin could afford to let Tannion go more than he could afford to bring the police to his house. Who was going to believe anything an ex-con said anyway? Besides, they knew where he lived and they only needed to get the car and go grab him. That way they were out of their own neighborhood. He told Mickey to get the car.

Tannion made his way down the street with only the occasional look over his shoulder. It took him a few minutes to get to a street where he could catch a cab, and a few more minutes to get to the halfway house. He noted that it had started to get dark as they were talking, and it was quite dark by the time he got to the halfway house.

Once there, he went to his room and quickly packed his bag and walked out of his room. Franklin knew where he lived, and although Franklin might just let him go, there was a good chance they would be at the house as soon as Mickey could get the car. Tannion wasn't taking any chances. He was going to be gone as soon as he could.

He took his bag and looked out of one of the front windows. He wasn't surprised when he saw the car he knew belonged to Franklin out front, and it looked like they were waiting for him to come out or eventually they would come in. They hadn't even bothered to park a little way down the block.

He made his way to the rear of the house and was about to sneak out the back door. He took a quick peek around the corner to ensure that he was alone. A small movement caught his attention, and revealed where one of Franklin's men had set up a trap at the back.

"That's what they were waiting out front for," Tannion realized. They needed some time for one of their men to get into a position in the back before they came in the front. Tannion's first thought was to make a run for it, but decided he would have a go at the guy first. He was hiding behind the bushes at the back of the yard and those same bushes would cover Tannion as much as they would Franklin's man, as long as Tannion could get to the one side.

He picked up one of his roommate's shoes sitting by the back door, and with a quick movement he threw it to the right side of the man hiding in the bushes. The shoe landed a few feet away and gave Tannion the diversion he needed to jump out the door and slide to the other side of the yard along the fence.

If the tough saw him, he didn't make any noise that indicated he had. It was just dark enough that Tannion would be hard to see and the house was dark, but it was light enough for Tannion to see everything very clearly.

Once Tannion made his way to the bushes, he slowly got down on his belly and slid the few feet around to the other side without making any noise at all. When he got behind and within a few feet of the man, he slowly stood up and stepped forward. Tannion recognized the man in front of him as Franklin's man Tony

He first grabbed Tony's right hand with his right hand, making sure that the gun was dropped without Tannion touching it. Tannion then held his left hand over Tony's mouth while at the same time lifting him off his feet. With a quick twist of Tannion's left hand Tony's neck made an audible and sickening crack, and he went limp.

Tannion used his jacket to pick up the gun and he placed it in the dead man's pocket, and carried the body with him down the back alley. He knew there was too much light at the end of the alley for him to carry Tony too far, but as long as he got him away from the halfway house, it wouldn't automatically look like the guy had died there. Having a dead guy in the backyard would bring suspicion down on him, but also on anyone else staying at the house and they didn't need that, not after what they had been through just to get there.

Tannion found a dark place between a couple of buildings halfway down the block, and dumped the body over the fence. With any luck it might look like he broke his neck when he climbed over the fence and fell. At least he hoped it would be enough to slow the cops down, if not completely throw them off the trail.

Tannion needed time to find that new place he had been thinking about. He ducked back into the house to grab his bag. On the way in he picked up the shoe he had thrown. He was over the fence and gone a moment later. He never did see if Franklin and his two men out front had moved.

It wasn't the way Tannion envisioned leaving the half-way house, but he suddenly wasn't given any other choice. Maybe he would drop in and say goodbye to Peter and a couple of the guys he had gotten to know, but it would have to wait until the FBI put Franklin away. The report Tannion would pass to Rallin was based on what he had seen, and what Mickey had told him. He felt sure it would do a good job of taking Franklin off the street, but for now he needed to find a place for the night.

15

"Where did this information come from, Mike?" Bill Pansloski asked as he was reading the report. "Is this from Tannion?"

"Yeah, that's his report."

"Nice. Well-written and concise. This guy writes a decent report, but how about the data? There's a lot of stuff here. If it's as good as the stuff he gave us last time, we should be able to get a few warrants and move on these guys."

"Read the whole thing, Bill. I think in this case there's more than there was in his last file. There are several houses noted, with times when customers arrive. There's a bar that looks to be where they handle the money, and at least one grow-op and a factory. He even has the name of what he calls Franklin's 'accountant'. I think we can get some of the uniforms going as soon as we get the warrants we need."

Bill took a few extra minutes to read the rest of the report. He was sitting in the chair across from Mike Rallin in Rallin's office. "This all came from his undercover work last week?"

"He was able to get out at the last minute, and this comes mostly from three days of riding around with one of

Franklin's men. Tannion said the man liked to talk, but he saw several places first-hand as well."

"Maybe Jeff and I were a little hasty on him then."

"I don't know, Bill. From what he told me I think he was lucky this time. He was able to walk away, but I've made a point of telling him not to get that close again. I don't mind him following people and getting the kind of information he's given us, but he's better off to stay on the outside."

"Did he agree to that?"

"I think so, but I don't know if Tannion ever shows his true feelings. He always seems to hold something back, if you know what I mean."

"Well, at least this file looks good. I'll get started on the warrants." Pansloski hurried out of Rallin's office with the report in his hand.

Rallin walked around his desk and made the short trip down to Tannion's office. He had a slip of paper in his hand, which he had received from administration that morning. As he sat down he showed Tannion the paper he was holding. "It says here that you've moved."

"Yeah," Tannion said. He handed the paper back to Rallin. "I needed a place that was a little closer to work. I can't afford a car yet, and I get tired of using transit. I would rather walk to work if I can."

"The timing of your move seems to correspond with your work with Franklin, which I can understand with them knowing where you lived, but there was something else that happened in your block last Friday. Know anything about it?"

"Not sure what you mean, Mike. What happened?" asked Tannion, pleading ignorance.

"There was a man found dead just a few buildings down from where you were living. He just happened to have a broken neck, possibly from a fall, and he just happened to be known to work for the same guy you have in your file. I don't believe in coincidences."

"I don't put much stock in coincidences either Mike, but do you think we can just let this one go?"

"As long as you fill me in on what happened off the record, we can probably forget about it. The uniforms aren't convinced that he wasn't murdered and the coroner's report isn't in yet. It isn't an obvious organized crime situation, so the file hasn't made it to my desk and it might never make it. I just happened to hear it from one of the uniforms, as the dead man was well known to them. The uniform even knew the guy's name and who he worked for."

Tannion knew that there was no sense lying to Rallin any more than he had already. The truth might be the way to go this time. Tannion took the time to completely fill Rallin in on what had happened, including what happened to the guy the cops found. Rallin was a good listener and waited until Tannion had finished before asking any questions.

Rallin had a few questions to clarify what Tannion had said, and then he felt he had a pretty good picture in his head as to what had happened, and more importantly why.

"Thanks, Jim." Tannion could tell that Rallin wasn't happy, but he was doing a good job of controlling his emotions. Tannion had already lied to him about how he got out of the house and why he moved, and Rallin didn't like to be lied to. "I get the impression that you never really intended to tell me anything if I hadn't asked. Correct?"

"I'm used to being on my own, Mike, and I haven't quite got my head around working on a team. In this case I thought, why open a can of worms if I don't have to."

"Well, it looks like that can has more than just been opened. If the coroner's report comes back telling us about there being bruises around the man's neck and on his arm, and the fact that a gun was found on him, but that it wasn't in his shoulder holster, I don't think they'll think he just fell. They might think that the gun fell out of the holster when he fell over the fence, but it wouldn't have ended up in his coat pocket. The coroner will know whether or not the dead guy got the bruises prior to him being dumped over the fence. These guys aren't dumb. They'll think there was foul play, if they don't already."

"I've given you a lot of info on these guys, Mike. Do you think it's possible that we can get the case transferred to us and then we can more or less lose that part of my involvement with the rest of what happens? I have to claim self-defense on this one, but no matter what, it would violate my parole and they would send me back."

Rallin didn't like to bend the truth any more often than he had to, but there was some room to move. "Leave it to me, Jim, and I'll see what I can do without opening that can any further. I understand that this sort of thing will happen as long as you're working with us, but can I ask you to keep it to a minimum? And please tell me when, or if, it happens again and try to stay out of these kinds of messes in the future. We've already talked about you not going into deep cover anymore. Remember, you're a civilian and not an agent."

"I'll try, Mike. I'll try."

"Just keep your surveillance from the outside and long distance. You've brought in some good information, but you need to be part of the team and not a one-man show. Remember that, please," Rallin told Tannion as he stood up.

Rallin left Tannion's office and Tannion watched him go. A thought went through Tannion's head. Maybe he wasn't so sure he really fit in with the team. He liked the work and he liked Rallin, but he liked to be on his own too. This job might not be what it was cracked up to be, but it was what he had for now. He only hoped things didn't change for the worse. He went on to the next file.

16

Somehow Tannion felt safe in his new place that evening, maybe safer than he had felt for a long time. Having an FBI agent like Mike Rallin on his side made him feel just a little more secure. Living in a place where no one knew where he was helped as well. Tannion knew however, that feeling secure was something that he always felt to some extent. Having a strong friend and ally in Rallin only helped.

Tannion's new apartment wasn't much to look at. After grabbing his suitcase at the halfway house he had made his way towards the office. It hadn't been too late at night, so when he saw an "Apartment for Rent" sign in a window of a low-rise that was within ten or twelve blocks of the office, he knocked on the door.

He took the furnished apartment on the spot, and paid the first month's rent and damage deposit up front. The land-lord was happy to have him. The bed was lumpy and old and the dresser was rather dilapidated, but they would have to do for now. He had to move out of the halfway house, and it looked like he would want to move again real quick, but this time he'd do a little more research. "Still better than a hotel room," he thought.

Tannion felt fairly certain that Rallin would be able to keep his name out of the file regarding the dead guy he had thrown over the fence, but he wasn't so sure if Rallin trusted him as much as he had before. Right now Tannion valued that trust.

His room came complete with a phone that could be used for local calls only. Tannion picked it up and made a collect call. When finally the voice he was waiting for came on, it was very familiar, with a slight Russian accent.

"Potenlikov."

"Hi, Vlad. Jim Tannion here. Glad I caught you at home."

Tannion went on to tell Potenlikov about moving and gave him his new phone number, which was written on the top of the phone, and his new address. Potenlikov was glad to hear from him as he had found out some more information on the John Doe case.

"The word out is that there's someone in New York who's trying to bust into the business and is being messy about it. The bullet in the back of the head with the guy on his knees and hands tied behind his back just doesn't happen that much anymore," Potenlikov told him.

The new guy was trying to look tough and make a name for himself, but as far as Potenlikov was concerned it would probably get the guy killed. There were a couple of families in New York who weren't too happy with the guy moving in on territory they considered theirs, and they also weren't happy that he might be bringing unwanted attention on to the scene. The families try to stay out of sight and out of mind.

Tannion wrote down a name and an address that Potenlikov gave him, as well as the name of the family that wasn't happy. Maybe this was a mob hit after all, but just a messy one from a relative newcomer. Potenlikov wasn't sure how accurate the data was, but he at least felt the guy's name sounded good. Tannion thanked his friend.

Before they said their goodbyes Potenlikov had to voice his opinion. "I don't know about you working for the feds, French. It just doesn't feel right. I don't think Mr. Philips likes it either."

"I'm sorry you feel that way, but after what I had to give up in Los Angeles, there's almost no place else I can go," Tannion told him.

"Maybe, but you could just get a job in construction or something and stay away from this business all together. There must be lots of jobs you would be good at."

"Probably, but this is what I know and I might as well put it to good use. Don't worry. I'll stay in New York."

Tannion suddenly had a thought. "But if there is someone out here who's giving you a problem, just let me know and I'll see what I can do. It could even be someone out there, too. I'm with the FBI now and we're not restricted to New York, so I could even be of help to you in LA."

"Slow down, French. Let's just say you'll stay in New York for now, if that's okay with you," Potenlikov told him.

"Sure, Vlad. That's probably for the best."

"French. I never did get a chance to say thanks from both me and Mr. Philips. You could have done us a lot of damage. As it turns out you did us a lot more good than harm."

"I consider you two to be my friends, Vlad."

"Thanks, French."

"I need to thank you for looking after Louisa."

"I'm sorry there too, French. We didn't expect to get close. It just happened after spending so much time together."

"That's okay, Vlad. I didn't have much to offer from prison, and she needed to move on. I'm just happy that you're both happy. You be good to her."

Tannion hung up and his thoughts were back in Los Angeles for a while. He looked at the names he had written down. Now he wasn't so sure about the John Doe. Was this really a mob hit gone a bit messy, or was it messy because the new guy wanted it to look messy, and in that way make it tougher on the existing guys?

Too many questions and not enough answers. "Might as well take a look at the name Vlad gave me," he said out loud.

17

Rallin picked up the phone on the second ring. The voice on the other end didn't give his name and expected that Rallin would know who it was. Rallin did.

"Morning, sir." Rallin didn't get too many calls from the director of the FBI, but it had happened a couple of times. It was usually when the director wanted something. Most of their communication was through email or messages from underlings, and occasionally, face-to-face in the director's office. Often as not, it was just a file showing up on Rallin's desk with a note from the director's secretary. It took only a couple of seconds for Rallin to find out what he wanted.

"I've got a job for you, Mike. I'm having the file sent over to you, but I wanted you to hear it from me first. This needs to be your top priority. Correction; this is to the point of being your only priority. Am I clear?"

"Very," Rallin answered. The director hung up without another word, and left Rallin holding the receiver wondering what the hell had just happened. He would have to wait for the file to arrive, but he already knew that he wasn't going to like whatever was in it.

Rallin's group had been given a lot of leeway when it came to picking files and setting priorities. Having the director suddenly dictate his priority didn't sit well with him, and it wasn't going to sit well with the rest of the team either. He was the director, however, and what the director wanted the director got.

The file arrived about twenty minutes later. The director had used the internal courier and it was as quick as the traffic would allow him to be. Rallin opened what appeared to be a very large file. As soon as he saw the name at the top of the file he knew the shit had hit the fan.

Jackson T. Philips; suspected Los Angeles crime boss, and the one person in LA Tannion hadn't fingered. This couldn't be good. The file was lengthy and it took Rallin several minutes to go through it, even without looking into it in any detail.

Philips had several priors, but nothing they had been able to make stick. All of the priors were more than five years old, meaning they were all prior to Tannion going to jail. There were names of suspected accomplices, with Vladimir Potenlikov at the top of the list.

Rallin had first heard about Philips and Potenlikov when he had chased and captured Tannion in Los Angeles. Tannion had left their names off the list he had handed over to the authorities back then, so Rallin didn't know that much about them. Today was different; the director had seen to that.

Philips had grown in size after Tannion was put away, and he had been on a watch list for Rallin and his team ever since Rallin's team had been set up. With their office in New York, and with there being enough work to do on the East Coast, the players in California had been left up to the locals.

Rallin called Pansloski and Martin into his office. They were both in the building that morning doing the inevitable paperwork. Some of the paperwork was a result of the warrants Pansloski had been able to get to look into the Franklin file.

As soon as they sat down Rallin shoved the file across the desk, and Martin picked it up first. A few minutes later he handed it to Pansloski. Martin didn't look any happier than Rallin.

"Why does the director dump this in our lap all of a sudden?" Pansloski asked, and then he answered his own question. "It has to be because of Tannion. It only makes sense. Once the director approved Tannion coming on board, and especially after he's given us a couple good leads, he dumps a file on us that he's probably had for a long time. Look at the size of it."

"Shit," Martin added. "I don't like this at all. This is probably just not what Tannion needs at this time."

Rallin jumped in. "I agree. Tannion kept his mouth shut regarding his friends in LA years ago. What makes anyone think he would do anything to help us at this point? It might even make him want to work against us. It's much too early to push our luck with his loyalty. I trust him for now, but this could easily eliminate any trust he has in us, and any he might have in the FBI. That is, if he has any at all."

The discussion went on for a few minutes. They came to the agreement that they would have to work on the file as the director hadn't made that an option, but for now they wouldn't include Tannion. This was a file that Tannion didn't even need to know about.

The director hadn't used Tannion's name and he hadn't told Rallin who he was to put on the case, so that meant it was Rallin's decision. For now, Tannion was definitely not on this one. The director might have thought he had simply not stated the obvious, but Rallin still felt as if he had some control. As long as the director left them alone for a while, at least.

They weren't too sure how they were going to hide it from Tannion, as it was going to mean at least one of the three or maybe all three of them flying back and forth from LA, and that sort of thing would be harder to hide. They would have to keep Tannion busy with other files, especially if it would get him out of the office.

Rallin asked Martin and Pansloski to hand the Franklin case off, but to ensure that it was a top priority. The two men didn't need to know about Tannion's additional role including the body found not far from where he was staying, but they needed to conclude the case to keep Tannion out of it.

Rallin knew that the director was expecting quick results, but without Tannion on the case that might not happen. He just hoped the director didn't demand Tannion be put on the case. Rallin wasn't so sure what either of them would do if that happened.

18

Tannion looked at the number on the house he stood across the street from. It matched the address Potenlikov had given him, but it seemed wrong. He was standing on a decent street in an obviously middle-class area in Queens. Ross Chambels was supposed to be the head of a crime syndicate in the area. Not a large one, but still in the business. This just didn't fit the type of place a guy like that would have been living in if he were in Los Angeles.

In Los Angeles it would have been Beverly Hills, or Malibu, or something in one of the many upscale areas, but not down in the valley or the hood. Maybe they do things differently in New York. Tannion was thinking a man in his position would likely be in Manhattan, probably the Upper West Side, but here he was in Queens.

It was late at night and there were no lights on in any of the houses on the street. A quick check around the back of the house, and he could see no sign of lights or life. Tannion checked for an alarm and didn't find one. A few seconds later he was standing inside the back door.

"I bet I'm going to find a little old lady in here who has nothing to do with anything crime-like," thought Tannion. He checked his ski mask to make sure it was over his face, and went down the hall. There were four doors along the hall, which looked to be three bedrooms and one bath, and the door to the bathroom at the end of the hall was open. The other doors were closed.

He bet on the master bedroom being where he had to go, but thought it best to check the other bedrooms first. The first door he opened was empty except for some furniture and a lot of cloth. It appeared to be a sewing room.

The second bedroom had a kid in it who looked to be about ten years old from the little he could see. She was mostly covered up, but Tannion thought probably a girl based on the posters on the wall. Most of them were of boy bands and what Tannion assumed were heartthrob singers. Tannion closed the door quietly and headed to the master bedroom.

The door opened easily and with Tannion's great night vision he could see a man and a woman sound asleep in a large king-size bed. Matching furniture was set against the two walls away from the window and the door. A woman's touch was obvious. The couple looked to be in their late forties or maybe early fifties. "A little old for a ten-year-old kid," Tannion thought, "Maybe she's a grandchild."

Tannion walked over to the bed on the wife's side and touched an arm that wasn't covered. He told her body to find a deeper sleep and knew she wouldn't be waking up, no matter how much noise her husband made. He then moved to the husband's side, touched his neck, and froze his vocal cords.

Chambels woke with a start. Tannion grabbed him by the scruff of his neck and dragged him to his feet. Adrenaline must have kicked in and the fear that was first in Chambels' eyes turned to anger, and he took a swing at Tannion, which missed. Tannion tightened his grip on his neck and lifted him off the ground.

"I'm going to let you down and as long as you behave yourself then I'm going to leave your wife and the kid alive. Fight me, and they might not be so lucky." Tannion released the lock he had put on Chambels' vocal cords, and as it looked like he wasn't going to do anything stupid, Tannion let him down to his feet.

Tannion took the man by the arm and dragged him out of the bedroom and into the kitchen, and sat him down on a kitchen chair. He didn't turn on a light. He didn't need to.

"Are you Ross Chambels?" Tannion asked.

"Who the hell are you? I suggest that you get the hell out while you can." At least he was trying to act tough, but Tannion could see more desperation than anything.

"I hold all the cards here, and I'll ask the questions If you know what's good for you and your family, you'll answer me. I ask again, are you Ross Chambels?"

A little of the light went out of Chambels' eyes and he answered. "Yes, I'm Chambels."

"Good. Now, what I have to ask is important, and how you answer will determine if your family lives or dies." Tannion knew his threat was empty, but he hoped that he sounded convincing. He had shown enough strength already, and as long as there wasn't a silent alarm going off somewhere, then he should be safe.

"A man was killed, execution-style, about three and a half months ago, and I think you know who he was and who killed him. Tell me a couple of names and I'll leave and you'll never see me again."

"How do I know you'll keep your word?"

"You don't. You also don't know what I might do to you and your family, and I think you would rather leave it that way. I know that you didn't kill this guy, so you have nothing to worry about. If you don't tell me what you know, then you do."

"Okay, but you'll leave us alone if I do?" He asked.

Tannion told him he would and Chambels continued.

"The man's name was Jason Wentworth. I don't know for sure who killed him, but I know who ordered it. Jason worked for me, and it's Peter Tong who wants to shake me up and move in. He put out the contract and tried to make it look like I did it. The only reason he failed so far is the cops don't know who Jason is and haven't tied him to me yet."

"Why haven't you hit this Tong yourself?"

"He's found some good backing. I'm just a small player and Tong is new, but he wants to be big time and he's worked his way into the Staguchi family by hitting Jason. Staguchi and I have been at each other's throats for years, and now it looks like he's won. I couldn't keep up. All of my guys have moved on. I knew I should have moved the family and hid. Now go ahead and do what you've been sent to do. I knew this day was coming."

Tannion thought that he had what he wanted. In the scheme of things these guys were small timers and that might have been why the hit was a bit messy, but Demetri Staguchi was the other name that Tannion had gotten from Potenlikov. Staguchi wasn't big time either, but he was big enough, and Tannion was surprised that he would have had any problems with Chambels unless Chambels had something on him.

If Tong had Wentworth hit in order to get in with Staguchi, then he had made a mistake in not getting the cops involved. An anonymous phone call would have done the trick. Things just didn't add up, but Tannion was pretty sure he'd gotten all he could from Chambels.

"I suggest you take your wife and kid and get out of town. I've got what I need, but things might get hot for you if things go wrong for Tong, and I think things will go wrong for him."

"Shit. You're a cop. What the hell?" Tannion saw that it was his cue to leave, and he quickly touched Chambels and saw him slump to the floor, out cold. It would be a couple of hours before either he or his wife came to. It would take a lot longer than that for Rallin to set things up, so Chambels should have no problem having enough time to get out of town.

Tannion didn't go home right away. First he went to the office, wrote out his report, and dropped it off on Rallin's desk. "Not bad for a night's work. Now it's up to Rallin to finish up." Tannion had given Rallin the dead man's name, but he didn't say in his report how he got it or any link to Tong or Staguchi. It was a pretty short report.

When Rallin got into his office he saw the report on his desk and wondered how Tannion had found out what he had. The name on the report matched one of the names from the homicide detective's list of missing persons. From here on in it would be easy. A phone call to the homicide detective in charge and Rallin passed the file on. It might come back to him eventually, but for now it was just a homicide and with the John Doe's identification they had enough information to get what they needed.

Rallin went back to Tannion's office to thank him and to fill him in on what he had done with the file, but he wasn't there. It was still early, so Rallin assumed he wasn't in yet. That was okay with Rallin; he was heading off to meet with Martin and Pansloski regarding the Philips case and it was just easier not to have to talk to Tannion. He would catch him later.

19

Tannion looked online to see if he could get addresses for Peter Tong and Demetri Staguchi, but got nowhere. He called directory assistance and found they weren't listed. He wasn't surprised. Jackson T. Philips didn't show up in a phone book anywhere in LA either.

Potenlikov had given Tannion the names and Tannion thought he would probably have more than that. A few minutes later and he was on the line.

"Potenlikov."

"Good morning, Vlad."

"French. I didn't expect to hear from you so soon. How did it go with the information I gave you?"

"That's why the call, Vlad. I found out who the John Doe was, and even who had him killed, but there are a number of things that just don't add up." Tannion went on to tell Potenlikov what Chambels had told him and why it didn't ring quite true to him.

"If Tong had Wentworth killed, then it was a gang or mob hit, but then why did he turn the body over? Chambels said that Tong was new, but then why would Staguchi care if Tong hit Wentworth? On top of that, why didn't someone call the cops and let them know who the John Doe was? If they were trying to set Chambels up then that would have been an obvious move. It doesn't make any sense," Tannion said.

"All I know at this time, French, is that there was some in-fighting and I had the names that I gave you. I'll check around and see if anyone knows anything else. Staguchi has some of his family out here and I can talk to them, so I'll let you know if I find anything."

Tannion hung up the phone and took a look at what was on his desk. He hoped Potenlikov would be able to get him some answers, as all he had were questions. If the homicide detectives went in the direction that Chambels thought they would, then the cops would be at Chambels' door. If he heeded Tannion's warning, they would be out of the country by now.

The files on Tannion's desk looked like they never ended, and after a few hours the work became exactly that. It was work. Tannion could spend time gathering the type of information the team could use to get the proper paperwork in order to allow for an actual arrest, but he wasn't feeling it. He wasn't enjoying it. He might eventually put someone behind bars, but it wasn't enough.

After a couple of days of not having heard from Potenlikov, Tannion was getting bored. He had been in the middle of whatever was going on for too many years, and now he seemed to be on the outside looking in and he didn't like it. Even prison he had to keep his eyes open all the time, but here it was so calm that it was getting to him. To top that off, the only person on the team who would approach him was Rallin, and he was never in the office anymore. To make it worse, it seemed to be a secret as to where he and many of the team went.

Tannion knew he couldn't last much longer this way and he didn't know how to get out, because this was the job his parole officer liked for him. He had only met Sarvo twice so far, having just had his second monthly meeting. A different job would mean a different meeting with Sarvo and Tannion knew it.

It was late on a Wednesday afternoon and Tannion was the only one in the office. That wasn't unusual these days. He needed to know where the rest of the team were heading to all the time, and especially he needed to know where Rallin was spending his time. Things were off, and it seemed as if Tannion were the only one not in the loop.

It had been at least a couple of weeks since he had given Rallin the John Doe report and he had hardly seen the man, or for that matter Martin or Pansloski since. They were out of town and Tannion didn't know where or what case they were on. He thought it was time for him to know more.

Rallin's door was locked, but the lock didn't stand a chance. Tannion could hear the mechanism well enough to know when the pick he was using would work.

Rallin's office was neat and his desk was clean. A look through the top drawer on the left revealed nothing, and the second drawer on that side was just as unrevealing.

The top drawer on the right side was locked, which drew Tannion's attention immediately when he pulled the handle. "What have we got in here, Mike?" Tannion asked no one.

The lock on the desk proved to be a little tougher than the one at the door, but eventually it yielded to Tannion's pick. The drawer pulled open smoothly and Tannion picked up the only file that was in it. The folder had the typical secrecy heading and the FBI logo on the outside, but Tannion had seen so many files just like this over the past month that he didn't even notice.

The file fell open to the initial page and Tannion's mouth fell open as well. As Tannion read what was on the page he suddenly realized where Rallin and most of the team had been going to and from for the past couple of weeks.

Jackson T. Philips had to be a big target for Rallin's team, and if Tannion had thought about it for a while he might have come to that conclusion himself. As it was there in black and white, he didn't have to. After all, it was the FBI. There were no state boundaries when it came to the FBI, and especially to Rallin's team, so why not California?

Tannion looked through the file quickly. There wasn't much in it but a few of what looked to be Rallin's notes; nothing of any real value in an investigation.

"Mike must have more than this on Philips," Tannion thought. Rallin had taken the main file to Los Angeles with him, but he had made up his own file for his notes before he had left, and had locked it in his desk for when he was back in New York.

Tannion put the file back the way he had found it, very carefully relocked the drawer, and then locked the office door behind him. Unless someone looked very closely there would be no way to tell that there had been anyone in that office. Tannion went back to his office to think. Philips could be in trouble. Rallin's team was good and had enough experience to do some real damage. As long as there was something to find, if they looked at someone hard enough they would probably come up with something, and in Philips' case there definitely was something to find.

If they got something on Philips then they would probably find something on Potenlikov, and that would have a detrimental effect on him and on Louisa. Tannion had gone to great lengths to ensure that Louisa was left out of the negative side of his being caught in LA, and although he was no longer the man in her life, he realized that he still loved her, and had never really stopped loving her. She had moved on as he had wanted her to, but still he didn't want anything happening to her.

Tannion picked up the phone and dialed the number. He knew what he was going to do, as much as he knew that it might bring his current situation to an end. The voice at the other end reminded him of what he had lost.

"Hello," she said.

"Louisa. It's Jim. Is Vlad there?" Tannion had to get right to the point. There was no place for his feelings for her at this time. She asked him to wait a minute.

"Hi, French," came Potenlikov's voice on the line. "I was just going to give you a call. I think I have the answer you were looking for."

"What answer is that, Vlad?" Tannion asked, having completely forgotten about the last conversation they had a while back.

"You know. I finally caught up to the Staguchi family here and they filled me in."

"Oh right, Vlad. Something has come up here and it had completely slipped my mind."

"What do you mean something has come up, French?" Potenlikov asked, suddenly having a bad feeling about Tannion's call.

"I need to talk to you, Vlad, but I don't think the phone is the best method. There's trouble coming your way and we need to talk."

"I can't get away from LA; can you come here?"

"I was afraid of that. I'll think of something. Meet me at the Round Table Restaurant at nine tomorrow night, but Vlad, it's almost certain that you and Philips are under surveillance. Make sure that you lose any tail that might be there. I can't be seen in LA."

"Can you wear a disguise just in case?"

"I don't think it would help unless it was very good. If they follow you they would be interested in whoever you meet with, so just make sure you aren't followed."

"I'll be there, and don't worry, I still know how to shake off a tail." Potenlikov hung up, leaving Tannion holding the phone and wondering if he had done the right thing, and wondering what Potenlikov was going to tell him about the Staguchi family. Potenlikov had forgotten about Staguchi as quickly as Tannion had.

Another phone call and Tannion had a plane ticket waiting for him at JFK for early the next day. He called Rallin's number, knowing that he would get the recording, and left a message that he was going to be undercover for a few days and would report in as soon as he could. At least that would give him some benefit of the doubt. The couple of times Rallin thought he had gone undercover, things had worked out well for the team, so Tannion knew it would work even if he had told Rallin he wouldn't go into deep cover again. Rallin would think that Tannion was just following someone around as he had done before.

Tannion reached into the files in front of him and selected one that he had already done some work on. It was going to be a busy night. Rallin was smart, and if Tannion told him that he was going undercover for a while, Rallin would be expecting results. He had given Rallin nothing but results, and anything less now would only lead to questions and possible suspicions. Best to get something to leave on Rallin's desk. It was time to get some results.

20

Mike Rallin had set up his offices in the Los Angeles Federal Building. It wasn't large, but it had three offices, a meeting area, an interrogation room, and access to the support staff in the building. Rallin had taken one of the offices and had moved two desks into each of the other two, so the team had to share whenever there were more than three of them there at one time. Today it was just Rallin, Martin, and Pansloski, as it had been all week.

Pansloski stuck his head around the corner of the door to Rallin's office. "Mike. We've made some headway, but it's slow. We know where Philips' office is, and the name of most of his closest advisors, and we have a surveillance team on most of them, but so far we haven't got enough to get anyone for anything more than jaywalking."

Rallin had been given access to several of the Los Angeles based agents to work with, and between Martin, Pansloski, and himself they had managed to create the teams and the assignments.

"Are you still working on the warrant for the phone tap on Philips' office?" Rallin asked him.

"Nothing so far, but we have a meeting with a judge in a couple of hours. I know the director wants us to get something on this guy, but there isn't a judge in the country who would think we have shit. I'm not too optimistic," Pansloski told him. "I don't think the judge is going to grant us a warrant, either."

"I understand, and I have to agree. We know this guy is dirty, but he's also good at what he does and he has legitimate businesses everywhere. He's friends with the chief of police, the district attorney, and maybe even one or more of the police commissioners. How do we compete with that? I bet he's even had lunch with the mayor a few times."

"Shit, Mike. It's not all bad. I'd like it better in New York if the weather were like it is here. That is, unless it gets too hot. I don't like the heat, you know."

"I know, Bill. I know."

Bill Pansloski withdrew his head from around the corner of Rallin's door and went back to his own office. Rallin could hear him mutter as he left, and had to grin. Pansloski was a good cop, but he wasn't always the most patient. A job like this was a lot of paperwork and a lot of patience.

Pansloski was right though. Members of the team had been in Los Angeles on and off for the last two weeks and Martin, Pansloski, and Rallin had been there most of the time. They had almost nothing to add to what they already knew.

The boys in the Los Angeles office weren't that happy to see them, either. They saw it as Rallin's team, or at the very least, the director, stepping on their toes. They had a large open file on Philips, and felt that eventually they would break the case open on their own. They didn't like having to turn the file over, even if it was to the director. The director had ensured their support and they were giving it, if grudgingly. Their agents weren't that happy working under Rallin's team, but they were at work.

Rallin had been there before and knew how they felt. It was their job, however, and the director had talked to the Los Angeles superiors and although the tension did ease a bit and was more aimed at the director, Rallin still felt it.

They knew what Philips was into and the break they really needed was to either get someone in undercover, or to get something on a wiretap. Either that, or get someone inside to rat him out, and so far that didn't sound likely. Tannion could probably get in, but then who would trust him? Would Philips trust him after what he had done more than five years ago, and then they also knew what he was doing in New York today, so why would they trust him at all?

On the other hand, if Tannion were to go undercover in LA, Rallin wasn't sure whether he could trust him not to go too deep and get lost. Rallin knew Tannion to be a good guy, but where did his loyalties run? Rallin wasn't completely sure. He was pretty sure that Tannion considered Potenlikov to be a friend, and that might apply to Philips as well.

For now, it was stick to FBI procedure and see if they couldn't come up with something, especially enough to get a wiretap in place, or a search warrant issued. That was all they could hope for. The file had a lot of data, but not enough in any one place for a judge to issue a warrant.

Philips looked to be untouchable on short notice. This was either not going to happen or it would take a very long time. Rallin wasn't sure what the director expected. If the call was because of Tannion, the director probably expected Rallin to use Tannion, but he still hadn't mentioned him. Rallin could only take one step at a time.

If the director demanded things happen faster, he might also demand that Rallin bring Tannion in. At this point, the director probably knew that Tannion was still back in New York, but he might think that Rallin was in touch with him or using his skills somehow. If things didn't happen soon enough, Rallin thought he might just have to bring Tannion in anyway. Not today, though. Definitely not today.

21

Tannion caught his flight out of New York the next morning on time, and everything went without a hitch. All he had was a carry-on, as he wasn't expecting to spend more than the one night, and maybe not even that. He hadn't booked a hotel, but he hadn't booked a return flight either.

He knew if Rallin had anyone in New York look, they might know he had flown to LA. He hadn't had the time or the contacts in New York to get fake ID made, and he had to fly under his real name.

Money wasn't a problem. After what had happened in New York years earlier, he hadn't felt that comfortable with banks. He'd had all his money in his bank account at the time he found he had to leave town quickly. He had been able to take his money out, but felt he had gotten lucky. He decided then to always have some cash on hand.

As a result, when he got to Los Angeles he stayed away from banks. He kept most of his cash in the house with Louisa when they were together. On one of her last visits to Tannion in prison, she shared out what was left and wanted to give him close to twenty thousand dollars. Tannion knew he couldn't hide that much cash in prison and asked her to keep it, but she refused.

They compromised with a safety deposit box in a New York bank, which she was able to get in his name with the help of Mike Rallin. Tannion cleaned the box out almost as soon as he was on the outside. Working with the FBI made Tannion feel more secure, and eventually he put most of the money into a savings account, but some vestiges of the memory remained, and he always kept a large sum either on his person or close by.

So when Tannion got to Los Angeles he had brought a supply of cash with him. He knew that getting a taxi or a room wouldn't be a problem. The taxi took him to the Round Table Restaurant and he found a table near the back so he could watch the front door. He got there at least a half hour early and ordered a cup of coffee.

At five to nine he saw Potenlikov walk in the door. Potenlikov saw Tannion in the corner, but instead of walking over to his table, he did a circuit of the room as if looking for someone, and then went out the back door. Tannion held the menu up high enough to cover most of his face and watched to see if anyone else came in.

After about five minutes of watching, Tannion was pretty sure no one had followed Potenlikov into the room, and then he came in from the back, through the kitchen. Tannion got up and held out his hand. Potenlikov would have nothing to do with a handshake, and grabbed Tannion in a bear hug, squeezing hard enough to have taken the air out of an ordinary man's lungs.

"Good to see you too, Vlad," Tannion said.

Potenlikov looked at Tannion and shook his head. "You haven't changed even a little."

"Neither have you, my friend," Tannion told him.

"You lie and I know it," Potenlikov said with a big smile on his face, but as he looked at Tannion the smile faded. "You're here and I don't think you have good news. Not when you have me looking over my shoulder like I haven't done in years. What's going on?"

"Okay, Vlad. Let me fill you in on why I came, and why I asked you to be careful. As you know, I've been working with the FBI."

"Yes, we know you're working with them. Why would you do that, French?" Potenlikov interjected.

"Hold on, Vlad. It isn't as bad as it sounds. I needed a job, and I got friendly with the FBI agent who brought me in. It seemed to be a good deal at the time. All I was doing was getting information on a bunch of small timers in New York, guys who really shouldn't be in the business."

"Okay. I think I understand, but what does that have to do with me or with Mr. Philips?"

"The FBI agent I mentioned is Mike Rallin. You might remember him from when he was here in LA. He's good and he has a good team. After he brought me in and after what I did here, he got a nice promotion and was set up in New York with a team that has one task, and that's to look into organized crime."

"We know all about Rallin and his team, but that's in New York, and for the most part they've stayed in New York," Potenlikov said.

"He's FBI, and you know that means they don't have any boundaries inside the US. The director gave him the job of looking into Mr. Philips, and it doesn't matter if he's in New York, Los Angeles, or in nowhere USA. His job is to get whatever he can on Mr. Philips, and that means on you too. I just couldn't stand for you or Louisa to run into a problem."

"I thought that Louisa might come up in all this."

"Don't get me wrong, Vlad. You and Louisa are a good thing, and I have no hard feelings, but I still have feelings. Feelings for Louisa, and for you, and I don't want to see either of you get hurt. So, I suggest if Mr. Philips doesn't already know that there's a team out for his hide then you had better tell him. That means they'll be using the usual FBI tactics and procedures."

Tannion went on. "They will try for wiretaps, and search warrants, and warrants to plant bugs. They will have Mr. Philips, and you, and probably several of your head guys under surveillance. They'll be taking pictures and gathering any information that they can put in front of a judge in order to get those warrants. They'll try to get someone on the inside, and it could be someone new or they might try to turn someone who's already inside. They can be relentless, so you need to be relentless too. Now is the time to be as clean as you can be. Nothing can look out of the ordinary. You got that?'

"I understand, French. What will you be doing?"

"I can't get involved on my own, and it looks like Rallin is trying to keep this as hush-hush as possible. As far as he knows, I don't know anything about it. I don't think that he trusts me in this case, and I've been kept away from it."

"Looks like he might be on the mark with that one."

"Maybe, but he might eventually need to call me in. If the director called this one, I suspect it was because he knows I'm part of the team. It's probably the reason the director went along with Rallin asking to add me to the team in the first place. I also suspect if Rallin's team comes up empty, eventually the director will demand that I get involved."

"If that happens, you'll be expected to show results and if I know one thing about you, French, is that you deliver. If your FBI guy knows you well enough, he'll know that you aren't giving it your all. What about until that time?"

"I'll keep my eye on what's happening as best I can, and I'll call you when I can. All I can do is try to call you at home, and then leave a message that will tell you to call a pay phone at a given time. I can't trust the fact that it looks like they don't have a wiretap yet. It will happen."

"Okay, French. I need to go before I'm missed too much by the guys who were following me. If they thought I lost them on purpose they might think their cover was blown, and we're better off having them think that hasn't happened."

"I agree," Tannion told him. "But I need to know what you were going to tell me about the Staguchi family."

"Right. I had almost forgotten. What I found out was that Peter Tong killed your John Doe himself, and it might have been the first kill he had ever made, which might be why he turned the body over. He had hoped that killing this guy would get him into the Staguchi family like I told you, but as it turns out, it failed. Staguchi had Tong killed almost as soon as Tong told him about the killing. That's why it never went anywhere. With your guy dead and the other group in disarray anyways, Staguchi didn't need Tong and got rid of him."

"As simple as that? That sounds too easy," Tannion said.

"As simple as that, French. It often is," Potenlikov told him.

Potenlikov told Tannion that he had better get going. Another quick hug and Potenlikov walked out the front door. A few minutes later Tannion went out the back door and got a cab back to the airport. "Might as well head back to New York," he figured. There was nothing more he could do in LA.

22

Tannion found himself back in his office late the next afternoon, typing his report on the file he had worked on before he left for Los Angeles. He knew he had enough data to give the team the ability to go in front of a judge and at least get a warrant for one of the buildings. Once that was done, he was sure that the rest of the operation would unravel.

He couldn't stop his mind from wandering back to Los Angeles. He had such a feeling of hopelessness, plus a strange guilty feeling. He thought he was feeling guilty because he didn't really know where his loyalties lay at that moment, but it might be guilt at not being able to help Potenlikov or Philips with any more than just a warning. Then again, it might be because he couldn't help Rallin either.

If someone with a gun were to try to shoot Louisa or Potenlikov, Tannion knew that he would stop him somehow, but he also knew that if that same gunman were shooting at Rallin that he would jump in front of a bullet for him as well. Tannion was in a deep quandary.

Sitting in an office in New York while all of the action was in Los Angeles was not Tannion's idea of fun. He knew he couldn't go to LA again, but he also knew that his report was done and that it could buy him a few days off, since pretty much the entire team were in LA.

The bar he stopped at that night wasn't one he had been in before. A few years back he had been in so many bars in the Bronx and in Queens that he was never able to remember them all. They blurred as each bar looked much the same. What didn't blur from his memory was what he had done.

At the time, which Tannion considered his black period, he had perfected a viral-looking disease that was deadly. As he went from bar to bar he released it into people who he thought were deserving. Maybe they deserved it and maybe they didn't. It was also the start of the end for him in New York.

As far as Tannion could tell it was the loss of too many lives from the virus that started the cops looking for a killer rather than a medical problem for the doctors to worry about. Too many of the same types of people who frequented the same types of bars were dying. Eventually the cops started to follow him and they almost caught him.

It was the bars, however, where Tannion did his best business, even if he left out his black period. He didn't like to even think about his black period. The seedy bars seemed to breed the type of guys Tannion liked to say were his. The first bar he went into that night wasn't much different from the bars he had gone into in the past, with one exception. Now he had the backing of the FBI. As long as he didn't do anything that would cause him problems, he could always use the FBI get-out-of-jail-free card. He had the ID.

He took a seat a little to the side of the bar, where he could watch the front door and see the bar. Unlike the undercover work he had been doing for the FBI in the past month or so, he wasn't looking for any particular face. This time he was working alone and working for himself.

A few minutes before midnight the bar was getting a little rowdy and Tannion knew it was about to burst. The bar had bouncers, and they were big guys, but two of them had just dragged a guy out back, and if what happened back there was what usually happened, they would be out of the bar for a few minutes.

It was at that time that a couple of guys over by the bar thought it would be great to hit on one of the waitresses. Tannion had noticed her much earlier, as she was by far the best-looking girl in the bar. Even a few of what Tannion took to be regulars were looking her over all night, and he had to assume that she was new.

She was probably only in her very early twenties, and possibly a college student working a few hours a week in order to get by. She had a few guys try to grab her ass, but the bouncers had an extra eye out for her, and anyone who tried anything usually got taken out back just like the guy who was out there now.

The two guys boxed her in over by the bar. The bartender was down at the far end of the bar and there were enough customers leaning on the bar that he couldn't see what was going on. Tannion, on the other hand, could see everything from his vantage point. As soon as the two guys moved in, Tannion stood up and worked his way towards the action.

When the first guy made a move to grab the girl in places his hands just shouldn't be, Tannion grabbed his arm. He took one look at Tannion and didn't say a word before he took a swing. Of course, that wasn't just his first mistake, it was his only mistake.

Tannion had used his right hand to grab the guy's left arm and the guy took a swing with his right. Tannion saw it coming and let it sail over his head as he ducked down. With his left hand Tannion grabbed the guy's friend, who was standing on the other side of the girl and wasn't sure what he should do and therefore hadn't moved. Tannion pushed him back against the bar. The girl pulled away and went to the side.

The force of the first guy's missed punch threw him off balance and Tannion simply threw him into his friend who was squashed against the bar. He threw him hard enough to have hurt the other guy against the bar, bad enough to take him out of commission for a minute.

Tannion didn't let go of the first guy's arm, but continue to swing him in a rebound off the second guy and the bar. Using the bounce momentum, Tannion swung him around and threw him against the wall about six feet away. Luckily the people who had been there only a moment before had moved out of the way as soon as they saw a fight was starting.

The guy hit the wall hard enough to have some cracked ribs and probably a concussion. He didn't get up. Tannion then grabbed the second guy again and threw him on top of his friend. Tannion went over and grabbed one of the guys in each hand, and dragged them to the back door and threw them through it just as the two bouncers were coming back in. All four went down in a heap.

The two bouncers weren't hurt and they were up fast. In a couple of steps they were in front of Tannion with their fists up, but the girl was even quicker. She had followed him to the back door and stepped in.

"It's okay, boys. He was helping me with a couple of guys who got out of hand when you were outside," she told them. She had to put a hand on them to physically restrain them. They had some adrenaline from what they had just finished in the back alley, and were looking for more.

Tannion had to admire her guts and her quick thinking, but he wasn't really too concerned about busting up a couple of bouncers if that was what they wanted. They both looked at her and asked her what happened and after she told them, they had a little more liking for Tannion.

Tannion went back to his table and sat down as if nothing had happened. He thought he might have a chance with the girl, but decided he was probably ten or more years older than she was and it just wasn't worth it.

A few minutes later he decided to call it a night. Somehow he felt better. A little physical action felt good after a lot of sitting and sneaking around. "I need to find myself a good gym to work off some of this aggression," he thought. There's nothing like a desk job to make a person fat and lazy.

23

Rallin looked over at his partner, who had just let out one of those snorts that's half snore and half a choking sound, which almost always wakes up the snorer. Pansloski's eyes fluttered and slowly opened.

"Good morning." Rallin told him, with sarcasm showing. Pansloski looked at him through hooded eyelids. Not wide awake, but awake enough.

"Fuck off."

"As I said, good morning to you. I can't believe how easy it is for you to nod off." Rallin and Pansloski had been parked in the same location for more than four hours. They were on a stakeout outside the house where Vladimir Potenlikov and his wife were. They had been there all morning and it was now noon.

"I didn't sleep that well last night. For that matter, I haven't slept that well since we got here. I miss my own bed," Pansloski told Rallin.

"I sleep better at home too," Rallin said. "But I can't just fall asleep anywhere the way you do."

"Your loss, you know. So what did I miss?"

"Absolutely nothing. They haven't moved. Doesn't this guy have to go to work? It's Tuesday, or doesn't he know it?"

"We'd have heard from the other team if they went out the back, and as they always take the car, they would've had to have come this way, so they must still be in the house. Must be nice to have a job like that."

"Better than this one you think, Bill."

"Guaranteed it pays a hell of a lot more."

At that moment, the garage door started to move, and as soon as it reached the top the light blue Jag started to back out. Rallin could see that it was Louisa behind the wheel, and that she was alone. A few seconds later and the black BMW also started to back out, and it was obvious who was driving. He filled the car by himself.

Rallin got on the radio and told the other team to follow Louisa and that they would take Potenlikov. Rallin assumed that he would be going downtown to where Philips had his office; finally going to work.

"I guess these guys do work some late nights, but shit, going into work at noon." As the car pulled away, Rallin pulled out of the little spot where they were concealed behind a fence. Rallin and Pansloski were in an old pickup truck that had a landscape company logo across the door. It was a good vehicle for sitting outside without arousing too much suspicion, but it wasn't the best to follow with, especially if they had to get up to any speed at all. The truck didn't have a lot of guts.

Rallin and Pansloski followed Potenlikov downtown. He never once broke the speed limit or did anything that would violate any traffic law. If they were going to pull him over for anything at all it would have to be bogus. It was almost as if he knew they were there.

Potenlikov parked his car in the underground parking at the building where Philips had his office. Of course, they hadn't been able to plant any listening devices or get any wiretaps yet. There wasn't a judge in town who would listen to them. Anything they planted wouldn't have been legal, and therefore anything they heard wouldn't be admissible in court or even used to get additional warrants. So far it was a dead end.

The judges might know that Philips was on the wrong side of the law some of the time, but they were either bought off, or they saw him as legitimate. Rallin thought that the judges probably saw him as someone with enough connections that unless the information was perfect they would be much better off leaving Philips alone.

The judges knew that since Philips had taken a stronghold on the city the amount of serious crime involving gang-type killings and murders had gone down to almost nothing. It was as if they were all one big happy family.

Rallin and Pansloski took up their spot in a hotel room across from the building Potenlikov went in. They had rented the room to be able to keep an eye on his comings and goings, and they hoped it would eventually house the electronic equipment they would need for a wiretap, but for now it pretty much looked like any other hotel room.

After waiting for a few hours they saw Potenlikov leave, and they went downstairs and picked up their truck. They left as if they were in no hurry, as they had done this before. It was time for Potenlikov to go home after only being at the office for three hours, as if he had gone in for a meeting and that was it for the day.

The call from the other group came through telling them that Louisa Potenlikov had come home from an afternoon of shopping and that they were camped in their regular spot watching the house. A little later Potenlikov pulled up to the house and parked in the garage. Another day coming to end for the happy couple.

"We can't go on like this, Bill," Rallin told his partner. "It's been all week like this and we're getting nowhere. We're no closer to having information that will lead us to a warrant or an arrest than when we got here, and I am pretty sure that they know we're here. Did you see him glance in our direction just as he closed the garage door? I'd swear that he looked right at us."

"I don't think we're the best at setting up a tail, if you know what I mean. Don't get me wrong, he might have seen us or he might have been tipped off, but I think you're right. This isn't working. I think we need Tannion. I can't see any other way."

"I know, Bill, but we can't do that. At least not yet, and the director hasn't demanded it yet, either. If we can't get anything concrete in the next week or so then we might have to think about it. Have the other teams checked in?"

Rallin had ten teams of men and women on the streets. There were tails on most of the senior staff, and three teams had gone in undercover and were trying to get in from the street level.

"Nothing, Mike. They all checked in last night and so far the tails have nothing to report. As far as they're concerned they might as well be following any and every businessman in LA. The undercover guys are getting stonewalled. They say it looks as if they know who they are and nobody will even talk to them."

"Shit, Bill. I don't like the way this is going. I would actually like to have a crime to solve, not hope to find one.

These guys can look so squeaky clean that nothing is going to show up under the best microscope."

"As I said, Mike, I think we're going to have to call in Tannion. It might be the only way. I don't like it either, but he might be our only hope."

"Shit, I don't like this. I just don't like this at all."

24

The meeting Potenlikov had gone to was just as Rallin had thought; it was his only work for the day. Philips and Potenlikov had shut much of the operation down as soon as they had heard from Tannion. The only things going were the hookers and some of the pushers who didn't need anything from Philips or his top guys on a regular basis. The guys on the ground looked after everything, and Philips had told them to store the cash for a while.

Everything else was pretty much business as usual for any legitimate businessman. Philips could look as legit as anyone in LA, and for a while that was all he was doing. Any discussion regarding the FBI was done face-to-face, not trusting any phone lines, and that was what Potenlikov and Philips were doing.

"Were you followed here, Vlad?" Philips asked.

"I was. They have a truck with some landscaping company on it that's been parked outside the house and I think they have a place in the building across the street as well."

"Any chance of them getting anything with a parabolic microphone or anything from across the street?"

"I asked that question when the guys last swept the room, and was told the building was too soundproof for that. The room was clean and we should be able to talk."

"Good," Philips concluded. "So where are we at?"

Potenlikov went on to tell Philips as much as he could about the operation and mostly about the shutting down of some of the more lucrative sections. If there was one consequence of the FBI watching the operation so closely it was that there was a lot less drug activity in the city.

Philips had shut down the labs and had stopped almost all of the imports. He didn't know who the FBI knew was part of his operation, or who they might be following or have turned. He was sure that the shortfall in supply was being picked up by some of his competitors, but there was nothing he could do about that for now.

The loss of cash flow might have been devastating to anyone not as big as Philips, and it had only been three weeks or so. Still, Philips was seeing the direction it was heading, and he didn't like it.

Potenlikov broke the silence. "There must be something we can do. If this goes on for any longer we're going to lose control of parts of the city, and it's hurting our bottom line. The guys are getting tired of staying home and they hate the idea that they don't know if they're being watched or if their phones are tapped."

"Have you heard from French?" Philips asked.

"No. Not since we met here in LA. That would mean that he hasn't been brought in yet, or that he's being watched. He doesn't think the FBI trusts him. They would either keep an eye on him, or they would just keep him in New York."

"You said he felt the FBI might bring him in eventually. Did he give any idea as to when?"

"No. He's waiting as much as we are. He thought he would be called in only if they got desperate, and who knows when that will be."

"We need French to come back and work for us," Philips said, more to himself than to Potenlikov.

"I can't agree more. It would be great to have French back and the FBI gone. Right now, especially the FBI gone."

"The FBI has always been there, Vlad. You know that they have a file on us and we always have to look as clean as we can, but I'd take the locals guys over this team that Agent Rallin has. Having French with us would make me feel a lot better. Having him with the FBI only makes me nervous."

"You can trust French," Potenlikov tried to assure Philips.

"I'm not so sure, Vlad. It's been years and he appears to have become quite friendly with the FBI and Agent Rallin in particular, and if he can become friendly with the guy who put him in prison, who knows what else might change."

"I don't think you're right this time. I've talked to him and met with him and he's the same old French. After all, he did warn us."

"You might be right, Vlad," Philips conceded. "But you can't be sure."

The two men talked for the better part of two hours, with lunch brought in so they didn't have to eat in public. They weren't just being paranoid, but they weren't taking any chances.

Philips said goodbye to Potenlikov and got on the phone. At least he had some legitimate business to run, and maybe he should have dinner with the chief of police or the district attorney. Maybe he should also talk to the mayor, but for now his call was directed to his lawyers.

Potenlikov left the building and as he was heading home he thought he saw a truck a couple of blocks behind that looked to be the same landscaping truck he had seen before. "Bastards," he said out loud.

Just as he was shutting the garage door he took a quick look at where the truck had been parked earlier in the day, and sure enough, there it was. The door closed all the way and he went inside. He hoped there would be a football game or something on television. He was getting very bored with this situation. He hoped something would break and break soon. He thought it best to give French a call. There wasn't much that they could do but wait, but maybe French had an idea.

25

Tannion's phone rang. He was in his office on a floor where he was the only inhabitant. The only other agent he had seen in the past couple of days had been Randy Silton. Either the rest were with Rallin working in Los Angeles, or they were on vacation. As far as Tannion was concerned they might as well be dead for all the contact he'd had with them.

Only Rallin, Martin, and Pansloski had ever come inside Tannion's office, and the rest either ignored him, or they might say hello at the coffee machine, but that was about it. There always seemed to be tension in the air whenever Tannion walked out of his office and there was someone else from the team hanging around. Tension that Tannion could feel, and he knew it wasn't going to go away fast. Even a few good busts attributed to Tannion weren't going to be enough. There would need to be something big. If anything, at least it was easier with Silton. He was too new to have the memory the other agents had.

Tannion picked up the phone on the second ring. The voice on the other end was very familiar to him, and it wasn't just because of the accent. Vladimir Potenlikov was someone people tended to remember, in person or on the phone.

"Vlad. I'm glad you caught me. Are you on a secure line?"

"We've swept the lines here at home and they're clean. How about your office phone? Would there be any reason they would be watching you?"

"I don't think so. The only agent who's been around for the past couple of days has been the kid, and I don't think they'd leave him here as a babysitter."

"I know this wasn't the way we had planned to talk, but I thought it would work if I called you knowing that our lines are clear here. Well, we aren't actually breaking any laws anyway, but if they find out we've been talking they might make it rough for you."

"Thanks for the concern, Vlad," Tannion told him. "That's something I don't think I'm going to lose any sleep over. How it is at your end?"

"They have a tight watch on a few of us. A couple guys you won't know, as well as Louisa, Mr. Philips, and me. They've been following us and as far as we can tell they've had undercover cops in some of our establishments. Mr. Philips has been keeping as clean as possible and making sure that he has lunch with a few respectable people. We've shut down a lot of the operation for now."

"I haven't heard anything at this end and they're still keeping me out of it. I'm pretty sure they still don't trust me."

"I would hope so," Potenlikov burst in. "Mr. Philips and I have talked about it, French, and you need to come back to work with us. We were good together. Mr. Philips doesn't like you working for the other side and would rather you worked for us. I don't think he trusts you as much as he used to. He sure doesn't like you working for the FBI."

"Thanks for the offer, Vlad, and tell Mr. Philips that he has nothing to worry about from me. I'm sorry to hear that he isn't sure that he can trust me. Try to reassure him for me. It would be nice to be back working with you again, but back then I was Victor French, and I was anonymous. Now they would know who I am and what I've done. On top of that, working with you and Mr. Philips would be a violation of my parole."

"Sorry, French. I hadn't thought of your parole. So what are you going to do?"

"There's not much I can do. If you keep going the way you are, it's quite likely they'll either have to give up or they just might ask me to help. I'm not sure what help they might think I could be. I'm also sure they know that I know things about your operation that might get them the go-ahead from a judge to set some surveillance equipment, phone taps, or even get search warrants. I'm sure there are a few places in town that you would rather they didn't get into."

"You've got that right," Potenlikov replied. "You haven't been around and we've changed our way of doing things and grown, as you know, but there are still some of the old holdings working and we would just as soon keep them that way, if you know what I mean. They just might put you in a tough spot, though."

"If that happens I can always quit," Tannion told him. "Rallin has already had a judge grant warrants here based on knowing that the information came from me, and I bet the director heard about that. If they asked me to get involved on this case, I just might have to quit."

"And then you can come and work for us," Potenlikov tried one more time. "That might be the only way that Mr. Philips would trust you again."

"I can understand that," Tannion told him. "I haven't seen him in years and I'm working for the FBI now, so I can see where he's coming from."

"I told him that it was you who warned us and that should have made him think differently, but it doesn't seem to have done the trick."

"That's okay, Vlad. He has his reasons for doubting me. I might doubt me too if I were in his shoes. Now, I think I should let you go, and I should get back to work in case Silton happens to show up."

"Okay, French, but please keep in touch. Anything that can help is appreciated by both Mr. Philips and me, and Louisa, too," he added almost as an afterthought.

With that, the line went dead and Tannion hung up the receiver. "I need to get a cell phone," he thought. It was just too risky talking over the line in his office. Tannion knew that things would eventually come to a head, and then he would have to decide where his loyalties lay. There was nothing he could do, and that was a foreign feeling. He could always do something before, but not this time. Frustration reigned supreme.

26

Jackson T. Philips was well known in Los Angeles. A few years earlier he was a midsize player in a big market, but big or small, he always looked like he belonged. Big, black, and beautiful was the way he was often described. Women loved him, and men knew to look the other way.

Philips and his right-hand man, Vladimir Potenlikov, were working LA as best they could before they met Jim Tannion, known to them as Victor French. Besides drugs and prostitution, they had illegal gambling and money lending, but they also ran to extortion when required. They, for the most part, ran a clean operation, and that was why Jim Tannion didn't finger them when he fingered almost everyone else in Los Angeles. That, and the fact that at least Potenlikov had become a friend, or as close to a friend as Tannion would allow.

Most people wrongly assumed that Tannion left Philips out of his information due to some sort of loyalty, or even friendship with Philips, but the real emotion behind the decision wasn't in that direction at all. Tannion knew that taking out a few or even all of the players in the criminal market in a big city like Los Angeles would only leave a gaping hole that would quickly be filled.

Very likely, the person or persons who would come in to fill that hole could and would be even worse. It was for that reason that Tannion left Philips alone. The clean operation Philips ran was what Tannion wanted.

Tannion also left word with Philips, in a rather cryptic message, that the reason he was left out was because he ran clean, and that he had better stay that way. Philips got the message and had run true to course, not so much because he was afraid of Tannion, although he had seen what he could do, but because it made good business sense.

That didn't mean he wouldn't break a leg or bash a head when it was required, but he had virtually eliminated any in-fighting, and he had also eliminated all sex slave traffic. A certain number of girls had been constantly on the move, often from Mexico, and they often went through Los Angeles on their way to wherever the product was desired, but the word got out that it wasn't to happen while Philips was around, and it ended.

Although there was good money in human trafficking, Philips found it distasteful and would not allow it on his turf. Anyone found trafficking young girls he quickly put out of business. It was this ideal that Tannion knew about and which had kept Philips out of the net that had captured most of the elite in Los Angeles' crime world only a little over five years earlier.

Now it looked like the FBI had come knocking, and Philips knew if they looked hard and long enough, and spent the money that could be spent, eventually they would find something. As legitimate as many of his businesses were, and as close to the top of the political echelon his friends might be, the FBI didn't care.

Potenlikov told him everything that Tannion had relayed to him and what had been happening on the streets. The tail wasn't always easy to spot, but often he saw what he thought was someone following his movements. It didn't matter if he saw them, as he knew they were there.

Philips made sure they saw some interesting sights like watching him having lunch with the chief of police or the district attorney, or going to the Lakers game and having front-row seats beside some of Hollywood's elite.

He only hoped that the FBI would get tired of chasing someone who looked as clean as he did and move on to easier prey. Every day that he had to keep some of his operation shut down was costing him money. Even worse was the potential loss of control in the city where his word was gospel. Shutting down made him look weak in the eyes of those who would love to take over.

Having Tannion on the inside might help, but Potenlikov told him the FBI were keeping Tannion out of the loop, so unless they brought him in, he might not be of much help. How much help he could be was an unknown. Then there was the question of where Tannion's loyalties lay. Philips knew that Tannion had become close to the FBI agent who hired him, and that Agent Rallin had visited him in prison often. He also knew that Louisa could be a wild card. Philips didn't think that the feelings between the two of them had ever really ended.

There were too many unknowns for Philips to feel comfortable, but for now there wasn't any way he could strike back. He was in Los Angeles and Tannion was in New York, but Rallin's team was too close. Potenlikov told Philips what Tannion had said about the job offer to come back and work with them and although he knew what the answer would be, he didn't have to like it.

Could he trust Tannion if the FBI did finally call him in? Could they successfully stay out of the FBI's grasp for as long as it took for the investigation to blow over? Philips didn't know the answers and he didn't like it. Philips always liked to be in control and hated that out–of-control feeling, and that feeling was coming on. Coming on strong.

27

Tannion was surprised when the knock at his office door was immediately followed by Mike Rallin sticking his head around the corner. "You got a minute?" Rallin asked. Tannion had no idea that Rallin was back in the office, but he was glad to see him and waved him in.

Rallin sat down in the only other chair in the room and looked Tannion in the eye. He didn't say a word for a few seconds, but Tannion wasn't biting. They might know each other well enough to withstand moments of silence, but Tannion knew it to be an old interrogation trick.

Most people don't really like the sound of silence. It makes them very uncomfortable, which often results in them filling the void with information they wouldn't normally have given out.

After the few seconds passed and Tannion had only given Rallin a look indicating that he should go on, Rallin knew he had to say what he had come to say. He was only hoping that Tannion would give him an easy out by asking a question. Almost any question would have done the trick.

"Jim. I need to tell you the truth about what has been going on around here. I assume you know that we've left you out of the mix for the past few weeks, but it's time to bring you in."

"I've kind of noticed that, yes," answered Tannion. It had been at least three weeks since he had warned Potenlikov.

"Well, sorry, but we didn't have a lot of choice. The director of the FBI has given us a high priority assignment. An assignment we couldn't say no to, and probably one that I should have been expecting if I had put any thought into it at all."

"You're going after Philips," Tannion said simply.

Rallin gave Tannion a quick, startled look, but almost immediately he composed his face and a small smile appeared. "I should have known you would know all about it," he told Tannion, and he reminded himself not ever to underestimate Tannion. That would be a great way to end up in the same place they were in a few years back, when they had no idea where he was.

"I have my sources," Tannion told him. "I understand you aren't doing so well, and that's why you have come to me, correct?"

"You might say that. The boss doesn't know I've done this yet, but I'm pretty sure that he waited until you had been working with us for a couple months before he sprang this on me. A couple months to see if you would be of any use to us at all, and I assume, based on the information that you have already supplied us with, he thinks you're on our side."

Rallin went on. "Am I correct in assuming that at this point anything to do with Philips would be touchy for you, and possibly a grey area as far as your loyalty is concerned?"

"I'm not so sure I can tell you that, Mike," answered Tannion. "I've thought about it and I still have feelings for

Louisa and I wouldn't want to see her hurt. Taking out the Russian would hurt her, and I consider Vlad to be a friend. On the other hand, we both know that Mr. Philips is just another crook. I could put him away, but then the person who would step in might be a lot worse than he is."

Tannion continued. "I bet if you ask for crime statistics in Los Angeles, you'll see that the number of major violent crimes has gone down since he took over more than five years ago. The number of gang-related murders and kidnappings at least, and probably even assaults."

"That might prove to be correct, Jim," answered Rallin. "But so what? Does that make him any less a crook? Is it only a matter of time before he falls into the same pattern of those who came before him? Frankly, I'm surprised that the power of what he has hasn't completely gone to his head already. It usually does."

"You might have Potenlikov to thank for that. If there's anything Vlad has, it's a steady, if not slightly lackluster, personality. If Mr. Philips had some funny ideas, it's likely Vlad wouldn't feel good about it and eventually talk some sense into him. Also, I did leave Mr. Philips with sort of a warning, and he knew that I would get out of jail eventually."

"So, let's say that we're able to keep Potenlikov and his wife out of the trouble, and only hit Philips. What would be your opinion then?" Rallin asked, hoping to find an angle that Tannion wouldn't have any problem with.

"I don't think that would be possible. When the shit hits the fan, it doesn't really care which direction it flies in, and I know for sure that you could never get Vlad to give evidence on Mr. Philips. They've been through too much together already for that. Any hit on Mr. Philips would include a hit on Potenlikov, and I can't see myself being involved in that."

"So what can we do, Jim? The director wants us to get something on Philips. It's almost as if he has a grudge against him. I can't see this case being closed if we fail. It would only be given to someone who doesn't know the same things that we do, and that would be worse. It wouldn't be good for Philips, but it also wouldn't be good for our team. This is what we're supposed to be good at."

"My guess is that you won't like my idea, but I'm going to tell you anyway." Tannion had taken some time to think, and he hoped what he had come up with would work. The first step was getting it past Rallin, and that wasn't going to be easy. "We need to bring Mr. Philips into the plan," he said.

"Christ, you're kidding me. God damn right I don't like it. How could I? Shit. Talk about setting us up to fail. If we did that and the director found out, we would all end up in jail. Besides, what good would it do?"

"First, if we do it right, the director never needs to know. Second, I'm not so sure that Mr. Philips would go for it anyway, but it never hurts to ask, and third, if it works, then we all win. Except for maybe Mr. Philips, who would end up with a bit of a mark against him."

"What the hell. I can't see us ever going in that direction, but talk is cheap. Fill me in on your idea. What have you got?"

Tannion took the better part of the next half hour filling Rallin in on what was only a rudimentary plan prior to the meeting, but had developed more and more as the meeting continued.

If they could talk Philips into it, it just might work. Philips would take a blow and maybe spend a little time in jail, but more likely he would just pay a heavy fine, get a suspended sentence, and be on the street as soon as his lawyer posted bail.

The reason Tannion liked the idea more as he told it to Rallin was that it didn't hurt anyone he didn't want hurt, and it left Philips in charge, or at least it might look to him as if he were in charge. It also left Philips with an even greater warning to keep it clean than he'd had before. It might just work. Now Tannion had to talk Rallin into it. Rallin hummed and hawed for a while and stewed over the plan, but in the end, he made the only decision that seemed to be available.

"It might work, Jim."

"Of course it will. As long as we all play our parts."

"I don't know Jim. It's got more chance of blowing up on us."

"Do you have anything else?"

"Okay. I'm not sure it will work but no, I don't have a better idea," Rallin said.

"This could be the only way."

"It goes against everything I've worked on, but I'm running out of ideas. I can't bring you in and expect you to do what the director hopes you will. At least a meeting with Philips can't hurt."

"No it can't hurt."

"Okay. Set it up."

"I'll call Vlad. That's all it should take."

28

Rallin knew that he had to keep tight-lipped about what Tannion had told him and what the plan had come to. He didn't like to keep his team out of the loop, and it felt very wrong to lie to Pansloski, his partner and friend. The consequences were worth the silence, however.

Rallin told Pansloski to work on a file that had come up in New York. He did tell him that he had asked Tannion for help and that Tannion had tentatively agreed to come to Los Angeles, which would allow Pansloski to stay in New York. Having Tannion in LA would free Pansloski up, and Rallin knew his friend was tired of the hunt and would jump at the chance to sleep in his own bed. That was as close to the truth as he could tell him at this time; not really a lie, just not the entire story.

Jeff Martin was still in Los Angeles and there was no story that Rallin could come up with that could get him out of the way. He could be brought into the loop, although Rallin thought that Martin might just believe that Tannion was willing to help, but that might be stretching it. Martin was a good cop with good instincts and would have real concerns with Tannion's loyalty.

When Tannion and Rallin landed at the Los Angeles International Airport, Jeff Martin was there to pick them up.

"Good to have you on this one, Tannion," he said, as he shook Tannion's hand. Tannion almost sent Martin to sleep, and would have, if they were back in a hotel room or where he could nod off without anyone, including Martin himself, thinking that anything was out of the ordinary.

"It might come to that eventually," Tannion thought.

Rallin wasn't aware of what Tannion might want to do or could do to Martin, and Tannion intended to keep it that way. "Maybe the stomach flu might be easier," Tannion thought.

Martin drove the three of them to the FBI building that contained the small offices they had been working out of. Once they got there, they met with the team members who weren't out on watch. They needed to understand where Tannion stood, and they would probably believe whatever story Rallin chose to tell. He gave them the 'I'm here to help' story, and they went about their routine business.

For Rallin, that meant time with Tannion in his office. Tannion made the call that would set up the meeting. Tannion called Potenlikov, and after a few moments he was speaking to Jackson T. Philips.

"French. Vlad told me that you would be calling. I didn't know whether to believe him or not. I should have known better than to not trust him."

"True, Mr. Philips." Tannion had never gotten past a boss/employee situation with Philips, even after they had worked very closely together. Mr. Philips was all that Tannion had ever called him, and it seemed appropriate at this time too. Philips didn't waste time with any further pleasantries. He was all business.

"Vlad tells me that you have a proposition for me that might work for both our benefit."

"It just might work, but a lot of it will be up to you. I can't talk about it over the phone, and there is the problem of you being tailed everywhere you go. We need to meet without the rest of the team knowing about it. There's a room at the Triple T Hotel under the name of Jackson Smith, and we'll be in it at eight o'clock tomorrow morning. I'll let Vlad know the room number after we are done."

"It will be just Mike Rallin and me. Bring Vlad and no one else, but make sure you lose your tail. It isn't critical, but best if they don't even know about the hotel."

"Why would I want to do this, French? What's in it for me?"

"Please, Mr. Philips. Bear with me for now and it will all come out when we meet," Tannion told him. He knew that Philips would probably be reluctant at first, but with the FBI on his tail, Tannion was sure that Philips would come around eventually.

Philips said they would be there. He gave the phone back to Potenlikov and Tannion filled him in on the details. They were to walk in as if they owned the place and not to let anyone at the hotel know what room they were going to. This included taking the elevator to two floors above their floor and walking two flights of stairs down, so anyone in the lobby wouldn't know exactly what floor they were on. Potenlikov would come first, followed by Philips.

The biggest problem would be to ensure that no one knew they were meeting, but even if they were followed, Tannion and Rallin would be in the room ahead of the meeting time and would leave an hour after it ended. Martin might be a problem, but he would be given a job to do that would take him out of the picture for a while.

Even if Philips and Potenlikov were followed, no one would know who they were meeting with unless they waited to see who left the hotel. Rallin would ensure that didn't happen. The consequences were too great.

29

Philips looked across his desk at Potenlikov. There were no smiles in the room this morning. Things were getting harder and harder with the feds looking over their shoulders all the time, and now things might have just gotten worse, if that were even possible.

French, aka Tannion, had been a good person to have around a few years back, but then he did what he did to the crime scene in LA. What did that mean today? What was he bringing to the table? Could he be trusted? All questions that Philips had, but answers he didn't.

Potenlikov tried to tell Philips that French could be trusted, but Philips wasn't buying it at the moment. Too many people were still behind bars because of him, and more than a few were dead after trying to kill him in prison. Philips had been the one to put an end to the hits on Tannion when he was inside. Not just because it was the right thing to do for Tannion, but because he knew that it was only going to get more people killed.

Tannion had nine lives, or so it seemed. Philips had seen Tannion in action and knew that Tannion's skills would likely keep him alive and would probably end the lives of whoever was sent after him in prison. Philips' control over any contracts might have ended when Tannion was released.

There were a number of people still in LA who would be very happy to get their hands on Tannion if they knew he was in town. The problem in prison was the choice of weapons that were available. There were no restrictions in the outside world. It wouldn't come down to a knife fight on the streets of Los Angeles.

Now Tannion wanted to meet and Philips was having a problem understanding what kind of outcome could possibly be to his benefit, especially when the other man coming with Tannion was an FBI agent, the same FBI agent who had caught Tannion those few years ago.

Philips left the office at exactly seven thirty. The limo was waiting for him downstairs, and he stepped into it with a look of going somewhere important. Two of Rallin's men watching it happen readied themselves to begin what had been for weeks nothing but a waste of time.

Philips would go to some office building for some unknown meeting, and after a couple of hours he would come out, get back in the limo, and go back to the office where he started. Nothing to put in a report worth reading, with no way of knowing who he met with or what was said. Their hands were tied.

Philips' car rounded the corner and without any warning the back doors opened. Philips got out of the left side, and they could see Potenlikov get out of the right side. They both walked a few feet in opposite directions, with Potenlikov coming directly back towards the car that the FBI sat in. Before he got there, however, he stuck his hand in the air and a cab stopped and picked him up.

At the same time, Philips was picked up by a car a few feet past the limo. With Potenlikov walking towards them, the men had taken their eyes off Philips for a second, and although they were able to spot him just as he got in the car, they couldn't follow them both.

Philips' car had already gone around the corner and was out of sight. They immediately radioed their backup, who were in position along the track that was expected, and were a few blocks further on. They gave them the number of the cab that Potenlikov was in and they then headed towards where they last saw Philips.

Philips had known the car would be there, and had jumped in as quickly as possible, but when the car went around the next corner there was a spot where he jumped out and he was able to duck behind a building.

He saw the FBI go by as it followed the car he had just jumped out of, and a minute later a second car, going in the opposite direction, stopped and picked him up. He was pretty sure that he was safe and not being followed, but he had the car take a circuitous route to the hotel where they would be meeting with Rallin and Tannion. He found he was having fun with the cloak and dagger routine; it had been a long time. Now he hoped Potenlikov was having the same luck.

Potenlikov went less than a block in the taxi, and when he jumped out he was immediately picked up by one of their cars and they headed in the opposite direction as well. If the second FBI car had been a couple of blocks earlier they might have seen the switch, but when they saw the cab coming towards them they could see that it was empty.

A quick call to the first FBI car confirmed the cab number and they knew they had lost him. As much as they were pissed at themselves for getting complacent and they were pretty sure that Rallin would chew them out, they were almost happy that finally something seemed to be happening. They were getting tired of chasing cars that went nowhere.

If Philips and Potenlikov were pulling these types of tricks, that meant that the word must be out and they knew they were being followed. Made sense, after all, the FBI had been at it for weeks and they were surprised it had taken as long as it had. Their report would be a little interesting for the first time since they had started.

30

The Triple T Hotel was small, with only seven floors, but it was out of the way, and not used by the hookers in the area. Although not a five-star hotel, it had been well maintained over the years. When Rallin asked for the key at the front desk, he could see the care that had gone into the lobby, the counter, and the computer system that sat behind it.

"I thought I was getting a seedier hotel," he thought as he walked to the stairs. He knew that Tannion was already on the floor, as he had walked in about ten minutes early, but he would be waiting for Rallin to pick up the key. It was still only seven fifteen. The hallway was empty when Rallin stuck the key in the door, but before he opened it, Tannion was standing beside him.

Rallin hadn't seen him standing in a doorway a few feet the other direction from the stairs, and he hadn't made a sound as he came up behind Rallin. Rallin looked at him and gave him an appreciative smile. If he could get up on Rallin as easy as that, he had to be good. Rallin had never really thought of Tannion in any police-like, or even criminal-like, capacity before. Rallin knew he was strong enough to lift a car off a kid, and maybe more, but that was about all he knew about Tannion's skills.

Tannion liked the feeling of putting Rallin off his game. Rallin might almost be Tannion's friend, but he was still a cop, FBI for that matter. That meant Tannion didn't know where he might stand in certain situations, and especially where he might stand if Rallin ever found out the truth about him.

Tannion knew that for the most part Rallin was a very stand up sort of cop, despite the issue Tannion had already gotten away with. Rallin had been able to hide the dead guy that was found close to the halfway house, so maybe he wasn't as by-the-book as Tannion had thought. Still, it was a good feeling to see the look on his face.

They both took a look at the hotel room to size up the meeting that was going to take place. Where would they sit? There was the usual queen-size bed, and there was a small table and a chair. There was another chair over by the window with a small desk that barely held the lamp that was on it.

Rallin quickly crossed the room and closed the curtains. The curtains were of a heavy material that would not only block anyone seeing in, but would block out all the light at night and even most of it during the day. The room was quite dark, and Rallin turned the lights on as soon as the drapes were closed.

A quick look at Tannion and the decision was made. Tannion pulled the two chairs together at the end of the bed and made them ready for company. Rallin and Tannion would sit side by side on the bed, and Philips and Potenlikov would get the chairs. There was just enough room so when they sat down their knees wouldn't touch. Neither of the spots were that great, but they had instantly decided to put

Philips at as much ease as possible, and that meant giving him the best chair. Then they waited.

At one minute to eight, according to Tannion's watch, there was a light knock at the door. He went over to open the door while Rallin took up a position with his hand on his gun. He didn't think there would be any need for it, but he wasn't taking any chances. From past experience he knew the type of people they were dealing with, even if Tannion had told him that these two were different.

Vladimir Potenlikov quickly took Tannion's hand in a firm handshake and almost gave him a bear hug. He knew that he was supposed to make it look like they hadn't seen each other in years, but as much as Potenlikov was a hugger amongst his friends, he couldn't hug Tannion in front of the FBI agent standing in the corner even if he were faking a first meeting. Tannion introduced Rallin to Potenlikov and they sat looking at each other, but stayed silent, as they waited for Philips to arrive.

Potenlikov knew that he would beat Philips to the meeting, as they had that planned. He told Tannion and Rallin that they had decided that Philips should be ten minutes late to ensure they were not seen going into the same building together, or even close together. Potenlikov had also used a back door that he was familiar with. Philips would use the front door.

At almost a quarter after eight, there was a loud knock on the door. Philips didn't do anything halfway, and that included his knock. Rallin quickly ushered him in and closed the door behind him. Philips saw Tannion standing over by the bed beside Potenlikov and greeted him with a large smile.

"French. I didn't think I would ever see you again," Philips told him. "I certainly didn't expect to see you under these circumstances. I expected I would end up going to your funeral."

"Good to see you too, Mr. Philips," Tannion replied. "I'm glad that we get to meet again, even under these circumstances." Tannion went on to introduce Philips to Mike Rallin.

"Agent Rallin. I know who you are and I know about your team, but I am not so sure what you think is going to come out of this meeting." The smile had disappeared from Philips' face as soon as he turned to Rallin. There might have been a slight hint of hatred flash across Philips' face, but he quickly controlled his emotions and went on in a business-like fashion. He showed no sign of fear.

Tannion showed Philips and Potenlikov to their chairs, and he and Rallin sat on the edge of the bed facing the chairs. Tannion could tell that Philips was almost physically holding himself in check. His first reaction was always to be in control and that meant he was the one to talk, but he obviously thought that it would be best to stay quiet at this time. Having the FBI in the room will do that to a person.

Rallin started. "Mr. Philips. I understand your concern, and frankly, I find myself in the same position as you do. Jim Tannion here has talked me into this meeting and I'm not so sure what he is going to say. I'm going to let him say it, but you do need to know that no matter what he says, I will back him up."

He directed his next line at Tannion. "I mean that Jim, but there's a line that even I can't cross. I'll let you know if you get close."

"Fair enough, Mike," Tannion started, and then turned to address both Philips and Potenlikov.

"First, let me say that we all know what's happening out in the real world. We aren't under any false ideas as to what kind of business either of the two groups in this room is in. With that said, we should be able to start at someplace that we all understand."

Tannion looked first at Philips, and then at Potenlikov, before finally looking at Rallin. The silence was loud to their ears as they all waited for what he would say next. "Mr. Philips, you're aware that the FBI is breathing down your neck, but you also know that they're getting nowhere. That is where they think I come in."

Rallin opened his mouth as if to say something, and then thought better of it. Tannion saw it, but went on.

"There are people in the FBI who think I know your operation here in Los Angeles well enough that I should be able to go in front of a judge and give them enough to ensure they can either get wiretaps or a search warrant, or at least enough to get the FBI started. At this stage they're struggling and have very little to go on."

"The fact is, it's been more than five years since I knew what was going on in LA, but I'm pretty sure they're right. There are a couple judges who want to get something on you, Mr. Philips, and they would jump at the right informa-tion. The problem is they won't do anything unless the info is perfect. I think I can give that to them. There are bound to be a few of your places that haven't changed in the last five years."

"But I won't do that," he continued. "I think of Vlad as a friend, and his wife is someone I don't want to see hurt, and hurting Vlad would hurt her. However, I know that the FBI won't just go away, and until they find something they will be on your tail, and I doubt that your operation can stand that kind of surveillance for too much longer."

"You're right there, French," Potenlikov piped in. Philips gave him a glare that told him not to open his mouth again.

"I thought I would be," Tannion told him, and ignored the look that Philips had given Potenlikov. "So with the FBI on your back but getting nothing, they're getting frustrated and with them constantly watching you, your business is suffering. Neither group is happy with what is happening. I think I have a solution."

Philips had grown increasingly tense during Tannion's speech, and with the last line he suddenly stood up. "Why do you think I would want to continue this conversation, French? The only thing you can possibly come up with can't be good for my operation. It can't be good for me."

Tannion stood up and put his hands out in a defensive position, although he wasn't expecting Philips to physically attack. "Wait, Mr. Philips. Just listen to what I have to say and then you can make up your mind."

With that Philips reluctantly took his seat and looked Tannion in the eye. "Okay. I'll do it your way for now, but it had better be good," he told Tannion, through tightly clenched teeth.

"Okay. I'll continue," Tannion said as he sat down, with calm back in the room. Rallin and Potenlikov hadn't moved, as they seemed to be entranced by listening to Tannion speak.

"First, Mr. Philips, there must be someone out there who's working around the edge of your business that you want or need to shut down."

"Yeah, there's more than a couple," Philips admitted. "There always are."

"Okay. So let's say that you supply us with enough information on one of these guys to allow the FBI to get a search warrant to go in and do some search and seizure, thinking that I gave up some information from my past about you. If they find out you had nothing to do with it, then I can simply say that it has been a few years and my information is a little out of date."

Philips' head was moving up and down and Tannion could see the thought process hard at work. If Philips was anything, he was smart. He could see a good thing a mile away, and all of a sudden this was sounding as least a little like a good thing. More than he had thought it would.

"If they don't find a connection to you, the FBI might not pull back, but it might just be possible that they'll be appeased enough to ease up on you and go on to different fish," Tannion continued.

Mike Rallin spoke up at that moment. "I don't think so, Jim. My feeling is if Mr. Philips doesn't at least have something on the books against him then the director won't be satisfied."

He then addressed Philips. "He would prefer to put you away for life, but he might settle for something on a rap sheet. He would really love some jail time."

Philips looked Rallin in the eye and a slow smile started to split his face. "I think I like this guy, French," he told them. "I see, however, where this is going, and it might just work. By putting the heat onto a competitor it will help me out, and after you scratch my back I can try to scratch yours."

The smile on Philips' face slowly faded. "I won't do any jail time, though," he stated firmly.

"But you see an opportunity, don't you, Mr. Philips? Might you have something in mind?" Tannion asked.

"I just might," was Philips' answer. "Let's meet here again in two days at the same time, and I will bring some information on the guy I would like you to hit, and I'll bring something you can use on me. It won't be big, and as I said, I won't spend any time in jail. I'll talk to my lawyers and then we'll talk. In the meantime, any chance of having your guys take some time off?"

"Afraid not," answered Rallin. "Anything outside of the routine we've set up will ring alarm bells, and I can't chance that. Martin and Pansloski are both good operators and they'd know something was up right away."

"No problem. Just thought I'd ask."

Philips and Potenlikov got up and headed for the door. They opened the door and Philips went out without a backwards glance or a goodbye. Potenlikov closed the door behind Philips and stayed in the room. Ten minutes later he shook both Tannion's and Rallin's hands and he left as well.

Tannion and Rallin looked at each other and knew they had an hour to kill in the hotel room before they could leave; an hour to discuss and postulate as to what and who Philips was going to bring in. Tannion had been out of the picture long enough to not even know the names of most, if not all, of the players in Los Angeles other than Philips, and as such he had no idea who Philips would give them. He told Rallin what he didn't know.

"It could be anyone, Mike."

"As long as he comes up with someone big enough."

"I know what you mean, but I have no idea who it might be."

"Maybe Potenlikov will give you an idea."

"Maybe, but I suspect we'll both have to wait until the next meeting."

"Can you talk to Potenlikov and push him to someone big enough?"

"I'm not sure I know anyone big enough anymore."

"Fair enough. I know a few names you could ask about."

Rallin wasn't that concerned with who the guy was as long as he was big enough to make a difference. Rallin was more concerned with what Philips would give of himself. He didn't have the same opinion of Philips that Tannion had, and as far as he was concerned, Philips was just another crook who belonged behind bars. He would concede one thing to Tannion though, and that was taking out someone only left a void that would be filled, and Philips would leave a big hole.

If Philips were anywhere near as good as Tannion thought he was, then having Philips to continue to fill the void would be as good as any, but the director wouldn't see it that way. Rallin had to catch Philips with something, and it had to be enough to convince the director to shut the investigation down.

Tannion thought that this just might work. Rallin wasn't so sure.

31

The phone rang in Tannion's room early the next morning. He had made sure that he was staying at a different hotel than Rallin, which went against Rallin's wishes, but it was the only way he could ensure that he could speak privately with either Philips or Potenlikov. Other than Rallin, only Potenlikov knew which hotel Tannion was in.

The large voice of Potenlikov filled Tannion's ear. Philips needed a little more time to talk to his lawyers and to ensure that he had enough information on the mark they were going to hand over.

Tannion called Rallin and told him the meeting would be the same time a day later than planned, at the same place, without stating any names. Tannion thought he was probably being paranoid, but he never knew who might be listening. Rallin should be the most trusted guy in the FBI, but that didn't mean that he couldn't be targeted.

When the day arrived, at about seven o'clock, Tannion let himself into room 305 of the Triple T Hotel. Rallin had left him the key after the first meeting. About ten minutes later, Rallin knocked on the door and before Tannion could open it, he walked in.

At almost exactly eight o'clock, Vladimir Potenlikov knocked on the door, and this time Tannion was ready for him and swung the door open just enough for him to squeeze his big frame in without anyone outside the door seeing anyone inside.

"Still being very careful, I see," Potenlikov noted.

"This has to go down right, especially now that we've gone this far. Word getting out would ruin the plan and would only lead to more problems for Philips," Rallin told him.

Tannion could tell by the look on Potenlikov's face that he wasn't impressed by Rallin's tone of voice and Potenlikov might have said something if Tannion hadn't jumped in.

"You know we have to be careful here, Vlad, and keep in mind that what we're doing is to the benefit of us all, and I include Mr. Philips in that."

At about ten after eight, a knock on the door was quickly followed by Philips walking in. The four participants sat in the exact positions they had three days earlier, but there was something different in the way Philips was acting. This time it was Philips who was in charge. It was Philips who spoke first.

"I've got a name for you and enough information that you should be able to put this guy away for a long time. There's no way he can be connected to me and that's just the way I like it."

Philips handed Rallin a slip of paper. Rallin took a quick look and saw a name and a couple of addresses. Philips picked up where he had left off.

"My lawyers and I have discussed this thoroughly, and after you pick this guy up and can't make the connection your boss wants, then this is what we have for you."

Philips continued. "First, according to my lawyers, I'll not spend any time in jail based on this information, and that's the way it has to be. I'll give you an address that you can walk into without a warrant and find the evidence that you need and then if you arrest me…" Philips hesitated for a second, and then went on to say that in no circumstances would he be subjected to handcuffs. He would only be asked to turn himself in at the precinct nearest to him.

Rallin was getting a little edgy, and Tannion could see that he was going to say something that might not sit well with Philips, so again he jumped in. "Okay, Mr. Philips. What are we going to find at that address?"

"You'll find it's a pet store, but when you look in the back you'll find some animals that are not legal to be imported into the United States. The pet store is registered to one of my companies and that will link to me."

Rallin couldn't take it anymore. "Illegal animals. Shit, you want us to have the director of the FBI take the heat off you because we caught you with illegal animals?"

Tannion was worried about Philips' reaction to Rallin's outburst, and was very surprised to see Philips sit back in his chair and smile.

"Agent Rallin," he started. "You needed a way in, and that's what I am giving you. With the fact that you supposedly have something on me, it should give you the impetus to get a search warrant for my house, my office, and the warehouse that the pet store uses."

Rallin looked at Philips and saw the logic in what he was saying. Philips went on and his tone changed. "You will find that I'm a well-respected, legitimate businessman in this town. When your men come to my house and office, you'll find nothing, as there is nothing there to find. The warehouse will have a few more of the same or similar animals, and the manager will bear the brunt of the search. He is willing to stand trial, and as a result I will not."

"If the district attorney decides to press charges against me, I'll deny knowing anything about the animals and at worst, even if convicted, I'll pay a fine. That's what you get. Take it or leave it."

Philips stood up and left the room. Potenlikov had nothing to say, and waited for a good ten minutes, then left as well, leaving Rallin and Tannion with a lot to talk about.

"Will it work?" Tannion asked Rallin.

"He's a smart son-of-a-bitch, Jim. There's no reason why it won't work. We get just a little on him and use it to find out that he is exactly what he says he is, and that's a legitimate businessman. After we search his office and house and find nothing, he'll come off looking even better than when we started. The director will have to back off. He won't have any choice, and if we do anything further, Philips can go to his friends and complain about FBI tactics. I'm not so sure his friends don't include the governor, let alone the mayor and chief of police. For sure we know he's in with the district attorney. The director will have to back off and we can go back to New York and the work we should be doing. Of course it will work."

"He's smart alright, but what if our guys actually find something in his house or office? What if the director wants to get a warrant for additional warehouses or something that's in Philips name, but is not as clean? You and I both know that he isn't that clean."

Rallin had to laugh. "Shit. That's an understatement if there ever was one. I think Philips and his lawyers will be able to look after themselves at that point. I also think that if Philips wants to look clean he can damn well look clean. Look at what we've found in the last month. Nothing."

32

Three days later an FBI team led by Rallin hit the home of Hank Pearsol. Tannion was left back at the hotel and was only aware of the time the hit was going down. He had never heard of Hank Pearsol.

Pearsol had come up from the ranks of another group on the east side, which had only grown big enough to be a nuisance to Philips. Rallin would have liked to have had a bigger name and he knew a couple that they could have been given, but the information Philips gave them was on Pearsol. Philips obviously had his reasons for wanting to have him off the streets.

The information was accurate, and Pearsol was picked up with a few of his men with enough guns and drugs to ensure that even a good lawyer wouldn't be able to keep him out of jail. Then came the raid on the pet store.

The raid on the pet store came as the result of an anonymous phone call that said there were animals in the back of the store that shouldn't be there. Someone who said they were from an animal rights group had made the call, and the police sent a car.

The two uniforms who went to the pet store found the animals they were supposed to find and the next day Rallin got a call. It hadn't taken long to track down the fact that the pet store belonged to a company owned by Philips, and the entire LA police force was aware that Rallin had been given the task of bringing Philips in.

Rallin made the call to Philips' office asking for him to come to the FBI building for questioning. He would have loved to send a car and put Philips in handcuffs, but that was not the deal they had made, so Philips was allowed to come in on his own. Even without the deal the best Rallin could do was ask him to come in. At three that afternoon a black limo pulled up outside the FBI building, and Philips and his lawyer walked in.

Rallin was called to the front and he had Philips and his lawyer follow him back to his office. Everyone played their part very well. The lawyer said his part, and Rallin indicated that charges might be pending against the store manager, and maybe against Philips.

After about twenty minutes Philips and his lawyer left the building and got back into the limo. Rallin made the call and put the paperwork in order to have a search warrant issued on Philips' house and on his office. At this point he wasn't supposed to be aware of the warehouse that was also up for a search. That would come later.

Rallin took part in the search of both the office and the house. By the time that was complete, the warehouse was discovered, a warrant granted, and an arrangement was made to search it as well. When nothing was found at Philips' office or home, and only a few additional illegal animals at the warehouse, Rallin had a meeting with the district attorney to determine what charges should be laid as a result.

The decision didn't surprise Rallin. The manager of the pet store had taken all the heat and was to be charged with a minor felony involving transport and sale of illegal animals. No charges would be laid against Philips, as he was an unknowing and unwilling partner to any crime that took place. His lawyer had done his job.

With that out of the way, the only thing left was to call the director of the FBI. The fact that Philips gave several interviews on television pronouncing his innocence and telling everyone how legitimate he was, as well as the television reporters talking about his generous donations to charity and extolling his virtues in general, left the FBI director no other alternative. He called off the hunt.

Pansloski and Martin found themselves on the next plane back to New York. Tannion was given a couple of days off when it was determined that they had something on Philips and didn't need his help anymore.

The plan had worked as well as could have been expected and it was back to life as they knew it. Tannion stuck around for a while in case he was asked to step back in, which was the official line, but Rallin wanted him there in case they needed to deal with Philips again. Officially, Rallin was the only agent still working the Philips file to clean up a couple of loose ends and to hand any information to the Los Angeles Bureau. It was over.

33

Tannion wasn't involved in any of the FBI action over the couple of days that it took place. As a civilian advisor he was not allowed to take part in any of the actual police work, and that was okay with him. He had a couple of days off in Los Angeles before he had to head back to New York and he was going to make the most of them.

As French, in what seemed another lifetime, he had seen a lot of LA and he saw a couple of days off as a chance for him to wander around and hit some of his old haunts. Most of the bars were still using the same names in the same spots, and he occasionally would see someone he knew from before. He didn't have the long hair and beard he'd had then, and he was a few years older, so they didn't recognize him from a distance, but he knew them.

He knew it was better to lie low, and even if he were visiting his old haunts, he couldn't just walk up to people and say hello. He also had to stay away from Philips, Potenlikov, and Louisa. They were likely being watched, and having Tannion show up might be taken the wrong way. The FBI, in their minds, had Tannion on their side and there was no reason to change that.

Tannion was careful to avoid people who might recognize him, that is, until he walked into the King's Head. It was as if the years had rolled back. Sitting over at the usual table was a small squirrely-looking guy who Tannion recognized immediately. Six might have gotten a little older, but he hadn't really changed a bit.

Tannion walked over to the table where Six was and sat down. Six immediately looked up to see who was interfering with his space, and, seeing a guy much bigger than him, he proceeded to get up and walk away.

Tannion grabbed him by the arm and sat him back down. "Six. Where're you going?"

Six sat back down, as he had no choice with Tannion's firm grip on his arm, and he was about to shout something when the voice he had just heard registered. "French. Is that you?" he asked.

"It is, Six, but keep your voice down. I don't need to broadcast that fact to the entire bar." Six suddenly remembered and realized why Tannion wouldn't want to be known there and he quickly dropped his voice.

"You're out of jail. I didn't think I would ever see you again."

"I didn't expect to be spending any time in LA either Six, but things just sort of happened."

"You mean like they did for you a few years back," Six stated, but leaned back just far enough to try to keep out of Tannion's way in case that was what he needed to do. He had seen Tannion in action and knew better than to get on his bad side.

Tannion saw what Six was doing, and he smiled at him and said, "Don't worry, Six. What happened back then was a long time ago, and not something that I truly wanted to do, but I wasn't given much choice."

Six grinned back, realizing that his old friend was still his old friend. "You sure as hell did a number on a bunch of guys, French, and your pal the Russian and his boss came out of it smelling like a rose. Nobody touched them and then they just walked in and took over. You can hardly spit on the street without asking them for permission."

"I didn't plan it that way, but if there is someone controlling the streets I would just as soon it was Potenlikov working for Mr. Philips, if you know what I mean."

"The streets have got a lot safer as a result, I have to admit, and yet they still let you know who's boss. A few heads still get busted, but nobody gets killed any more. There hasn't been a real turf war in a long time."

"Have you had your head busted lately, Six?"

"You know how it is, French. I do what I got to do."

"You've been gambling again haven't you, Six?"

"Only a little, but I'll get it back, no problem. I always do."

"How much, Six? How much do you owe, and is it run by Philips?"

"Hey, don't worry. It's nothing," Six told him, but Tannion was having nothing of it. He grabbed his friend by the shirt collar and pulled him close to look directly into his eyes.

"How much?"

"Three thousand," Six finally said, and then he couldn't look Tannion in the eye.

"And it's Philips, right? Does he still use the stooges?"

"They were around yesterday and I was able to give them a couple hundred to keep them off my back for a couple of days and then I can get the rest. He's really not that bad, French. Philips, that is. He lets me pay a little at a time as long as I pay, and he never sends the big Russian anymore. Just the stooges."

"That's awful nice of him," Tannion told him with enough sarcasm that even Six caught it.

"No, French. I mean it. Things have been pretty good since you left. Not that bad at all."

"Maybe you should get smarter, Six. Next time you see them, tell them that French said you need a job."

Tannion had brought a fair amount of cash to LA, but not enough bail Six out, and he would need some to get back to New York. He dropped five hundred bucks on the table when he said his goodbye. He noticed the two men sitting a couple of tables away from where he was talking to Six, but paid them no attention. If he had thought more about them at the time he might not have let them leave the bar.

As soon as Tannion left, Six was paid a visit. The money Tannion left on the table wasn't what they wanted, but information was. Six didn't see any way around it and as they were willing to pay, they got what they were looking for. Six knew he was ratting on his friend, but then he reasoned that they were going to find out anyway and it was better they found out by paying him than by hurting him.

34

Victor Mercido was one of the names Tannion had left on a list he gave to the FBI a few years back, when Rallin and Pansloski had gotten their hands on him. There were a lot of names on that list and Mercido's wasn't at the top, nor was he the biggest name, but he was on it. When the busts went down, Mercido had a knock on his door the same as the rest.

Mercido, however, was one of the lucky ones. First, he seemed to be prepared and he cooperated with the police when they came to search his property. He was also one of the smart ones and he didn't have any incriminating evidence at his house. They did manage to find some cocaine and other street-ready drugs in one of his warehouses, but with a good lawyer the FBI couldn't prove that he knew anything about it and only the warehouse manager went down.

Tannion had given the police the whereabouts of several of Mercido's places and although they were shut down and drugs, guns, and money were confiscated, none of it was traced directly back to Mercido and he was able to get away without prosecution. However, he lost a large portion of his action.

Mercido wasn't happy with the shakedown or losing several thousand dollars' worth of goods, but there were a few of his friends who weren't quite as lucky and found themselves looking at four grey walls. Mercido swore to get even, and told his friends that he would look after it.

Mercido knew who was responsible and took it upon himself to get revenge. He placed a contract on Tannion when Tannion was in prison. All, of course, were failures, and the men Mercido sent died a quick death. He would have gone for another hit, but it was about that time that Philips made a deal with him, and part of that deal was to leave Tannion alone.

When two of his men, who just happened to be sitting in the King's Head, reported to him that they had seen Tannion in town, he thought of Philips. The deal with Philips was simple. Mercido had agreed to leave Tannion alone in prison, or better yet, the agreement was that he wouldn't send any more hit men after Tannion in prison. In return, Mercido and Philips would work together on a few deals that would be beneficial to them both. Now that Tannion was out and walking around, the agreement was over. Tannion was fair game.

One of the two men had called Mercido while the other followed Tannion. He was pretty sure he knew who he was following based on what he had heard in the bar, but he wasn't willing to do anything just yet. When his cell phone rang and his friend told him what Six had finally let out, he knew he had hit pay dirt. He knew that at least a few guys had died in prison trying to kill this guy, but even that was not going to be enough to stop him from trying.

Mercido's man knew there would be a reward out for whoever got Tannion, but if he hit him before he knew what the reward was, the reward might simply disappear. He knew how Mercido worked. Once Mercido named the price on Tannion's head, then he would be sure to be the first one taking a crack at him. It looked to be so easy and would be too good to resist. His friend was going to Mercido to find out what Tannion was worth and then it would be time to cash in.

Tannion had seen the two men paying attention to him and Six while they were in the bar and hadn't thought that much of it, but he wasn't that surprised when one of them followed him out of the bar. At first Tannion ambled down the sidewalk going no place in particular, but heading into an area that he knew very well.

After he had walked a few blocks, Tannion knew for sure he was being followed. He looked for an appropriate place and found it. He turned a corner he knew was a blind corner, as it opened into a back alley that turned more than ninety degrees. Because the alley angled back somewhat towards where he had come from, it gave him a good spot to stop and wait for whoever was following him.

As soon as Tannion ducked around the corner, the guy following picked up his pace, but then his cell phone rang. Tannion could hear one side of the conversation and knew enough from what was said to know that they knew who he was. He couldn't blame Six.

When the guy finished with the call he quickly hurried to catch up, and when he got to the corner he stopped and stuck only his head around to see where Tannion had gone, hoping he would still be in sight. That was all Tannion needed, as he quickly grabbed him by the shirt collar and dragged him back into the darker alley. As soon as Tannion had him, Mercido's man started to talk. He wasn't going to get himself killed by covering for Mercido. Tannion didn't have to hurt him, or barely even threaten him, to get him to talk. All he needed to do was grab him.

He told Tannion all about his partner having talked with Six, that he would be talking to Mercido, and that a contract would be out on Tannion no matter what he did to him. Tannion could tell he was telling the truth. The first fact was that he was talking too fast to be lying, and the second was that with Tannion holding his arms behind his back as he held him a foot off the ground, most people would talk. He didn't have to hurt him, but he did.

First Tannion made sure that he would be able to take a message back to Mercido. Tannion told him very clearly that if anyone tried to hit him, or anyone Tannion knew, he would come after Mercido and may God help him if that happened. After Tannion was sure he was understood, he took him back into the street and had him call a cab. As soon as the cab got there he put Mercido's man in and directed him to head to Mercido with the information. It was all he could do for now. Mercido would know he was out of prison and in Los Angeles, and that couldn't be helped, but he would also know it wasn't in his best interest to pursue Tannion. Or at least he hoped Mercido did.

A quick phone call to Potenlikov and Tannion knew what he was up against. He found out that Philips had stepped in once and made a deal with Mercido, but he wouldn't be able to do it again. Philips was the larger player and he could use force against Mercido if he wanted to, but that would escalate into a full-scale turf war that neither Philips nor Tannion wanted. Even the smaller players could put some hurt on the big guys before they were beaten down, and

Mercido wasn't a small guy. Tannion told Potenlikov the word that he had left with his would-be killer, and told him that he meant it, but he also told him goodbye. It was time to get out of Los Angeles.

He knew he would have to be careful. He knew he was better off not telling Rallin anything about it, and to just get back to New York. At least there he had some distance between Mercido and his men, and that could be an advantage. Also, there was the fact that he knew New York as well as he knew Los Angeles. He hoped that Mercido's men wouldn't have that familiarity, and that might be another advantage.

He also hoped Mercido would believe that it would be in his best interest to leave Tannion alone, but he didn't think that was very likely. He also hoped that Philips might step in again, but Potenlikov made it sound like that wasn't likely to happen, either. The first time was easy as Mercido was hurting and was getting his operation off the ground again, but this time Mercido would not be as easy to stop. Mercido had grown considerably, thanks in large part to the deal he had made with Philips, and he was no longer easy pickings. Not even for someone as big as Philips. Tannion was pretty sure he would be back in Los Angeles a lot sooner than he hoped to be.

Tannion had the late flight back to New York and he made sure that he was on it. Rallin was coming out in a day or two, after he found out what the director was wanting him to do, but assuming that everything went the way they had planned, then he should be back in New York within a couple of days.

There were a number of files sitting on Tannion's desk and Rallin had made sure to remind him that he wanted a report on his desk when he got back. Tannion knew exactly which file he would be writing a report on, and he knew that the information would be easy to gather. He only hoped that if Mercido decided to do something he would do it sooner rather than later.

35

Vladimir Potenlikov knocked and stuck his head around the door. Jackson Philips looked up and waved him to the chair across from him and asked him what was up.

"I just got off the phone with French," Potenlikov told him. "It seems that he went down to the King's Head and was talking to an old friend of his, and it appears that a couple of Mercido's men heard him."

"So they know he's in town. I'm not surprised. He was pretty well known after he turned state's evidence, even if it was over five years ago," Philips told him.

"I'm not so sure they recognized him at first, but if you remember the guy they call Six; he was the one French was talking to."

"Still owes us some money, if I'm not mistaken."

"He's paying it off slowly, but he's good for it."

"Okay, so French talks to Six and these guys overheard him."

"And then they talked to Six to make sure that he really was Jim Tannion, and Six dumps on his friend."

"Should we do something about that?" Philips asks. "You know this Six character. Maybe we should make an example of him."

"No. I don't think so. They would have beaten it out of him if he didn't give it up, so nothing would have changed. Besides, he's a friend of French and he wouldn't like us getting on him. If you remember it was because of Six that I first met French."

"That's right. I do remember. So what else did French tell you?"

"He caught one of the guys from the bar and made sure he took a message back to Mercido to try to get him to lay off, and now he's heading back to New York tonight."

"Good plan," Philips said. "But I doubt that Mercido can be stopped with just a warning. I don't think he has any idea as to how good French is. If Mercido puts out a hit and it fails, then I wouldn't want to be in Mercido's shoes."

"Yeah, I agree, and French hopes that the distance will help, but he wants us to know about it because he knows that you stopped Mercido before in prison."

"How does he know that?"

"I don't know. I didn't tell him, but he seemed to know." Potenlikov didn't lie to his boss often, but this was one time when it was best he didn't know everything. "He mentioned that you stopped him once and maybe you could stop him again."

"That won't happen, Vlad, and you know it."

"I told French that. Mercido has grown and he was pretty pissed back then, and now with French out of jail, he'll think our agreement is over and he'll feel free to go after him. If we try to stop him now there could be a real turf war. The kind of war that we agreed with French that we will stop, not start."

"We should have knocked Mercido down when we had the chance. He's been growing steadily, taking over for a few guys when he could, and stepping in where he shouldn't as well."

"Wasn't Pearsol one of his?" Potenlikov asked.

"That's why I gave him to Rallin. He wasn't big, but he was becoming a key player in Mercido's operation and taking him out was good for us. I had Johnny Rayborn step in and take over part of the area, and it seems to be going okay. He wasn't big enough for Mercido to get involved with either and Mercido won't give us any problems about it."

"You hadn't told me that before, and I never knew you were getting worried about Mercido."

"Some things I don't tell even you, Vlad. I won't say I'm getting worried about Mercido, but it's always prudent to watch your enemies, and if you can hurt them without them knowing about it, all the better."

"So I told French that he was on his own with Mercido, but you might have other ideas?"

"I can't say right now, but I've seen French in action recently and I don't think we need to worry too much. He's a big boy and he's forewarned."

"I hope you're right, Mr. Philips."

36

New York the morning after looked the same as it had when Tannion left. Rallin wasn't expected back in town for a couple of days, and it was just Tannion and the kid in the office. There were files on his desk, but he wasn't in the mood.

A quick look at the files told him that he could repeat what he had already done before and have the report that Rallin wanted on his desk when he made it back from LA. The file that he had thought would be the one to work on was at the top of the pile, and he might as well get started.

A couple of days later and Rallin was back in the office. He stuck his head around the door to Tannion's office and said hello, then set a lunch date for the two of them plus Pansloski and Jeff Martin. Rallin needed to fill them all in on what had finally happened in Los Angeles.

Lunch was at the small diner a couple of blocks from the office. It was a cop and FBI hangout, and Rallin had to say hello at a couple of tables before they were able to sit down. The four of them had walked to the diner together.

They put in their order as the waitress wrote down what they were having. A couple of sandwiches for Tannion and Pansloski, and both Rallin and Martin ordered salads.

Tannion knew that would be more their wives' doing than theirs, but they both could stand to watch what they ate. Pansloski could too, but somehow it didn't seem to matter as much to him.

Tannion decided not to give them any grief over their salads, and also to let any discussion be led by one of them and not by him. It didn't take long before Rallin started the conversation. Tannion thought they were there for a meeting, and not just lunch, and as Rallin had called it and as he was the boss, he was expected to speak first. Tannion wondered if Rallin would pick up the tab.

"Okay. First I want to talk about what happened in Los Angeles." Rallin started the meeting, and the tone told Tannion that he was right and it was a business meeting.

Tannion wasn't sure who knew what, but after the next few sentences from Rallin, he knew that Pansloski and Martin didn't have access to everything that went on. It was probably killing Rallin to keep things from his old partner, but in this case Tannion didn't think Rallin had any choice. Rallin hadn't mentioned anything about the meetings with Potenlikov and Philips. As far as this meeting was concerned, the other meetings just hadn't happened.

"Based on the tips we got we were able to pin a good case on a small timer by the name of Hank Pearsol." He looked at Martin and Pansloski, and then back to Tannion. "We got enough on him to put him away for a while, but as it turned out, he wasn't connected to Philips."

Rallin went on to make sure they all were up to speed on what they did get on Philips. "Jim, you're the only one this is news to. Both Jeff and Bill know what went down, but not the final results. None of you are aware of what the director said after we got the information on Philips. That's mostly what I want to make sure you hear from me."

"Philips won't stand trial," Rallin told them as he jumped right to the point, and he knew that Martin and Pansloski would not be happy.

Both Martin and Pansloski let out a sigh as if that was what they expected, but certainly not what they were hoping for. They'd been on Philips' trail, and they had wanted to catch him in the act and pin something big on him. They were both happy it was over though, so not too heavy a sigh.

Rallin went on. "The manager at the pet store and at the warehouse will stand trial and will probably get a fine and parole, but no jail time. The key piece of information I want to pass on to you is what the director has decided and, as much as we might not like it, it is what it is."

Tannion looked over at Pansloski and Martin and although he knew they would have liked to pin something on Philips, they also knew that they would rather be working out of New York and not LA. There was enough crime on the East Coast to keep them busy for the rest of their careers, and they knew it. They also knew that the fact they were back in New York meant the director had called the operation completed, at least for the time being. They just didn't know the details.

"The director wasn't overly happy with the minimal bust on Philips, but I think he must have been getting pressure from somewhere to let this one go. Philips looks like a legitimate businessman as far as many people are concerned. As you know, we found nothing in Philips' office or at his house. We did hit a warehouse that contained additional illegal animals, but the store manager is taking full responsibility for them. Philips will not be indicted for anything and his record remains clean."

Pansloski had to say a word and interrupted Rallin. "Are you kidding?" he started. "We know he's dirty. How can he pull the wool over everyone's eyes?"

"He gives a lot of money to charity. He pays his federal, state, and municipal taxes on time, and he employs a lot of people in several legitimate businesses. There are several people in high places who are willing to look the other way when it comes to Philips. That seems to include the Chief of Police, the district attorney, and maybe even the mayor."

Tannion knew he would have to put his few cents in, and it was time for that now. "You all know in a city the size of LA there is going to be crime, and from my experience, Jackson Philips is a lot better guy to have at the top of that food chain than almost anyone else. I would hate to see who would replace him."

"Did you talk to Philips when you were in LA?" asked Martin. It had to be Martin who would have the suspicious mind, and certainly he was smart enough to see things from every angle. If what Rallin and Tannion worked out with Philips were ever known from within, it would be Martin who would work it out. Not that Pansloski was slow or anything, but he was more likely to look at what his partner did or hear what he said, and take it at face value and not ask questions. Martin would ask the questions, including the hard questions.

They all knew that Rallin had brought Tannion in to help and that Rallin had him stick around just in case, and then sent him back to New York a couple of days before he came back. They might have thought that Tannion was the one who gave them the tip on Pearsol, but he wasn't around long enough to be of much help. The tip came in and Rallin didn't expressly tell anyone that it didn't come from Tannion.

"I didn't talk to Philips," Tannion lied. "But I did talk to Potenlikov. Everything that Vlad told me makes me feel that leaving Philips in charge is the best thing we could do. He's branching out into more and more legitimate business and is keeping the lid on any violence, and certainly there were a lot of turf wars and gang violence in LA before he took over."

"I'm still not sure that's the best thing we could have done for the city. I can't argue the point you make, but I still think our job is to put these guys behind bars and not to let them walk the street."

Rallin broke in. "Okay, Jeff. I understand where you're coming from and I tend to agree, but at this point we've left Philips in Los Angeles and the director has told us to pull back and leave him alone."

"To finish off, I can tell you that the director indicated that it was a job well done, and with the backing Philips has and the fact that the newspapers are calling him something close to a saint, the director didn't have any choice but to pull us off. He did add that if there was anything that came up anywhere that would link to Philips that he would still like to catch this guy, but for now we can't go looking. The file has been passed to the local guys and they'll probably sit on it. Personally, I'm glad to be off that case and back in New York. We have enough to do in our own backyard."

The meal went on to the end in relative silence, and when the four walked back to the office it was obvious that not everyone was completely satisfied with what went down in Los Angeles, but they were happy to be back in New York. That, and they knew that life and the work would go on. Tannion might have been the only one with a smile. Rallin had picked up the tab.

37

Victor Mercido wasn't in a good mood. The news from one of his men might have been the reason, but Mercido didn't need a reason to be in a foul mood. It was just the way he was. Anyone looking at him might think he was still a poor, out-of-work punk from upstate New York where he grew up, but that was almost thirty years ago and it had been almost as long since he had moved to Los Angeles.

He got into trouble at home when he was young, and knew he had to leave. His parents couldn't handle him, so at the age of sixteen he left home and moved into New York City. After working at odd jobs for a couple of years, he joined a small gang that almost got him killed. At first he was doing all right, as he was running a small numbers game and pimping for a small string. Things were looking good.

New York would have been a place where he could have lived out the years of his life, but a disagreement between two rival gangs ended up in gunfire with a couple people dead, and Mercido with a gunshot wound in his leg that gave him a limp and occasionally the pain to go along with it. After the two gangs squared off it was only a matter of time before the cops started to round up everyone involved, and with Mercido lying in a hospital bed, he was going to be an easy target. If the rival gang didn't get him, he was sure the cops would. One of the dead had one of Mercido's bullets in him.

At the age of twenty-three Mercido limped out of the emergency ward of Mercy General Hospital. He had no idea where his steps would take him. He couldn't go back to what he was or where he was living. The cops didn't know for sure that he was involved, but they assumed that he was and would have brought him in as soon as they found him. His gang had ended up on the losing side and the rivals controlled the streets. If he went back and the cops missed him, the rival gang wouldn't. He knew he had to leave.

A couple weeks later he found himself in Los Angeles, California, and he found a fresh start. The wound in his leg had healed, but would give him pain and a slight limp for the rest of his life. When Mercido got to Los Angeles, it wasn't New York. It would never be New York and he was pissed off from the get-go. His attitude never went away, and after almost thirty years, and after accumulating several million dollars, he never appeared to be a happy man.

"Bring Dorno back in here," Mercido bellowed at whoever was close by. Peter Dorno was the man who had ended up in Jim Tannion's clutches, and he counted himself lucky to be alive. He was standing outside the door and moved in as soon as he heard his name.

"Yeah, boss?" he asked. He didn't like to be in the same room as Mercido, and it was clear from the look on his face. Especially when Mercido was in an even worse than usual mood, which was what he saw on his boss's face.

"Dorno. Tell me what he said again," Mercido told him. There was no mistaking the authority in his voice.

"He told me to tell you that if you went after him again, or any of his friends, then he would come after you and God help you if he did." Dorno didn't like being the bearer of bad news, but even worse was that he let Tannion catch him, a sure sign of incompetence in Mercido's eyes.

"Bullshit. Fucking bullshit. That asshole almost had me in jail and I lost a lot of money because of him. Friends of mine are still in jail because of him. He's one man. He can't touch me. He should already be dead. Why should I be scared of him?"

Dorno looked at his boss and based on the color of his red face, he knew better than to answer his question. He might not have known that it was a rhetorical question, but he knew better than to give Mercido a target to vent his frustrations on.

After a couple of minutes Mercido had taken a few deep breaths, and started to issue orders again in a relatively calm manner. At least, calm for Mercido.

"I want him dead. One hundred thousand dollars for whoever hits him. Make sure the word gets out. Someone get hold of Bellows. I want to talk to him."

Dorno took it as his time to leave and he hurried. Before he got out the door Mercido called him back and made sure that he understood that the word was to go out to all his men, and in particular to the one man who Mercido thought could do the job.

Damon Bellows was that man. He had done a few jobs for Mercido in the past and he scared the shit out of Dorno. Dorno knew where he could find him and he headed for Bellows' favorite bar. As soon as he got there, he saw Bellows, passed the information on, and got the hell out of there as fast as he could. He wasn't sure if he were more afraid of Mercido or of Bellows. When he had a chance to think about it, he decided that maybe he was more afraid of Tannion.

One hundred thousand dollars was a lot of money, but Dorno wanted nothing to do with it. He saw what Tannion could do in the brief time they had been together. He had heard about what had happened to the people who tried to kill him in prison. He had seen and heard enough. He was thinking of moving. Mexico maybe, but if they were going to hit Tannion and missed, God have mercy on their souls. Mexico might not be far enough.

38

Damon Bellows took the news as if it were something he was expecting. The money was good, but not as much as he had made on other jobs. It was good enough to take the job, though. Mercido wasn't the only person Bellows worked for, but Mercido didn't need to know that. Los Angeles had been pretty quiet since Philips had taken the majority of the control, and there just wasn't enough demand for Bellows' line of work there, so he had looked elsewhere.

All Mercido had known was that Bellows had taken a long vacation and had gone out of the country, which probably meant Europe. The fact was that Bellows had gone to work for one of the head drug cartels in Northern Mexico. After putting a few of the cartel's enemies out of business, and having been paid very well for a couple hits on local government officials and a chief of police, he shut it down.

Bellows had enough of Mexico and ended up back in Los Angeles as if his vacation was over. He even knew enough about Europe to talk about a couple of spots that he had never seen if anyone ever asked. Not too many people asked. Most people stayed a long ways away from Bellows. "One of the perks of the job," he thought.

Bellows made a couple of calls to contacts he had in New York, and within a few minutes he had the start of a picture. Jim Tannion's name was well known to most of the organized crime heads in Los Angeles, if not to all their underlings, and Bellows was aware of the name as well. The name wasn't the person however, and if Bellows was anything, it was careful. He would do his homework.

He found out about the hits that were attempted inside the prison, but other than the fact that they failed, he was unable to find out why. What were Tannion's strengths, and even more importantly, what were his weaknesses? All men had weaknesses and almost all of them included a good-looking woman, and even better if she were in a short skirt.

Bellows wasn't against using anything he had to do the job, including hookers or anyone in a skirt. No one he used would know what the end result was going to be or even know that the result was his. No loose ends were best. If they knew too much they became a casualty as well.

Bellows was good at what he did and leaving behind any witnesses who could finger him was never going to happen, not as long as he had control, but he found it better to manipulate people from afar to ensure they never knew who he was. Less messy that way, with fewer people to worry about. In this case he had to get himself to New York, but not as Damon Bellows. No disguise would be necessary as the identification was that good.

Bellows had been to New York on many occasions, and had his favorite hotel where the concierge knew him by name. Not by Damon Bellows of course, but still by name. He checked in, got one of the better suites, and settled in to find out what he could. A phone call and he had the address of the FBI unit involved in organized crime.

Bellows was a little surprised that the team wasn't housed in the same building as the rest of the FBI, but he was quite pleased, as it should make his work that much easier.

All he had to do was go down to the area and keep watching the building until Tannion walked out. Bellows had looked at a picture of Tannion for long enough that his features were imprinted on his memory. He would know Tannion when he saw him. He had also gotten the names of the rest of the FBI team who worked with Tannion.

Bellows remembered hearing three of the names before. Mike Rallin who headed the section had been instrumental in capturing Tannion in Los Angeles. He also remembered the names Jeff Martin and Bill Pansloski from the same time. "Wouldn't hurt to take a couple of them out as well," he thought, "as long as Mercido is willing to pay."

A taxi dropped him off about three blocks from the FBI building and he made his way on foot until he had walked past the building. There was a café conveniently located a couple of blocks away that he was sure would be a hangout for most of the local workers, including the FBI, and he wasn't wrong. At about ten after noon Tannion walked into the restaurant with two men who looked like cops. Bellows knew that one of them was Rallin and thought the third man might be Pansloski. They were the right age.

Bellows had a light lunch of a tuna fish sandwich and coffee, and kept an eye on Tannion and his friends. About an hour later Tannion's table paid their bills separately and made their way back to the FBI building. Bellows knew that he could have killed all three of them right there in the restaurant, but that would mean witnesses and that just wasn't the way he did things.

Guns blazing wasn't his style. A silenced gun in a parking garage, or a garrote behind a darkened building were more his style. He didn't like to use the high-powered rifle from hundreds of yards away. There were too many chances to fail, and there was a large gun to haul around. It was much better to find a place where he could get up close and personal and do it right. Even better if he could get someone else to do it for him, but he wasn't against getting his hands dirty.

He knew that his chances would be better after work when the cops split up and went their separate ways home. Once he found out where Tannion lived, he could make his plan. He knew he had a few hours to kill and if there was one thing that his job had taught him, it was patience.

Bellows settled in to wait. First, there was a bench in a park about halfway down the block, which allowed him to see the front door. He bought a newspaper at the corner and sat with one eye on the FBI building as he read the entire paper. How little real news there was in any newspaper, he decided, including a city the size of New York.

After a couple of hours he went back to the café for a coffee to go, knowing that he probably had at least a couple more hours to kill. He was out of sight of the building for about ten minutes, but he knew the game well and was feeling very confident. Tannion would come out and he would see him.

Finally, about five o'clock Bellows saw Tannion walk out of the front door. At that time Bellows was standing at the far corner drinking his second cup of coffee. Tannion looked both ways before crossing the street, and headed across the street and directly towards Bellows.

Bellows saw him coming and decided that Tannion wasn't going to live long enough to worry about having seen him at least once, as long as he didn't see him the second time. As Tannion walked past Bellows they caught each other's eye and they each nodded half a hello and, without slowing, Tannion walked by.

Bellows waited until Tannion got to the end of the block and then he crossed the street. Making sure to stay just a little more than a block behind, he was able to keep Tannion in sight. It was obvious that Tannion wasn't in a hurry and that he wasn't worried. After a few blocks Tannion turned into a brick, three-story building and stuck a key in the lock.

A few seconds later and Bellows was across the street looking for some sign as to which room Tannion was in. He wasn't worried, as even if he didn't find out tonight he would find out after Tannion went to work the next morning. Tomorrow would be a different day and New York was one of his favorite cities. Tomorrow might be Tannion's last day.

39

When Tannion left his apartment building at seven thirty the next morning, Bellows was watching from his vantage point across the street on the second floor. He had managed to find a place where he could see the front of Tannion's building without being seen. He was there about six in the morning, knowing full well Tannion would be leaving later than that. Cops like him weren't likely to get to work early, Bellows had thought. After all, Tannion was only an assisting civilian and not a real cop. He wouldn't get a call in the middle of the night.

Tannion walked the few blocks and went into the FBI building, and Bellows followed for a half block and then went back to his hotel. He had learned what he had needed to learn, and now it was time to make a plan and decide where he would do it. He had several options and it was only a matter of picking the one that was the best for him. Not that any one of them would be a problem. He knew he could do the job.

Tannion stuck his head around Rallin's office door as he rapped on the window. Rallin looked up and waved him in to sit in the other chair.

"Morning, Mike," Tannion started. "I need to talk to you for a minute, if that's okay." After Rallin said sure and sat back to listen, Tannion went on.

"I might have picked up a tail. I can't be sure, but I think there was a guy across the street last night who was in the restaurant when we had lunch yesterday. I think I saw him again this morning. I don't believe I'm being paranoid, but after being back in Los Angeles it's possible that some of the guys back there haven't forgotten about me."

"I wondered if that would happen after you got out. The warden told me there were a few tries in prison, but obviously they all failed. Not as easy to kill a guy in there as they thought it was. It might be a lot easier to get to you now, though."

"Oh, they tried alright, but some people are just easier to kill than others. I can't get too paranoid now that I'm out either."

"Are you sure you recognized the guy from the restaurant?" Rallin asked.

Tannion told Rallin he was pretty sure, but he didn't tell him why. With Tannion's abilities he'd developed the physical aspect where he was probably the closest thing to Superman this side of the comics, but he had also been working on other attributes as well. Humans might use less than all their brain's ability and Tannion was trying to expand that use.

Tannion was hoping to find things like telekinesis or levitation, or possibly telepathy, but so far, none of those seemed possible, at least not for him. The one thing that he had been able to work on was his memory. He thought that it was possible he had perfect recall, but the one item he had been working on was recalling faces. He wanted to be sure that if he saw someone at any time and then saw them again, he not only would recognize them, but he would also be able to remember when and where he had seen them before.

As it was, he was completely sure that the man he saw as he crossed the street had been eating a sandwich with coffee in the restaurant, and then had shown up across the street. This morning he thought he got a glimpse of him as he was leaving his apartment, but that was only a partial sighting so he wasn't too sure. Add up the first two sightings, and he was at least sure enough to be careful.

"So what do you want to do, Jim?" Rallin asked him. Rallin knew that Tannion could take care of himself, but had no real clue how good that care could be. "Do you want some company later to see if we can spot him?"

"I don't want to get you in the line of fire if there is a contract out on me, but with two of us working together we might be able to spot him. If we're sure he's a tail, then we grab him and ask him what the hell he's doing." Tannion had thought Rallin might want to help and he was glad he did.

"Okay, Jim. When you leave tonight, I'll follow about two minutes behind. If you have a tail I should be able to see him. What does he look like?" Tannion gave Rallin a very detailed description, right down to the clothes he had on that morning, assuming that the partial sighting was the same guy. Tannion knew that Rallin was a professional, but he also knew that if it was to be a hit, then the guy on the other end would be a professional too. He didn't want Rallin to get hurt.

"Thanks, Mike, but make sure if you see him that he doesn't see you. No need for you to get in the middle of something."

About five o'clock Tannion left the cop shop and walked across the street. Bellows was not there and neither was he anywhere to be seen. He didn't have to be. He had made his decision. Rallin followed about two blocks behind until Tannion got to his building. He hadn't seen anything out of the ordinary. Tannion waited outside while Rallin walked the two-block difference.

"Nothing, Jim." Rallin told him. "Must have just been your trip to LA making you spooked."

Tannion wasn't so sure, but if Rallin hadn't seen anyone then he was pretty sure there was nobody there to see. At least not this time. "Need a beer, Mike?"

Rallin was getting off a little early that night because of having to follow Tannion to his place, and Arlene wasn't expecting him home until about seven. That would leave lots of time to have a beer, then walk back to the office and pick up his car and drive home. "Sure, why not," he told him.

Tannion put his key in the lock and opened the front door to the apartment building. His apartment was on the second floor and the building only had stairs. The door was open to the stairs and he waved Rallin through, telling him it was only one floor. When they got to the second floor landing it was Rallin who stepped through first, with Tannion just a step behind.

The bullet hit Rallin high in the chest, spraying Tannion with Rallin's blood. There had been only the small sound that a silenced gun makes when it's fired, but it was loud enough for Tannion's sensitive ears. Tannion was moving before Rallin had hit the floor. The shot had come from the doorway at the end of the hall. The door led to the fire escape.

Bellows had made his decision and he knew it would be a good hit. He knew when Tannion was going to be heading home, as long as he stuck to the pattern he had established the day before. One day wasn't long enough to be a real pattern, but if he didn't come at that time then there was only time lost.

A window that looked out of the first floor told him all he needed to know. Tannion was on his way and when he stopped to talk to Rallin at the door Bellows knew he was going to have to take them both out. "Bonus," he thought. Maybe Mercido would throw in a little extra for Rallin.

Neither Tannion nor Rallin had seen Bellows slip up the stairs ahead of them as they came in the front door. He quickly went to his spot in the doorway at the end of the hall, which would give him just enough cover. It was the last apartment before the fire escape door. If all went well, then he would simply leave by the front door, but if there were any unforeseen problems then he had the fire escape as a secondary escape route. He always had to be sure to have a secondary escape plan.

The first shot had hit Rallin in the chest and Bellows thought that it might not have hit the heart, but unless he got help immediately, he would probably bleed out in a matter of minutes. The second shot was supposed to hit Tannion in about the same place, but he watched as it only hit the wall at the end of the hall.

Tannion had moved, and Bellows had never seen anyone move that fast. Before he could squeeze off another shot, Tannion was more than halfway down the hall. "Still not fast enough," thought Bellows.

Tannion was moving fast, but he was watching the hit man the entire time. He saw his trigger finger start to move again and knew that Bellows was about to shoot. Tannion threw himself to the side just in time, and the bullet went by him close enough he could feel the breeze. The slight diversion wasn't enough to even slow Tannion down as he put his right hand on the wall and used it as extra leverage. Before the hit man could take a fourth shot, Tannion hit him.

The force of Tannion's fist hitting Bellows' chest stopped his heart. Blunt force trauma can do that sort of thing if it's hard enough, and Tannion had hit him hard enough. His heart didn't explode or anything that dramatic, but it certainly quit. Bellows slumped to the floor and within a second or two his eyes glazed over.

Tannion looked back and saw Rallin lying on the floor near the stairwell with a pool of blood starting to form beneath him. As quickly as he had gone the length of the hall in one direction he now did it in reverse. Tannion took hold of Rallin by the neck to feel for a pulse, but at the same time told his body to quit bleeding. He had lost a lot of blood up to that point, but it might not be enough to kill him.

Tannion dug into Rallin's pocket and pulled out his cell phone. He called 911 and gave the woman who answered his name and the address. He told her that he had an officer down, and told her Rallin's name. The operator was very efficient and within ten minutes there were cops and paramedics coming in through the front door.

She was almost too efficient, or else the ambulance had been close by. If they had been a minute sooner they might have seen Tannion heading down the fire escape at a speed that defied human skills. Luckily no one saw him. The fact that Tannion lived in the building was going to be enough for any cop to want to ask him questions when they found out.

He took one last look at Rallin to see that he was still breathing and hoped that he had been quick enough. He could hear sirens in the distance as he headed towards the fire escape. Tannion wasn't worried about being caught and charged with killing the guy at the end of the hall. He was only worried about being slowed down.

It might take a while for anyone to realize that the guy who made the 911 call worked for the FBI and also lived in the building, making him a person of interest. By then he hoped to be well on his way. If Rallin lived, he would be able to piece together what had happened and then Tannion would be safe from the police, but until then they would probably hold him.

That was something he couldn't afford right now. He had warned them in Los Angeles and they hadn't listened. A contract was out on his head and that meant they would try again. This time they had tried to kill him and had shot a friend. That was something he wasn't about to let go without hitting back. They had been warned and now it was his turn.

40

The ambulance crew got to Mike Rallin just in time. He had lost a lot of blood, but they were able to get some saline solution into him as they were heading to the hospital, and ordered a blood transfusion as soon as they got there. Rallin would live, but the attending doctor was puzzled. When Rallin woke up a few hours later, Arlene was allowed in and a little later it was the doctor who asked the questions, even before the police could.

"Agent Rallin. My name is Doctor Collins. I was the attending physician when you came into emergency. I need to ask you a couple of questions if you feel up to it."

Rallin was feeling a lot better than he thought he should and he knew he was going to have to answer questions before too long, so it might just as well be the doctor first. He nodded for him to go ahead.

"Do you remember anything? Can you tell me what happened?"

Rallin thought for a moment and in a voice that was strong, but felt like it hadn't been used for a while, he answered. "When we came up the stairs he must have been waiting for us. I never saw or heard the shot, but I assume that was what hit me. I passed out after that. That's really all I remember until I woke up here."

Rallin suddenly remembered Tannion. "Was Jim Tannion brought in here too, and do you know how he is?"

"You were the only one brought in alive. The other guy went straight to the morgue," the doctor replied.

Rallin let out a moan. He was happy to be alive, but it really hurt to know that Tannion hadn't made it. He was starting to think of him as a friend.

The doctor went on. "When they brought you in, you had lost a lot of blood, Agent Rallin. We gave you a blood transfusion and stabilized you. The bullet hit you high in the chest. It went right through, and you should have needed surgery to repair whatever damage the bullet did internally and externally, but there didn't appear to be any need. We cleaned out the wound and took a close look. There was no bleeding and the tissue was healing very quickly. Your vitals were strong and you didn't show any signs of shock or distress. We applied a bandage and waited for you to wake up."

The doctor continued, "The bullet might have hit your left lung, but it either missed it or the damage was minimal. You had blood on your lips and mouth as if you had been shot in the lungs, but by the time you were in emergency your breathing was strong and normal. This morning the entry and exit wounds look as if they have been healing for a week. What can you tell me Agent Rallin? Why are you healing as fast as you are?"

Rallin couldn't tell him anything more except to tell him that he had been shot in the hallway and that was all he could remember. After he was shot he had passed out and had not been awake until that morning. Now only a few hours later he was able to talk well enough to answer questions.

"With the blood loss you suffered, you should have a terrible wound, but you don't, and you shouldn't be able to be talking today, in fact, you probably should be dead. Yet here you are, healing fast and in a couple of days, based on what I see happening, you'll be able to get out of the hospital and go home. I'm not writing you up as a medical miracle yet, but that's probably only a matter of time."

The duty nurse walked in and told the doctor that Rallin had a visitor. The doctor excused himself for now, but told Rallin that he would have more questions and would be back. Arlene told Rallin that she was going to get a cup of coffee.

Rallin should have known who the first cop to walk in the door would be. Arlene passed him at the doorway as Bill Pansloski walked in. Bill had been waiting patiently after Rallin had come out of the coma the doctors had told him Rallin was in. He was expecting the worst, but when he walked into the room he was greeted by the smile on Arlene's face as they passed and said hello.

"Hi Bill," Arlene called out. "I knew you would be here as soon as they said Mike could have visitors."

"Hi Arlene. How's he doing?"

"Why don't you ask him yourself?" and with that she went for her coffee.

Pansloski moved around to the other side of the bed and he took a good look at Rallin. Rallin wasn't a hundred percent and he could tell that by looking at him, but he didn't look like someone near death, either. Rallin had some color in his cheeks and he was sitting up.

"Are you sure you're good enough to be sitting up? I was expecting you to be nothing but tubes," Pansloski asked.

"I'm fine Bill. I don't know why and it has the doctors a bit stumped, but I'm feeling pretty good, all things considered. It mustn't have been nearly as bad as it looked at first. I just wish I could say the same thing for Tannion."

"What do you mean, Mike? Do you know where Tannion is?" Pansloski asked.

"What do you mean do I know where he is? He's in the morgue, isn't he?"

"Morgue? No way. We haven't seen him since he left the office last night. We've been looking for him and the director is thinking about putting him back on the most wanted list. We aren't sure what happened and we've been waiting for you to wake up so you can tell us what you know."

"What time is it Bill?" Rallin asked suddenly realizing that he didn't know if he had been out for hours or for days.

"It's a quarter past ten in the morning. You were shot at about five thirty last night and have been out cold for hours. Can you tell me what happened?" The local cops had wanted the case, but as it was an FBI agent who was shot, it was left in the FBI's hands and Pansloski had made sure that it would be him doing the questioning.

"All I know, Bill, is that Tannion thought he had picked up a tail and that it might have been someone from Los Angeles. There might be a hit on him based on his being there last week. He thought he might have been seen and reawakened old hard feelings. He asked me to follow him home to see if a tail existed, and when we got to his place, with no tail in sight, he asked me in for a beer. We walked up the one flight of stairs, and when I got to the top something hit me hard in the chest and then I woke up here. That's all there is. I thought the gunman got Tannion too."

"No, Mike. He certainly didn't get Tannion. The gunman's name was Damon Bellows. He's known to the FBI from previous activity, but there's never been a charge against him. He's thought to be one of the best hired guns on the West Coast. He had a nine millimeter Berretta with a silencer in his hands, and ballistics matched the bullet that went through you and embedded in the wall, as well as two additional slugs pulled from the wall at the end of the hall," Pansloski told him.

"So Tannion's alive?"

"There was no sign of Tannion when the uniforms got there. He was long gone. It looks like he must have hit Bellows hard enough to kill him. The medical examiner says he has never seen anything like it before unless they were hit by a car or a train. Not even a baseball bat could have done that kind of damage."

"The bruising indicated that Bellows was hit in the middle of his chest, probably with a fist, but any heavy rounded object might have done the damage if it were thrown at him hard enough. There was nothing like that at the scene, and we haven't seen anything like it anywhere around. The examiner isn't sure, but there looks to be marks from the bruising that are pointing to it being a closed fist. He's doing some testing to determine if he's right. If he's right, then it looks like Tannion might have killed him with one blow from his fist."

"So Tannion somehow manages to get to the killer before he can shoot him, and then hits him hard enough to kill him. Have I got that right?" Rallin asked. Pansloski could tell by the look on his partner's face and the way he asked the question that he didn't believe everything he was being told.

"Believe me Mike, if there was anything else that might have happened we haven't come up with it yet. Remember how hard he hit Inspector Leed. He was dead at the scene with a broken neck. This sounds very similar if you ask me."

"Maybe," Rallin noted. "Who's handling the case?"

"Started with the NYPD, but when it was known that you were one of the victims and that another of our team was missing, we took over. I think the locals were glad to be rid of it. They also think it looks like a pretty much open and shut case once we find Tannion."

"Okay, so fill me in on the rest," Rallin told his partner.

"Hold on, Mike. You just came out of a drug-induced coma after a severe gunshot wound less than twenty-four hours ago. The doctors say that you'll be fine, but it might take a while."

"Bullshit, Bill. I already feel fine. Take a look at this." With that Rallin pulled up the front of the hospital-issued nightshirt they had put on him and showed him where the bullet had gone in. Except for a little puckering around the wound, which looked like it wouldn't even leave much of a scar, there wasn't anything to see.

Turning his back to Pansloski, Rallin told him to check it. Healing was already occurring where the exit wound had been much larger than the entry. The extent of healing was almost the same as the front, which meant it was almost healed, with no sign of infection or anything that might be problematic.

"That's not possible, Mike. The amount of blood at the scene should have been enough to kill you, and that bullet must have hit a lung, broke a rib, caused internal damage, or done something that would take a while to heal, let alone the outer damage. What the hell happened?"

"I don't know, Bill. The doctors don't know. They didn't even operate on me. They think I have some special healing properties, but I've been hurt before and I know I took a long time to heal, and with me getting older it seems to take even longer. I don't even have any pain."

Rallin went on. "I need to talk to Tannion. He should know what happened, and maybe he can shed some light on both parts. He must know what happened to me and what happened to Bellows."

"He's out there somewhere and we haven't heard from him, but based on what he told us before, I bet he's out for revenge," Pansloski said.

"If he's heading for Los Angeles he could already be there and God help whoever put out the contract on him. I just hope he doesn't make things worse by doing something he'll regret and that we can't get him out of."

"The director thinks he's running just like he did years ago. He still isn't convinced that Tannion wasn't the one who shot you."

"I know Tannion didn't shoot me, as he was behind me in the stairway, but I don't think he's running either, Bill. It's different this time, but we need to talk to him soon. Real soon."

41

Tannion knew he had to get out of New York as soon as he could. He also knew that what had happened in that hallway would be considered self-defense. He also knew that no matter what they called it, he would have been stuck in the city for days and possibly weeks if he had stayed and talked to the police. He couldn't afford days, let alone weeks.

As soon as he knew Rallin was on the mend and that the gunman was dead, he went into his room and quickly packed a bag and grabbed the cash he kept handy. He hurried to ensure he was out of there before anyone else came into the hall. As soon as he got outside the place, he could hear that the police and an ambulance were on the way. The sirens were getting close.

A taxi was waiting down at the corner and Tannion jumped in and told the driver to take him to the airport. He thought he would have at least a few hours. By the time the police got to the apartment building and determined what had happened, an hour or so would have gone by. It would take even longer for them to realize that Rallin and the guy who called 911 worked together at the FBI, and that Tannion's apartment was on that floor. Only after that would they start looking for him and even then they wouldn't close the exits to the city. He had a little time and he was going to use it.

Tannion was feeling a little déjà vu as he stood in the lineup to get on a small commuter plane to Baltimore. It was the next flight out that a ticket was available on.

How long had it been since the last time he had done this exact same thing? Kill someone and then run like hell. This time it was different. It felt different. He wasn't just running, he was going somewhere on purpose. He had told them in Los Angeles that there would be hell to pay if they came after him, and that was exactly what was going to happen.

The first thing he had to do, however, was get to Los Angeles without being on the run. He didn't want to be held up by the police investigation, but he didn't want them after him either. He had already gone down that route and it hadn't worked out that well.

He had left a trail that the police would be able to follow to Baltimore, but he thought it was best that they didn't follow him any further. As Tannion waited for his flight to be called, he found a pay phone and placed a call to Rallin's home phone number. When the fourth ring ended, the voice mail kicked in and Tannion left a message.

He thought that Arlene would probably be on her way to the hospital, or she would already be there, but if everything went the way it should, Rallin would be all right and back home in a couple of days. Arlene at least would get the message even sooner, assuming she went home.

Tannion told the machine that he was following a lead and would be in touch with Rallin as soon as he could. He didn't have a cell phone number to leave, so the best he could do was to tell the machine that he had hit the gunman in self-defense and was going after the person who put out the contract on him, and he asked Rallin to cover for him.

Tannion got off the plane in Baltimore and caught a taxi to the bus terminal, where he bought a ticket to Los Angeles. He needed some time to think and a bus trip would be the best way. Unlike the last time he did this sort of thing, he didn't have the feeling that he was running from someone. Rallin would be able to watch his back and he wouldn't feel the hot breath of the cops behind him. All he needed to do was focus on what he was going to do when he got to Los Angeles.

Almost a couple of days later Tannion could see the familiar big city smog that is always there when you come in from the northeast side. He was still a ways from where he was going, but he was getting closer. The two days riding the bus had been easy, but it had been a bit boring. Not like the last time.

This time he had relied on the bus, and he still paid in cash to be somewhat anonymous, although he knew the FBI would be able to follow him. Rallin would know where he was going, but he didn't want anyone else to know, not as long as Rallin could cover for him.

The bus had given him plenty of time to think out what he needed to do. First, he needed to find a place to stay. He quickly found an area where he felt comfortable, saw a small hotel, and booked a room.

After a few minutes, he decided that sitting in his room wasn't the best place for him in his frame of mind. It was too quiet. He needed a little background noise. He decided to see if the hotel had a bar.

As it turned out, there was a small bar just off the lobby of the hotel. He was always comfortable inside a bar. He ordered a beer and sat back in a corner with his thoughts. He knew that he could probably wait until dark, walk into Mercido's house and kill him, and anyone else who might get in the way, but he had come up with a couple of problems with that idea.

First, he wasn't a hundred percent sure that the gunman was working for Mercido. The guy he caught in Los Angeles had worked for Mercido and said that Mercido had a contract on him, but there could be more than one contract out. Tannion was that disliked in Los Angeles.

Second, he wasn't sure anymore where Mercido lived. It might be better if he gathered a little information first. He thought it might be best to give Potenlikov a call in the morning, but then he thought about Rallin.

"He should be getting out of the hospital soon, if he hasn't already," he thought. "That is, if he made it."

Tannion knew that if he hit Mercido it was likely to get him thrown back in jail. No, not likely; it was a sure thing, but only if they caught him.

He wasn't sure that he wanted to spend the rest of his life as a civilian assistant to the FBI, but he was real sure that he didn't want to be on the run again. If Rallin were able to hold off the troops, maybe he would have an idea on how to proceed. Also, there might be a way that the FBI could do the dirty work for him.

Tannion's thoughts were all over the board, but they seemed to be starting to come together when things suddenly got interesting in the little pub. Over next to the bar it looked like a fight was going to break out. He had nothing to do with it, but when it started it quickly spilled over to the rest of the bar, and as he wasn't in a good mood at the time, he decided to put an end to it. He stepped in and picked the two main combatants up by the scruffs of their necks. With their feet dangling in the air he took them outside and threw them on the ground.

Of course, that only makes two enemies the best of friends. One of them pulled out a knife, and as soon as they could get back on their feet, they both came after Tannion. Tannion barely moved when the one closest to him took a swing. Tannion moved just enough to ensure that the punch missed. A quick slap from Tannion's hand alongside the guy's head and it was lights out. The one with the knife was further away, and had only gotten a step closer before his new best friend was sailing towards him. They collided with enough force to take them both to the ground. Tannion stepped forward and stood on the guy's knife hand before he could move. A short kick to the guy's head with his other foot and Tannion was the only one awake. The fight had taken less than ten seconds.

Tannion went back into the hotel, paid for his beer and went to bed. He had paid cash for the room and had used a different name, but he knew with the two on the street that it wouldn't matter. They would have had enough. They were both drunk enough that they would wake up with headaches and not remember much of anything.

The next morning Tannion had the time to finish the thinking he needed to do. A decent night's sleep had helped. Now it was time to go to work. He caught a cab and told the driver the destination. About a half hour later he got out of the cab and looked up at the sign over the bar. It read "The King's Head".

It had only been a few days since Tannion had met Six at the King's Head, and he was pretty sure this was where he had been spotted. Six would never have ratted him out unless he was going to get hurt, and then he would have eventually spilled everything and Tannion couldn't blame him.

The guy who had followed him must have been sitting in the bar when they had been talking and might have heard what he needed to know. It was probably the guy he caught at the time and Tannion would recognize him again. Tannion thought it might be interesting if the guy was in the bar, but it didn't really matter.

The gloom inside was always the way Tannion remembered it. The last time he was there was different than this trip, and somehow it hadn't brought the memories back that this visit did. A quick look around and he could see that neither the guy who had tailed him nor Six were in the bar. He ordered a beer and took a chair in the back of the bar where he could watch the door, and he waited.

Tannion had left New York without a plan of any sort except to get to Los Angeles. He knew that it would be relatively simple to get there and then he would find Victor Mercido, if he was behind the hit attempt, and make him disappear, but that would be too easy. He wanted to take revenge, but not the old-fashioned kind.

Tannion knew he had turned a corner and life would never be the same. After going to work with the FBI, and Mike Rallin in particular, he knew that the criminal life, or anything on that side of the tracks, no longer appealed to him at all. When he was in Los Angeles a few years previously and working for Philips, he had almost lost himself and gone down the road where Philips could lead him.

Tannion's need to rid the world of killers and rapists had led him into a version of life where he could get rid of a few, but keep more than a few working for him even if they really worked for Philips. He knew that wasn't going to happen again.

Tannion left the King's Head after paying for the one beer he had drunk, and caught a taxi to a better part of town, a part of town that was usually full of tourists, and that was about all. It was the perfect place to make the phone call he knew he had to make.

It had been three days and Rallin should have healed well, and with what Tannion had set in motion that should have been more than enough to have him at home with Arlene, if not back at work. He didn't think the amount of time would be long enough for anyone to think that Rallin was well enough to be back at work though, and that would especially include Arlene, so he would likely be at home.

When the phone rang it was Arlene who answered. She had been a cop's wife for too many years to ask any questions when the caller asked for Mike, and this time was no exception. She told Tannion to hang on and in a few seconds Mike Rallin's recognizable voice came on the line.

"Rallin," Rallin answered. He'd had many such calls since he had gotten out of the hospital. People had phoned wanting to wish him well and telling him that they were glad he was okay. There had even been a few reporters wanting to talk to him about how quickly he had recovered. The doctors were still buzzing about it.

"Mike. It's Jim Tannion."

"Tannion. Christ, I thought you were dead, but then Arlene got your message. Where the hell are you? No. Don't tell me. Los Angeles, right?" Tannion didn't miss the use of his surname and knew that Rallin wasn't exactly happy with him at the moment. Then again, how could he blame him?

"Yeah, Mike, I'm in LA."

At that point Rallin cut him off. "What the hell are you doing in LA? Do you know that the FBI is looking for you, or at least we were until I got your message? I was able to shut off the search and keep it inside our group so you aren't on the FBI's most wanted list again. I think that's where the director would have you if he hadn't been talked out of it. Half the guys in the group think that's where you belong too. No matter what you said in your message, it still looks too similar to what happened the last time you ran from New York."

Tannion took a few seconds to think. "I know, Mike. I thought of that too, but it's not like it seems. I didn't run because I had done something wrong. Killing that hit man was self-defense."

"We know that, Jim, so why did you run? You mentioned you were after the one who put out the contract, but we could have helped you."

Tannion noticed the use of his first name this time, and felt a little better. Rallin had calmed down after the first shock of hearing who was on the other end of the phone, and it sounded as if he were ready to talk.

"I knew if I stayed there I would be caught up in the investigation, and I didn't want to spend the time. I needed time to think things through and I wasn't going to get that in New York."

"Come on, Jim. You know who you're talking to. Come clean and tell me what the hell you're planning to do. I'm at a loss here."

"Okay, Mike. When I was in LA with you, I went to see a friend, and I was seen by someone who recognized me. That was why I was being followed in New York. I caught the guy in LA and informed him in no uncertain terms that if anyone came after me, or if anyone I knew got hurt, then there would be hell to pay. They didn't listen and now I'm here to raise a little hell."

"I understand that, Jim, but I wish you hadn't run. I'm okay now." A thought suddenly popped into his head. "You killed the guy who shot me, and by what the doctors said, I probably should have died on the hallway floor too, but not only did I not die, I'm already at home making a full recovery. The doctors are stumped. What do you know about that? I get the feeling that you know what happened in that hallway."

"Not much I can tell you."

"Bullshit, Jim. I know something happened in that hallway that I can't explain and the doctors can't either. I think you know more than you're telling me."

Tannion knew that his secret was very close to being exposed and that there was probably little chance that Rallin would let this one go until he knew the truth. He decided he had held onto the secret too long, but he needed to hang on to it just a bit longer. Rallin might be in a need-to-know frame of mind, but it could wait until they were face to face.

"Mike. Meet me in LA. I'll fill you in. Stay at the same hotel we were in before. Make it three days from now. I'll pick you up at the airport."

"Jim. You need to tell me what you have planned. Don't go turning vigilante on me. You've been down that road before and you know how it turned out."

"I'll fill you in when you get here, and don't worry. Everything I do will be in an official capacity only. I'll wait until you get here. Can you hold off Sarvo and the rest of the team?"

"No problem, Jim. I've already told the team and the director that you're on a special assignment for me and they just might buy it. I was out of the loop while recovering from the gunshot, so they might think I wasn't aware of you running off. Pansloski and Martin know, but they'll be okay. I'll talk to Sarvo, too. He shouldn't cause any problems. I'll fill you in on how that went when we see each other, but for now you're just going to have to trust me."

"I can do that, Mike. You might be the only one I can trust." With that, he hung up, leaving Rallin looking a little sheepish and not knowing what to say anyway.

"Three days. They might be the longest three days of my life," Rallin thought. At least he had some time to finish healing. He wondered what Arlene would have to say.

42

The next morning Tannion had only two days left to do what he needed to do. He wasn't sure that would be enough time, but he had to start somewhere. He also intended on keeping his word to Rallin and to not do anything that would be out of line with the law. At least, not too far off the mark.

First things first, and that was to get hold of Potenlikov. Of course, that would be in violation of his parole, but that was part of what would be off the mark. It had already been done before. Tannion was glad that he had called Rallin; it was nice to be back in the FBI's good books, and it sounded like Rallin had performed a miracle on that end. Now it was his turn on his end.

Potenlikov answered the phone on the third ring. Tannion told him who it was, and was met with silence on the other end of the line.

"Vlad. Didn't you hear me? It's Jim Tannion. You know, French."

Potenlikov finally spoke and Tannion could hear relief in his voice. "I heard you. I wasn't expecting to hear from you. Last I heard was that a hit was put out on you and that something had gone wrong. I've been calling you for three days and I thought the worst. Louisa and I thought you were dead. We've been worried sick. Mr. Philips said that the shooter was dead in New York and that it was Damon Bellows. Out here he's known to be the best there is, so we weren't sure."

"As they say, Vlad, the reports of my death have been greatly exaggerated. Was there anything in any of the papers?"

"Not a word. That sort of thing might not be common in New York, but the FBI must have closed the scene down quickly. Must have kept the press away. We checked the papers all week and there was nothing."

"That's good. What did Mr. Philips say about Victor Mercido?"

"Word is that Mercido put out the hit, and that all Mercido knows is that he hasn't heard from Bellows. We think he assumes that Bellows is dead, same as we do, but it's quite possible that he also thinks that you're alive, but he won't know for sure."

"Shit. I was hoping he would be thinking that we were both dead. It might have made my work a lot easier. I was pretty sure it was Mercido who put out the contract."

"That's the only contract we've heard of and if it was Bellows, he's known to work for Mercido," Potenlikov said.

"So Mercido might be expecting me."

"I would think so, French. Mercido has been hiring a lot of new muscle and has tightened his security, so it's safe to assume that he's expecting you. You did tell his man that you would be back if he tried. Too bad he didn't believe you. Either that, or he had too much faith in Bellows."

"Too bad for Mercido, for sure, but we're not going to do it the old-fashioned way. I'm with the FBI now and I gave my word to Rallin, and I intend on keeping it. I'm going to get Mercido, but not like he thinks. I'm not going to hit him. I'll let the FBI take him down, but I was hoping you and Mr. Philips would lend a small hand."

"What do you need, French? Just name it."

Tannion told him what his plan was and how Philips and Potenlikov could be of help, but he also wanted Philips to know that after it was over he expected him to move in and take over Mercido's area, including any men who might be left on the streets. That is, as long as Philips was still willing to do things the way Tannion had told him to.

Potenlikov let Tannion know that Philips was doing even better than Tannion could have expected. Any drugs they were moving were clean and good. Hookers were looked after, and, as far as they knew, the trafficking of kids for sex had left the LA area. There were enough young girls who wanted to make the kind of money that hooking could make without their pimps having to resort to drugs and violence or stealing them off the streets somewhere.

Philips made sure the girls were clean and healthy, and given a good share of the take. He found that his profits had actually gone up, as the girls were pulling more tricks, and that had helped to solidify the process in Philips' mind. A happy hooker, so to speak.

Tannion hung up the phone. His phone in New York must have a hundred messages on it, he thought, but that was okay, except he would need a cell phone. That would be the first thing on his to do list for the day, followed by the better part of three days' hard work before Rallin got there.

Tannion thought that Rallin would probably be back at work this morning, and picked the phone up again. The phone only rang once and Rallin's familiar voice was on the line. As Tannion had thought, he was already back at the office. He quickly filled Rallin in on parts of his discussion with Potenlikov.

After he hung the phone up he wondered why he had made the call. He really didn't have much to tell Rallin, and wondered if he only needed to talk to someone he trusted, or maybe he was just checking to see if Rallin were well enough to be back at work. It was good to hear his voice.

43

Rallin was a little distracted when Bill Pansloski stuck his head around the door and knocked on the wall. Having just gotten off the phone with Tannion, he wasn't really sure what had just happened. Maybe he still wasn't feeling one hundred percent. It probably was too early to be back at work. After all, it had only been four days since he was shot.

"Come on in, Bill."

"How are you feeling, Mike? You look a little red-faced. Do you really think you should be at work so soon? What does the doctor say?"

"I'm fine, Bill, but I just got off the phone with Jim Tannion," Rallin told his friend, completely ignoring his questions.

"Our Jim Tannion?" Pansloski exclaimed.

"Yeah, our Tannion. Who the hell else would use that name? More than likely to get him killed if he did. I already talked to the boss and assured him that Tannion is still on the payroll, and that I sent him out into the field to do a little research. Thanks for backing me up on that one, Bill."

"Sure, Mike. If you think that was a good idea. What did Tannion tell you?"

"Not much, but we're going to meet in LA in three days and then he'll fill me in. He knows a lot more than he's told me. I think not only does he know what happened in that hallway, but he also knows why I'm not lying out in the cemetery with you crying over my grave. It's the only thing I can come up with. He had to have done something. Either he injected me with something or…hell, I don't know. I'm just damn sure that he did something. He must have done something."

"Okay, Mike. Don't get all in a state now. I doubt the doctor likes you being back at work so early, but to have you have a stroke over why you're feeling so good would be the icing on the cake. I'll continue to back you up from here, and I'll talk to Jeff as well. There shouldn't be any problems. I've got to run down to the locals and look into that bike gang case I've got, so I'll see you tomorrow, and for Christ's sake, take it easy."

"Thanks, Bill. I will."

When Pansloski left, Rallin called the director's office and had to wait for about five minutes before he heard the distinctive voice on the other end of the line. Rallin told him again what he was doing with Tannion, or at least that Tannion was gathering information for him and that he had just had an update. He needed to ensure that the director didn't still feel like Tannion was at large and should be hunted down.

The director wasn't happy, but then he never was, so Rallin was just pleased that he seemed to buy the story. He was also pretty sure that the director would cover his bases and check Rallin's story, if he hadn't already, which meant he would have someone talk to his guys. Martin and

Pansloski were the only ones who might know about what Rallin and Tannion were doing, and Bill said they would back him up. Tannion should be okay. Now the only thing to do was to meet him in three days.

Tannion might be okay with the team and the director based on the story they concocted, but they both knew that he would still need to tell his story about what happened in the hallway. It was well known that he had been there, and he had to be debriefed if nothing else, but Rallin also knew that it could wait. Rallin knew his status with the FBI was still good enough to allow Tannion the time.

Tannion was on Rallin's mind. What was Tannion doing in Los Angeles? Rallin knew the attempted hit would have come from someone in LA, but did Tannion know who had ordered it, and if he did, what was he going to do about it? Was it Victor Mercido who put out the hit and if it was, would Tannion hit him back?

Rallin thought he could trust Tannion, but he wasn't sure. Tannion had told him he wouldn't do anything outside the law, but would he stick to that?

He just wished Tannion had stuck around. There was also what had happened to him. Something wasn't right, or maybe everything was more right than it should have been. The doctors were baffled and as far as they were concerned Rallin should probably be dead. He had lost enough blood in the hallway to have almost died anyway, but he should have bled out more than he had. The bleeding had stopped and the doctors couldn't understand why.

Although the bullet seemed to have missed most of his major organs, the doctors thought it must have hit at least a lung. The bullet had done a lot of damage, including hitting some larger blood vessels that should have caused him to bleed out internally as well as externally. Something had simply stopped the bleeding. Something had caused any damage to heal.

The doctors also couldn't explain any of the healing process. There was no way they could explain why or how he had healed so quickly. Not only had the outside wound area healed far more quickly than they knew was possible, but the doctors didn't do anything for the wound on the inside, either. There was no need. By the time they got Rallin to the hospital and looked to see how badly he was hurt, his wounds were already healing.

There was nothing for them to do but run tests, and when they came back it looked like he was fine. An MRI showed nothing to be concerned with. The bullet was a through and through, and an X-ray showed no fragments in the wound. After a couple of days in the hospital they released him, and a little more than a couple of days later here he was back at work. It made no sense, but he was sure that Tannion had an idea of what had happened. He had to.

Rallin couldn't wait to get to Los Angeles. Tannion knew something and he was damn well going to tell him. If Tannion didn't, he'd beat it out of him.

44

Tannion knew as soon as he hung up the phone from his call to Rallin that his next order of business was a visit to Philips' office. Vlad had filled him in as best he could, but there were some things that could only be done face-to-face, and dealing with Philips was one of those things best done in person.

Tannion stepped out of the hotel and hailed the first cab he could get to stop. "Not like New York," he thought. The taxi dropped him off at a very nice high-rise in the downtown area where he knew Philips had moved a few years back, not long after he had hit the big time. Potenlikov had told him all about it when they first talked after Tannion had gotten out of prison.

Tannion knew that not having an appointment would be a problem, but he also knew that it wasn't going to stop him. It might not even slow him down a lot. Philips would see him, he just didn't know it yet. When he walked in the front door, the big desk over by the elevators was the obvious choice. Tannion didn't know what floor Philips was on, but he had a guess.

Tannion walked over to the desk and took a look at the board over the receptionist's shoulder. The receptionist probably wouldn't appreciate anyone calling him a receptionist. He was not a particularly big man, but he had the look of someone who was in Philips' employ, and that could only mean he was the first stalling tactic.

As he looked at the board, Tannion could see that there were offices on all the floors, with the exception of the thirty-eighth floor. There was no indication of Philips even having an office in the building. The building only had thirty-eight floors and Tannion knew that Philips would probably want the penthouse for his office. The guy behind the desk was staring at him, waiting for Tannion to either make a move or to ask him a question. Tannion decided to make a move.

As Tannion started towards the elevator, the guy yelled out after him. "Hey, wait a minute. Who do you want to see? Do you have an appointment? Come back here."

Tannion pushed the elevator button and turned to look at the guy behind the desk. The elevator next to him opened up, and without saying a word he stepped in and pushed the button for the top floor. He was only a little surprised that the button was there at all, but it was an office building and Tannion knew that Philips was trying to look as respectable as possible. That, and the fact that the building was built before Philips moved in.

As the door closed, Tannion took a last look back towards the desk and wasn't surprised to see the receptionist with a phone in his hand, talking very quickly. Chances were that there would be company at the top when the door opened on the thirty-eighth floor, and Tannion wasn't wrong. There were three rather tough-looking guys standing at the door waiting for him.

Tannion took a quick look and didn't recognize any of them. That would have been too easy. If Potenlikov would have been there it would have been easier still, but Tannion was glad he wasn't. This was a business call, but Tannion didn't want to hurt anyone. At least, not too much. He took the first step to get out of the elevator, and the biggest of the three men stepped towards him.

"Just stay in the elevator and take a ride down. If you want to see Mr. Philips you can talk to Ben at the desk and make an appointment." He took a step into the elevator and pushed the button for main. Tannion let him say his piece and push the button, but then took his own action.

Tannion grabbed the man by the shoulder of his jacket, and with a solid jerk he threw the man against the back of the elevator hard enough to knock the wind out of him and take him to his knees. Tannion took a step out of the elevator, and as quickly as he stepped out the doors closed.

The two toughs standing in the hallway were as stunned as the guy in the elevator, but it only lasted for a couple of seconds. The one closest to Tannion reached to grab him as he stepped out of the elevator, while the second guy came around from the side to get his hands on him as well. Tannion reached through the first guy's outstretched arms, took hold of his neck with his right hand and lifted him off the ground.

The second guy was just a little slower, and a second later Tannion had his left hand around the guy's neck and he lifted both men off the ground. He thought there was a very good chance that they were both carrying guns and if they wanted to, they might reach into their holster or waistband, or where ever they carried them, and that would spell trouble for everyone, including anyone who might happen to be close by.

Tannion turned one hundred and eighty degrees and with a flick of his wrists he threw both men against the elevator door. When they hit the ground Tannion was on them, he took about three seconds to find their weapons, and then pulled them to their feet.

"Okay, boys, let's go see Mr. Philips." They both blustered and one of them told Tannion that Mr. Philips would kill him or something like that, but Tannion wasn't listening. He frog-marched the two men to the door, then tossed them to each side, opened the door and walked in.

The look on Philips' face was worth it. Tannion knew that by going through channels, Philips' men would have given him the run-around without Philips even knowing about it. Potenlikov could have gotten him in, but that would have taken time. The look on Philips' face was enough to assure Tannion that, given any other choice, this was still the way he would have chosen.

"What the fuck? French. What the hell are you doing here?" Philips had been in the game too long for him to be caught at a loss for more than a quick outburst. "I mean, Jim Tannion. Come on in. It's good to see you."

The two men Tannion left outside came into the room as fast as they could, and Philips put up his hand and told them it was okay. Reluctantly they both left, closing the door behind them. Tannion chose the chair closest to the desk that Philips was behind and sat down. Philips had been standing and he sat down as well.

"How are you, Mr. Philips?"

"Mr. Philips. Come on, French. After what we've been through and with that entrance, I think you can call me Jackson. You've earned that right."

"Sorry for the way I came in, but it was the quickest. I needed to see you and I needed to see you now. Your men would have only slowed me down."

"That's fine, French, but I'm a busy man, so why don't you cut to the chase and tell me what's so dammed important that you needed to get the better of my men and bust in here." Tannion went on to tell Philips of the near hit in New York, and wasn't surprised when Philips told him that he was aware of it.

"I heard about it," he said. "I wasn't sure if you would make it here."

"I knew you would be up to speed. Vlad filled me in a little, but I need a little more from you. You know that it was Victor Mercido who put out the contract on me, and I need some starter info. I'm going to take that stupid shit down," Tannion said.

He went on to tell Philips that he was going to do it with the help of the FBI, and the main reason for the visit was to get Philips' word that he would take over as much of Mercido's operation as he could, without anybody getting killed, and that he would continue to do his business in what Tannion liked to call 'the Philips way'.

Jackson T. Philips was the big man about town, but he still liked to have his ego stroked now and again, and he liked how 'the Philips way' sounded. The fact that it was working so well for him and he was way ahead of everyone else in the city made it a lot easier to understand why he would like it.

Philips told Tannion that he would do what he could and would take over everything he could if Mercido went down. He passed Tannion as much information on Mercido as he could recall, and promised to have Potenlikov pass on more info if he could come up with any.

Tannion could tell that Philips would be more than happy to have him take Mercido out for him. Mercido had grown and probably had the largest operation in town, next to Philips. As someone got bigger they always wanted more, and the clash between the two of them seemed to be inevitable, which went against the Philips way. Having Tannion take Mercido down was about the best Philips could hope for.

Tannion left the office and went down the elevator, but before he got in, Philips made a point of getting the three goons outside the door to come in. He introduced them to Tannion, although he introduced him as French. Philips made sure that each one of them understood that Tannion could have killed them all without working up a sweat, even if they had their guns pointed at him, and that the next time they were to escort Tannion to his office when he came, even if he didn't have an appointment. Especially if he didn't have an appointment.

Tannion wasn't sure whether he had made three friends or three pretty tough enemies. At this point, he really didn't care. He didn't expect to be in Los Angeles long enough to find out.

45

Tannion was thankful that he'd been able to get the missing information from Philips. All he needed were a few starting points, and he had at least that and maybe Potenlikov might give him even more. He knew what building Mercido worked out of, but that was just the office he used mostly for show, to make him look as legit as he could. What Tannion didn't know, and what Philips had given him, was where the majority of Mercido's holdings were. If Tannion was going to put him away for a long time the FBI way, then he was going to have to stay within the law. That meant no break and enter, or any data gathering that came from it. Surveillance was the name of the game.

A quick stop at the nearest camera store and he was equipped with a good camera with a telescopic lens, along with some nighttime equipment that the dealer wasn't so sure Tannion would need. The dealer only needed to know that Tannion was spotting owls and other nightlife, and that was good enough. Tannion's eyesight was almost as good as the lens, but the lens caught things much more permanently. Now he only needed to get enough information so the FBI could take the next steps required to bring Mercido down.

Tannion knew that he did his best work at night, and he also knew that Mercido's best work would be after dark as well. That meant a few hours' nap before it was dark enough to hit the streets. Tannion didn't think he would be getting much sleep in the next three days, so a nap would be good. The sun was nicely down when Tannion walked out the front door of his hotel. This time, however, he didn't look like Jim Tannion.

A little hair dye, a fake mustache, and the camera around his neck and he was just another tourist in downtown LA taking some night shots. As soon as he was outside he caught a cab and took it for only about ten blocks before he had it drop him off. He walked around the corner, and was lucky enough to catch another cab at the taxi stand and had it take him to an area he knew well.

He had the cab take a few unnecessary turns and he kept a sharp eye on his rear. When the taxi dropped him off he knew he wasn't being followed, but when he stepped out of the cab there was a car waiting for him. Vladimir Potenlikov was sitting behind the wheel. Tannion got in the passenger side and with a grin said hello to his friend.

A few minutes later Potenlikov stopped the car in what was an almost deserted parking lot and got out beside one of only a handful of cars sitting there. He tossed the keys to Tannion and told him not to wreck it. Tannion got behind the wheel and was gone before Potenlikov was back in his car.

Tannion had a few places he could start with, but he had wanted to make sure that he had talked to Potenlikov before he did. He had assured Philips that nothing would get back to Mercido to indicate that Philips was helping him or even be aware that Tannion was in town. The car was rented to Mr. Victor French. If Mercido wanted to check, it would look like Tannion had just rented a car under his old name; still nothing that would alert Mercido to Philips' involvement. Potenlikov didn't have much to add to what Philips had told Tannion, but it was good to know they were working together again.

Tannion parked the car several blocks from the warehouse he had chosen to be his first point of surveillance. Philips had told him about the warehouse and Potenlikov had filled in a little more.

There were always drugs being smuggled in from Mexico, and as long as anyone was close to the waterfront, they could probably get their hands on some. That was where so much of it came in, and in this case the warehouse was also where it was cut and bagged. The drug of choice for Mercido was usually cocaine, but it could be heroin or anything that didn't need a lab. The lab was somewhere else, and Philips had given him that address as well.

Tannion found a hiding spot and he waited. About three-quarters of an hour into his wait, he saw what he was waiting for. A truck rolled up to the door and honked once. It was a three-ton delivery truck with advertising on the sides, but Tannion had seen enough of these types of transactions to know what this kind of truck could be used for. More often than not it would haul fresh produce all day and turn into something not quite as legal at night. The smell of tomatoes and whatever had been hauled all day still hung around the truck.

Tannion took a few pictures, but he knew he was going to have to get closer and get some shots of what was inside the warehouse. He was worried about getting caught only because he didn't want to warn Mercido as to what was happening. Mercido couldn't go to ground like a common thug, but he could pull in his operation to the point where Tannion would have a hard time getting anything on him. Tannion remembered how good of a job Philips had done with the exact same problem when Rallin's team was after him only a little while ago.

Tannion made his way around to the back of the warehouse and found a door in an area that was very dark. Philips had told him that Mercido kept the warehouse guarded in front on the inside, but there were no guards on the outside. Guards walking around outside would be hard to explain and with the locals on payroll, Mercido had no reason to worry.

He grabbed the doorknob and found it was locked, and with just enough pressure, the lock gave way, but the door didn't. The deadbolt was still holding tight. Tannion was able to place a small bar he had brought for just that purpose between the door and the casing, and with a little pressure the deadbolt was hanging in air as useless as Tannion needed it to be. Well, maybe a little break and enter.

Tannion pulled the door open and made sure that it was shut, but not locked. If anyone happened to find the door they would notice the deadbolt unlocked, but that was a chance he would have to take. He couldn't be locking his escape route and making it more difficult than was necessary.

The warehouse was very large and the door Tannion had used was far in the back corner, a long way from where the action was. There were crates of what, based on the signs on the outside, were supposed to be auto parts, but

Tannion wouldn't even guess as to what was really inside them. They were perfect for hiding behind and that was all that mattered. Tannion climbed up to the top of the pile and found that he could move forward just enough to see what was going on in the rest of the building.

The lights were on only in the back half and Tannion didn't even need the night equipment. The pictures he took included the unloading of what looked to be pallets of potatoes, but between some of the bags were much smaller bags that looked to contain a white powder that could have been cocaine, but could also have been sugar. Not enough to get the FBI going, but that wasn't all there was to take pictures of. The pallets were being unloaded off to one side and there was an entire workforce taking the powder from the small bags and making even smaller bags; just big enough to sell on the street. Tannion wondered how many millions worth of cocaine were sitting there and how much would go through the warehouse in a year. The numbers were astounding.

Tannion also knew that Philips had a couple of warehouses just like this that he could be taking pictures of, and unless Philips had moved them in the past few years, he could probably be doing the same thing to Philips as he was doing to Mercido. Philips knew it too, and that was one reason he kept his word to Tannion. Drugs, gambling, money lending, and prostitution were enough to make a person really rich or really dead, depending on your luck and your position.

It was important to Tannion that Philips didn't run young girls unwillingly. That was how he had met Louisa and the girls that were with her, and he was not going to let it happen to any other young girls if he could help it. Philips knew how serious Tannion was on this issue and he had kept his word.

Tannion got enough pictures and knew the place would be easy to take down. After climbing down from the top of the crates, he went out of the door he had used to come in. He used the same bar to slip the door apart and lock the deadbolt. The door lock was still busted, but with the dead-bolt locked, no one would care. Tannion had used a cloth to ensure the bar didn't make a mess of the door or the casing, and he made sure that he had gloves on so his fingerprints wouldn't show up if they dusted. He was being careful.

He decided to leave the car where it was, walked a few blocks, and caught a cab in front of a small hotel where there was a taxi stand. He gave the cabbie an address and got out in much the same type of area he had just left. The cab ride only took a few minutes.

Tannion walked the last couple of blocks towards a second warehouse Philips had on his list. This time it was supposed to be a storage facility and probably not drugs, but Philips and Potenlikov weren't sure what might be there.

He got close enough to see that there were no lights on, in, or near the warehouse, but Philips hadn't been sure if Mercido would have guards out or not. After a few minutes watching from cover, Tannion decided that the warehouse was unguarded and went in for a closer look. If there were no guards then the chance of there being anything valuable inside was slim.

A quick look told Tannion that there were no windows, but the roof style made him think that there might be a sky-light. A few seconds later and Tannion was on the roof. A couple of crates leaning against the wall and the ability to jump, grab, and climb made it easy for him. Once on the roof Tannion was glad to see that he was right. There were two skylights.

The roof was flat and the skylights were about six feet square and raised about a foot off the roof, but with a flat window. Tannion took a quick look over the edge and with his enhanced night vision he could see what Mercido was hiding. The warehouse was the storage area for what would probably be a drop spot for a chop shop operation.

There were at least a dozen cars lined up on the warehouse floor. He could see that all the cars were high-end and most likely stolen, unless Mercido had suddenly become a car collector. Tannion took a number of pictures with the night scope, trying to ensure that the picture included the license plate. The cars must have been freshly stolen and waiting to be taken to where they would be chopped.

A few minutes later Tannion was off the roof and ready to call it a night. It would be daylight in an hour and the city would start to come to life. He knew he had enough information for one night, and after walking a few blocks before he could catch a cab, he finally made it back to his car. He drove to a different hotel he had booked on the other side of town. The first hotel was still booked under an assumed name and as far as they were concerned he was still there. Victor French was living on the other side of town, and for Tannion it felt good to be back in action. The name seemed to fit as well.

46

Vladimir Potenlikov knocked on the door before he entered. Jackson T. Philips was on the phone, but he had heard the knock and saw Potenlikov's big head peek around the doorframe, and he waved him to a chair.

Potenlikov knew Philips about as well as any man did, or for that matter, any woman. They had been together for several years and had seen the worst of it, and now they were experiencing the best. Philips was the biggest player on the West Coast and everyone knew it. That included the FBI and the locals, but they also knew that he ran a very large legitimate business as well.

Philips was proud of the legitimate side of his business. The trucking line that had once belonged to the Santos brothers was a big part of it, but he had added wholesaling and warehousing, and had even bought into some shipping companies.

In all, Philips' companies had over fifty thousand employees, with most of them in the Los Angeles area. He was a well-liked and well-respected member of the community. The slightly seedier side of his business was now only just over half of his income and the legitimate business had become much more than just a way to clean up the dirty money. He thought of himself as a businessman and never as a criminal.

Philips knew that he had Potenlikov to thank for much of his success, and also the man he knew as French, but now knew as Jim Tannion, but he would never call him that. He would always be French to Philips. Tannion had taken the fall when he got caught and had taken so many of Philips' rivals with him that he had left the door wide open for Philips to walk right in and with Potenlikov by his side, in they had walked.

Potenlikov almost filled the easy chair that Philips waved him to. Because of his size he was known as the Big Russian, and the nickname had made him look like muscle, which of course meant all brawn and no brain. In his case that wasn't true, but it had taken a while for Philips to understand it and thanks again to Tannion, Philips did finally figure it out.

Philips put the phone down and looked over at Potenlikov. He broke out in a grin that took up a large portion of his face. "Good to see you, Vlad. Guess who paid me a visit yesterday."

Potenlikov had been running some errands for Philips that had taken him away from the office the day before, and therefore he wasn't around when Tannion had come in, but he had heard about it as soon as he walked into the building. He had taken a look at the surveillance video before he had come up to Philips' office, as well as talking to the men who had put up only a token opposition, despite their obvious size and ability. Potenlikov knew Tannion well enough to know that his men didn't stand a chance, but they didn't need to know that and he told them of his displeasure, but that was to be the end of any disciplinary action. The men felt bad enough without any encouragement.

"Let me think, Mr. Philips. Might it have been our friend French, by any chance?"

"God damn right, Vlad. You should have seen him. I looked at the surveillance tapes and it was quite the show. The guys didn't have a chance, and there were three of them and they were armed. Tannion was unarmed and he didn't even work up a sweat. It's been too long since I saw him in action and it was great to see. Christ, but we need to get him back working for us, Vlad."

"That's not likely to happen, Mr. Philips. He seems to like the FBI game and plans to stay there. Besides, working for us would be a parole violation for him. There's also a chance that having him with the FBI might even be better than having him work for us."

"You might have that right, Vlad. Did you know he was in town?" Philips asked.

"He called a couple of nights ago, just before I went to San Diego," Potenlikov told his boss, deliberately leaving out the quick meeting that he had with Tannion in a parking lot. He didn't want Philips to think that him and Tannion were doing anything behind his back.

"I didn't think he was going to pay you a visit. What did he want? He told me about wanting to get his hands on Mercido, but he didn't give me any details."

Philips went on to tell Potenlikov what he had discussed with Tannion, including the data that Tannion had asked for. "He wants us to take over as soon as we can, but he wants to ensure that we do it in what he calls 'The Philips Way'. I kind of like the way he put that. It has a nice sound."

"What did he mean by it?" Potenlikov asked.

"Just a continuation of what he wanted when he went down years ago, but didn't finger any of us. It's been working so well for so long I'm pretty sure that none of us want to go back there."

"No, sir. Not if there's any way not to, and certainly not while French is on the outside keeping his eyes on us. When does he expect to hit Mercido?"

"He said within the week, but he's doing it by the book, so the FBI will be involved, as well as the locals, so it will drag out. We'll wait and see, and take over when and where we can. I'm not so sure how deep he'll be able to dig into Mercido. Mercido tends to cover his tracks pretty well. French might hit him in a few places that I mentioned, but even then he might not be able to actually hang anything on Mercido himself."

"Knowing French the way we do, nothing would surprise me," Potenlikov said.

"You said that right, Vlad. Just have a look at the tapes and you'll know that he hasn't lost anything."

"I'll do that, boss. I'll do that," omitting the fact that he already had.

"It sure would be nice to have him working for us again, though. He might be of help working for the FBI, and he proved that when he was here last, but he knows stuff I don't like anyone at the FBI to know."

"I know, Mr. Philips. Remember, it's French. He didn't turn on us back then, and I don't think he'll turn on us now."

"Not even if his FBI pals put pressure on him? They didn't last time, but they could try again. He could do us some serious harm."

"No, Mr. Philips. We can trust French." Potenlikov sounded very sure, but Philips wasn't as confident.

"I hope you're right, Vlad. I'm not so sure, but I hope you're right."

"I'm certain I'm right."

"I told French that I would ask you to talk to him and pass him anything you can about Mercido. I gave him what I could."

"No problem," Potenlikov said. He knew he would be talking to French again soon, and now he had the boss's blessing.

When Potenlikov left Philips' office, Philips picked up the phone. The call was to one of his men he knew to be loyal to him, but who wasn't on the best of terms with Potenlikov. He was also good at what he did. Philips told him to pick three men and wait until he called him again.

The four of them should be good at tailing someone, and if he decided it was necessary, then they would be able to make a hit as well. That was where their skills lay. If Tannion became a problem, Philips might need to get rid of him, as much as he hoped he didn't have to. If Potenlikov was right and Tannion could still be trusted, then there was no harm done in just watching him, but if he was wrong, then it was always best to be prepared.

Philips saw what Tannion had done to his men and as much as Potenlikov seemed to trust him, he wasn't so sure. If he could take Mercido out of the picture, that would be a bonus, but if it looked like he might turn on him, Philips needed to be ready.

He found it fun to watch Tannion in action again, but that just showed that he hadn't lost his touch. He would be an incredibly tough foe and Mercido had better be very careful. If Tannion did decide to look in Philips' direction, no matter what Potenlikov said, Tannion could cause him a lot of harm. Philips knew that he needed to be ahead of the game, no matter what game it was. This was his town.

47

Tannion's second night went much the same as the first. He met Potenlikov in the same parking lot as before, making sure that he wasn't followed. Potenlikov told him about his meeting with Philips and gave him a couple more addresses to look into. Tannion went to take some pictures. One of the places was supposed to be another drug operation, but the better of the two was what Potenlikov called a gambling hall.

Tannion drove back to his hotel and went to his room for a shower, and when he came out he didn't look the same. He didn't want to take his car and had the bellman call him a taxi. He had the cabbie take him to the address of the gambling hall Potenlikov had given him. Tannion was able to walk in as if he were just there to play for a while, and after losing a few dollars he decided to leave, or at least look like he was leaving, but instead he went looking for a nice spot to hide and take a few pictures.

He worked his way upstairs in the hotel, where more than illegal gambling was taking place. Along with the gambling were the usual perks, and the girls were expensive. This was not a low-end place. Either people went to Las Vegas or Tahoe, or they went to Mercido's. It was well known around town, but it kept moving and the cops could never nail it down.

Vlad had told Tannion that the hall had been in this hotel for over a month and was probably going to move in the next week or so. Mercido was always looking for the next place. The regulars got the address of the new place by registered mail.

Tannion was able to take a few pictures when the cameras were not able to see him. It had taken a couple of hours of playing to get the layout in his head and part of that was where the cameras were, and better still, where they weren't. Tannion went back upstairs, and this time was immediately approached by more than one of the hookers. He needed to know for sure that what he was told, and expected, was actually going down.

This would be a good coup for the cops. It might not directly tie to Mercido, but putting this place out of operation would hurt him. Tannion thought it might be best if he gave the collar to the LAPD. That way it would hurt Mercido right away, without tipping Tannion's hand by using the FBI.

As he left the building he knew he was going to wait until Rallin got there and let him make the decision. It was Rallin's game only because Tannion gave it to him, but Rallin didn't need to know that. Rallin would do a good job, and as long as the location hung in for a couple more days, then the local cops would hit it.

Tannion left the gambling hall and had a taxi drop him off a couple of blocks from the next address on his list. It turned out to be a warehouse. There were no lights on and there didn't appear to be anyone nearby, but Tannion was careful in case there was a guard around somewhere. Tannion found a good hiding spot, close enough to see what was going on, but far enough away so as to not be seen by anyone passing by.

After waiting for less than ten minutes a car with two men in it pulled up. One of them got out and went to the warehouse door and made sure it was locked. He then walked to one side of the warehouse and took a look and then did the same on the other side. Seeing all was okay he got back in the car and the two men drove to the back of the warehouse and repeated the movements.

Based on the guards' activity, Tannion knew there had to be something in the warehouse. He waited to see when the guards would come back, and he found they were there at almost one-hour increments. As soon as he saw them leave for the third time, Tannion cut across the street and walked up to the front doors. A small door beside the large main door was easy to pick and Tannion was inside.

A quick look around told Tannion what he needed to know. There were several cars sitting to one side, and a full chop shop in the back. The warehouse was obviously another stolen car operation, but this was the place where the cars were broken down into parts, and either sold or shipped. Tannion took a few pictures and let himself out before the hour was up and the guards came back.

As the night was over, Tannion made his way back to the hotel to wait out the day and get some sleep. The third night found him staking out a warehouse that Potenlikov said was one of Mercido's, but he hadn't been sure what it was being used for. He thought it was probably drugs and might even be the location of a meth lab setup. Tannion was there to find out.

Tannion set up shop in a building across the street that happened to have a door unlocked, and as it was empty, it appeared that nobody was going to mind if Tannion took a few pictures from the second floor. He used it to get as close as he could to the warehouse without walking in. He had cased the warehouse as soon as it was dark out, and other than the large front lift door and a small door beside it, the warehouse was locked down.

There were no other doors and there were no windows. Whatever was to go on inside was not going to be seen by anyone on the outside. That meant that Tannion was going to have to take pictures of the comings and goings and hope that it was enough for Rallin to get a warrant to bust in. It was either that or a front door assault, and that wouldn't keep things quiet at all. So pictures it was.

About two o'clock in the morning a truck pulled up to the warehouse and was let in immediately. Tannion took a couple of pictures to capture the truck and the license plate, but he had no idea what was inside. A couple of minutes later and the truck pulled out again, and Tannion heard rather than saw what was going on inside.

A woman screamed, and before the door shut Tannion heard what he thought were other women crying. His highly sensitive hearing could not pick up anything more from across the street and he wasn't able to see anything inside. The sounds that Tannion heard brought back very vivid memories of when he had first met Louisa and the girls she was with, girls who had been stolen off the streets and who were destined to be sold back on to them. That was, until Tannion stepped in.

Tannion knew immediately that he couldn't just sit across the street when the one thing he had told Philips he was strictly against appeared to be happening within his range of hearing. Tannion was ready to bust in and let whatever happened happen, but first he stopped to work out some semblance of a plan rather than letting his emotions control his actions.

The two front doors were the only ways in, and he knew they were both manned outside for sure, and probably inside as well. In each case the men had guns, and he had seen at least six of them, but there were bound to be more inside. The sounds that were coming from inside might mean that Tannion had a slight advantage, assuming that they were busy at the moment.

Tannion went down the stairs in the building across the street and looked out the window, where he could see the two men standing guard outside the doors to the warehouse. They had been left behind by the truck and weren't there when Tannion had arrived. Two men wouldn't be a problem as long as he could get to them and then keep them quiet. If they got a shot off or made any noise that brought the rest of the men outside, then they would be only a small part of Tannion's problem.

Tannion had tried the drunk routine once in the past and it had worked, but at that time he had a bottle to share. This time he didn't have a bottle, but he thought that it might still work. As long as they let him get close enough to shut them up, then he could worry about the inside of the building later.

He opened the door and went to walk outside, making sure to trip over the doorframe. He landed on his side, facing away from the other side of the street. Cursing under his breath, he worked his way almost back up to his feet, but with a slip he went down again. This time he made sure to bash the side of his face against the pavement hard enough to bleed. It had to look real and Tannion made sure that it did.

He had turned the pain receptors off, and he knew that hitting the pavement wouldn't hurt and he would heal any damage as soon as he was done. As soon as Tannion had opened the door the men across the street were on alert. They both reached for the guns they had holstered under their left armpits. When Tannion fell the second time they both laughed and their hands went away from their guns. They started across the street and were already giving Tannion the gears for being so drunk.

"Hey, asshole. Drunk as hell, aren't you?" one of them called out. "You got any left?" the first guy asked, and the second guy had to answer for Tannion.

"He's so fucking drunk he can't even stand up. Hey, pal. He asked you if you've got any left."

At that point Tannion had gotten back to his feet and was starting to walk away from the two guys coming across the street, as if he knew they were trouble and even as drunk as he was he knew better than to walk into trouble. The two men had decided to have a little fun with the drunk and to check to see if he had any booze on him and maybe some ready cash, or whatever they might be able to find.

Tannion took a couple of unsteady steps in the direction he was heading, but he fell again and the two men were on him. They grabbed him under the arms, one on each side, and stood Tannion up. The guy on Tannion's right took a quick check of Tannion's pockets to see what he might be holding. Tannion was wearing jeans and a short-sleeve shirt under a blue jacket, with the shirt half pulled out of his jeans. The pockets of the jacket were the only possible hiding spots for a bottle and they checked there first.

As soon as the first guy stuck his hand in Tannion's pocket, Tannion grabbed them both by the neck. Using a similar move to the one he used on Philips' guards, he held them with one hand around each of their necks, but he knew these guys wouldn't have any concern about grabbing their guns as Philips' guards had. As soon as he had them lifted off the ground, Tannion stepped forward and slammed them both to the pavement. Using his considerable strength wasn't required, as gravity would have done enough damage, but use it he did.

Tannion took the bodies into the building he had just vacated. He checked to see if they were alive, and not finding a pulse for either of them he didn't bother to tie them up. He opened the door and dumped them inside, pulling the door closed behind him. He then crossed the street and stood before the smaller of the two doors.

Tannion opened the door, but stood to the side so anyone looking out wouldn't see him. It only took a moment or two before someone inside noticed the door was open and came to investigate. Tannion's luck was holding, as the man stuck his head out the door without telling anyone what he was doing.

As soon as the guy's head was out far enough for Tannion to reach him, he grabbed him by the collar and hauled him around the side of the building out of sight. A quick right and he was out cold. This time Tannion checked to see if he had killed him, and was happy to note he was still breathing. The first two had to be silenced, but this guy was too easy. Killing these guys wasn't exactly the FBI way and as a result this guy got lucky and got to live.

Tannion went back to the door to wait to see if it would work again. After a couple of minutes it looked like his luck had run out, as no one was coming out to investigate. Tannion stuck his head around the corner and as far as he could see there were only a half dozen men left inside with probably a dozen girls. The girls weren't happy to be there and they weren't exactly happy to have the six guys trying to get into their pants. As Tannion could see, more than a couple of the guys had succeeded.

Tannion didn't have a weapon of any sort, but he knew he wouldn't need one. A couple of quick steps and the first punch landed, and now there were five. One of the girls screamed when Tannion hit the guy beside her. Tannion was big and he scared the hell out of her, but after he hit the guy hard enough to render him unconscious the girl realized what he was doing, and the screaming turned into yelling and fighting back. The second and third guys were down and out before they could move.

That left three men and they had finally noticed what was going on. They were pulling their pants up and looking for their jackets where their guns were. The guy who peeked out the door was supposed to be watching their backs and their guns, and all of a sudden they found this big guy in amongst them, and then they found out that the girls had their guns. Two of the girls had run over to where the men had left their jackets and each had grabbed a gun out of its shoulder holster.

Tannion stepped back and headed for the door, as he knew what was going to happen next. The first gunshot was a gut shot into the last guy to get up, and the next two weren't any better. Tannion quickly stepped to the door and was outside just after the third shot rang out.

He had already been through a situation like this in the past and the result was either the best thing that ever happened to him or the worst. It was a situation like this when he had met Louisa and then eventually lost her. He wasn't going to have that happen to him again. The girls had things well under control and they didn't need him anyway.

Tannion heard a half dozen more shots as he stepped out of the door. He knew that the cops would be there in a matter of minutes. That many gunshots would be heard and someone would call. He hoped the girls would be smart enough to get out and run like hell. The girls all looked to be young and black. They might have been picked up in the area, and from their looks, and from what they had on, they had probably already been working girls. They didn't have a Spanish look like the girls he had rescued when he met Louisa.

Mercido wouldn't like what had happened, but it would look like the girls had ended things without help and it might not come back to haunt Tannion. As long as the girls got away there wouldn't even be a mention of the helping hand they had. There were the two guys dead across the street that the cops might have a hard time explaining, and there was the guy out cold, but that was a worry for a different day.

Tannion thought it best to call it an early night and get back to his hotel and get out of sight. Suddenly Rallin's idea of lying low was sounding like a good idea.

48

Tannion met Rallin at the airport the next morning. Rallin's plane was on time and Tannion was happy to see that Rallin had brought enough luggage to mean he was planning to stay a while. Obviously he had taken Tannion seriously when he said he was going to let the FBI take Mercido down. The luggage meant that Rallin was coming to LA to work.

After they said their pleasantries, Tannion led Rallin to the car and tossed his luggage in the trunk. He drove back to the hotel where he was staying under the name of Victor French. They didn't exchange many words on the trip, but as soon as they got in the hotel room, Rallin wanted answers. They sat down at the small table that was in the corner of the room.

"What the hell happened in that hallway, Jim?" The words almost exploded out of Rallin's mouth. Tannion knew that Rallin had been waiting a long time for the two of them to get to a place where they could talk privately, and that wasn't in the car. Rallin didn't want any interruptions.

"Hold on, Mike. Not so fast. I think you know what happened. The hit that was meant for me hit you first and then I took him out. I called in the troops and an ambulance and then hit the road. I wasn't thinking very straight at the time. I had flashbacks of the last time the same sort of thing happened in New York and I had to leave. I even made sure that no one knew where I was going at first, but mostly I wanted revenge."

"But you ran."

"After I was on the road and had a chance to clear my head I thought about going back. I wasn't worried about clearing my name this time, but I was centered on getting to Mercido. I thought if no one knew where I was then Mercido might think I was dead, or at least missing, and he wouldn't be following any of you guys and not getting anyone else shot."

Rallin was listening, but trying to get a word in as well. When Tannion finally took a breath, Rallin jumped in. "That makes sense Jim, but that's not what I meant. What did you do to me?"

"Oh, that. Right," Tannion stuttered, not sure exactly how to explain, or if he should explain. "I can explain, Mike, but I'm not sure that you want to know."

"Trust me, Jim. I want to know. Hell, my doctors want to know. Arlene wants to know. Pansloski wants to know. Now what the hell did you do?"

Tannion could tell that Rallin was like a dog with a bone and there was no way he was going anywhere until he knew the truth. Tannion suddenly felt as if a weight were about to be lifted off his chest. His secret was coming out.

"Okay, Mike. You deserve to know what happened. This is a secret I've carried for years now and it's time someone else knew. I need you to keep this just between us though, Mike. Not even my mother knows. Do you swear that you can and will keep this a secret? Your doctors can't find out, and not even your wife."

"Christ, Jim. What are we, back in grade school? Just tell me what you know."

"I mean it, Mike. Swear to me that you'll keep it a secret, or I can't say anything," Tannion said, and Rallin could tell that he was completely serious.

After a few seconds Rallin gave his answer. "Okay. I swear that I'll keep your secret between only you and me. Now do you feel better? Now tell me. What the hell did you do?"

"First, Mike, before I tell you what I did to you, I have to explain what happened to me. A few years back I was hit by lightning and as a result, some kind of molecular change took place inside of me. It might be that it removed a block, which allowed my mind to do things that all of us might be able to do if we were able to use a different part of our brain. I don't know. It might be something strictly at the molecular level, but the only way to find out would be to dissect me and I'm against that, if you know what I mean. That's why it has to be our secret."

Rallin was a good cop, which meant that he was trained to listen and to pick the truth out of all the bullshit, but this time he wasn't sure what he was hearing. "Come on, Jim. What has this to do with me and what you did to me?"

"Right. Let me jump ahead. As a result of the changes to my body I'm able to adjust my body and through contact, I can adjust the bodies of others. The short story is that I simply told your body to heal itself and it did."

"Shit, Jim." The look of total disbelief on Rallin's face told Tannion what he needed to know. It was going to be tough to prove it to Rallin, but he knew that he could.

Rallin went on. "You want me to believe that you told me to heal, so I did. That's not possible. How can I possibly believe you?"

"I know it's hard to believe, but I've come up with a couple of experiments to prove to you that I can do what anyone else would think was impossible. Do you remember that car I picked off that kid that caused us to meet the first time?"

"I remember. Pansloski thought it must have weighed a thousand pounds. You said it must have been the adrenaline pumping and I've heard of that happening before."

"Maybe, but I could have picked up a lot more weight than the end of that car. Let me start with this."

Tannion reached into his pocket and pulled out a small pocketknife that he had bought the day before. He usually didn't have a need for something like a small knife, but he knew he was going to have to prove himself to Rallin.

Tannion took the knife and told Rallin to watch as he cut the base of his thumb about a quarter inch deep. The wound didn't bleed, and Tannion didn't feel a thing. As Rallin watched the wound slowly closed up, and in a matter of a couple of minutes there was nothing left that even looked like a scar.

The look on Rallin's face had changed and it told Tannion what he needed to know. There was a look of fascination with a small amount of fear. Fear that he couldn't possibly believe what he had just seen, but fascination in having seen it. Tannion suddenly reached across the table and grabbed Rallin's right hand. Rallin jerked his hand back, but it might as well have been held in a vice.

Tannion went to work immediately. Through the contact he gave Rallin's body a few instructions. First was to stop movement. Rallin tried to move, but found that he was held as if he were frozen. The knife appeared over Rallin's hand, and Tannion plunged it in deep and pulled it forward for more than an inch.

Rallin's eyes were as big as saucers. He saw the knife enter his hand and could do nothing about it. He couldn't even scream. He noted that there was no blood to speak of and there was no pain. A few seconds later and he could see the wound physically healing, and after a couple of minutes he could tell there was nothing left that had been caused by the knife. At that moment Tannion released him from his grip, both on his arm and on his body. Rallin almost fell out of his chair backwards from the force of the pull that he had made almost five minutes earlier.

"What the hell?" was all Rallin could say. He kept looking from his hand to Tannion and back to his hand. Tannion went on to tell him what he had done to his body to immobilize him, and how he had stopped the bleeding and blocked the pain receptors. He also went on to talk about what he could heal and how he had changed his own body.

Tannion looked to be a big man and Rallin would not have doubted him if he said he weighed in at two-twenty or two-thirty, but Tannion told him he was over three hundred pounds. He also told Rallin that he could bench press almost a thousand pounds and he could run at over forty miles an hour for an extended period. He also told Rallin that he could kill him in a thousand ways just by touching him. He could also just as easily kill him with his bare hands.

Rallin sat speechless for several minutes and when he finally did get his voice, he only asked one more question. He might still be somewhat in doubt of Tannion's skills, but he had seen what he had seen. It might not make complete sense to him, but he was going to need some time to think. His question to Tannion was, "How are we going to catch Mercido?"

49

Victor Mercido was not a happy man. He was never overly thrilled with his situation in life in the first place, but that wasn't what was making him unhappy today. Mercido was in his late fifties and although he was considered to be very rich by anyone who knew him, it wasn't enough for Mercido. It would never be enough. He wanted more and he also wanted his bad leg to stop aching. Arthritis had finally caught up to his leg and it was almost always giving him trouble.

Mercido was even less happy today than he was in general. He had just found out about a bunch of his men who had been found dead in one of his warehouses. The warehouse had been used to switch trucks that were carrying girls picked up locally. Girls that were picked up would either be sold and placed on a ship to somewhere in the east, or they were placed somewhere closer and put into the sex trade. These girls had been heading for San Francisco.

Some of the girls had been easy as they were picked up off the street already hooking, but some would need a little help. They would be shot up with heroin or crack and eventually they would hook for a fix. The girls who came off the street simply disappeared from a competitor's string and would be back to work in a couple of weeks in a different city. Mercido liked the idea of hurting his competition as he feathered his own nest.

That night a shipment had been picked up locally, but now the girls were gone and his men were dead. It looked like somehow the girls had gotten the jump on his men and had shot them with their own guns. All his men were dead except for one. That one was in the hospital with a broken jaw and a concussion.

Two of the dead men weren't found in the warehouse. Mercido couldn't figure out why they were found in the building across the street. Apparently they had been killed by some form of blunt force trauma. The coroner had said the cause of death looked to be a blow to the head, and in each case it looked like they had fallen on the pavement. Small bits of asphalt and the usual grit found on the pavement was imbedded into their skulls.

That didn't jive with the girls getting hold of the guns and shooting six of the men. These guys had their heads driven into the pavement hard enough to kill them. The coroner said it was equivalent of a five or six story fall.

Two of the six men who had been shot to death had been hit hard as well, and he just didn't think the girls could have hit that hard unless they had a baseball bat, but the coroner said it looked like they had been hit by a fist. That meant they must have had help and whoever it was had to be strong. Very strong.

Losing the girls was a big deal. It was money lost and Mercido hated to lose money, but he took the loss of his men even more seriously. He was in the hospital waiting for his one injured man to wake up. The cops were there to question his man as soon as he came to, but they had told Mercido that he could talk to him first. As far as the police were concerned Victor Mercido might be a big-time crime figure, but he was also a rich businessman who was known to be a friend of the chief of police and many others in high-profile positions. As a result he got to see the coroner's report, and he got to talk to his guy even before the cops could question him.

When the doctor gave his clearance, Mercido went into the room along with two of his obvious-looking bodyguards. The guards stayed by the door while Mercido went over to the bed. The man in the bed looked a little roughed up, but mostly he was scared. He wasn't sure what Mercido was likely to do. The punch to the face he took outside the warehouse hadn't killed him, but it was quite possible that Mercido would.

One quick question from Mercido and the story came out. The kid described how the men were having a little fun with the girls before the next truck arrived to take them the rest of the way. He had been set at the door to keep an eye out, and there were the usual two guards outside. He was to watch the door and their backs. When the door to the warehouse opened and no one came in, he had gone over to investigate and the next thing he knew he was in the hospital.

Mercido walked out of the hospital feeling only a little better. He made sure the kid knew what he could tell the cops, but that didn't worry Mercido. When the kid got out of the hospital he would find himself having an accident. Just as well that the other men were all dead, as Mercido would have killed them himself. The girls were part of the business and not playthings for his men, and his men had been told that on numerous occasions, but they were just too stupid to get it. Either that, or the temptation was just too much. Mercido would have to ponder how to stop it from happening again.

Mercido also was sure the girls had outside help, based on the dead men in the building across the street, but that was unconfirmed. Someone had killed the two guards outside, and then had hit the kid when he came out to investigate, and it wasn't the girls. The girls might have been given the guns and finished the job off before they left, but they had help. That meant that something was happening and he needed to get to the bottom of it.

Word had made it back to him about the failed attempt on Tannion in New York and that Bellows had been killed. Might Tannion be back in town to get his revenge? He had told Mercido that revenge would be his if he tried, but Mercido never reacted well to threats. Somebody was going to pay for what happened in that warehouse and he was going to have to find out who it was.

Tannion was known to be strong, but was he that strong, or had there been several men there? That could mean that someone other than Tannion had it in for him. Mercido wasn't a happy man and in this case he felt he had good reasons not to be happy.

50

Jim Tannion and Mike Rallin talked well into the night. Tannion had to show Rallin a few more demonstrations, but when Tannion made Rallin's heart stop for a few moments and Rallin thought he was going to die, he finally had enough. He didn't want to believe Tannion, but he had no choice. The evidence was too strong and as a good cop, Rallin understood the value of solid evidence.

After Rallin came to his inevitable conclusion they talked about Tannion abilities and how he had improved upon them. These included his strength and endurance, but just as important were his vision, hearing, and even his sense of smell. His memory was almost photographic and he had taught himself to speed-read. It all seemed too much for one man and Rallin told him so.

That was when the discussion got into what the future had in store. Tannion made sure that Rallin understood that if the scientific community found out about his abilities they would want to take him apart to see how he could do what he did. After all, he could cure any disease. Or at least he thought he could.

Rallin suddenly had a thought. "Back when I first ran into you I had a case with two people who were suddenly cured of cancer. I thought you looked a little like the composite sketch. Was that you?"

Tannion had to laugh. "That was me. I was so scared when that sketch was shown on TV, and then you showed up at my door. I thought for sure you were there to take me away. That was the first time I had really used the skill beyond friends or family, and even with them, it was only little things they might not have known about. It did give me a sense that I could do anything, though."

Talk finally got around to the job at hand. "Where are you at with Mercido?" Rallin asked.

"Not too far yet. I haven't had enough time to get much. Philips and Potenlikov gave me enough to get started and we could probably make a couple of busts, but nothing would ever go high enough up the food chain to hit Mercido. He covers his tracks too well for that. I have a couple of drug warehouses, including a meth factory. There's illegal gambling and prostitution, and I did bust up a sex slave setup, but nothing big enough yet. I'm not done, though."

Tannion went on to tell Rallin about the sex slave ring that he had put a dent in. Rallin wasn't happy, but he knew there wasn't much that Tannion could have done differently. Rallin was concerned that one of the girls might recognize Tannion. After all, it wasn't the FBI way to kill two guys and dump them in an empty building.

"Will any of the girls know it was you?"

"I didn't know any of them, and I was in and out so fast that they probably barely saw me. All they would have is a general description. I think I'm still okay. I'm not sure any of them would have hung around or would be that willing to talk to the police."

"We're still working from the element of surprise, as well as trying to keep you alive. If Mercido gets wind of you being in town he won't wait. He'll send all he has at you," Rallin said.

"I agree, but I'm not sure he doesn't suspect that I'm here just because I told him I would be. The dead guys might only confirm what he's already thinking."

"Better to leave him guessing than having him know," Rallin surmised.

"I agree." Tannion said again, and then continued. "I was thinking that the gambling and prostitution unit should be hit first and hit fast, as they move it around a lot and it's due for a move. It might be best to get the LAPD on it as soon as possible."

"Why the locals? Shouldn't we hit it?" Rallin asked.

"First, I think they'll be able to get to it quicker. My understanding is that they're aware of it and are constantly looking for it, so an anonymous phone call might be all it will take. Second, if the FBI hits it, it might look like I had something to do with it, and Mercido will be warned. I don't want to do that just yet."

"Makes sense, Jim. I agree, if all it takes is that phone call. Go ahead and make the call, and I'll keep an eye on what happens."

"Also, Mike, if Mercido knows that you're in town he might think it's because of me. Can you keep out of the loop for a couple days?"

"What the hell am I going to do if not my job? I came here to work."

"I'm glad you asked. I have a couple more locations where you can probably dig up some more crap on Mercido. As long as it's done at night and you don't get caught, we should have a couple more days before we need to make a bigger move."

"Shit, Jim. Undercover has never been my game, but we still have the equipment we were using on Philips, and as long as I can get my hands on it without alerting the entire force, then I should be able to help." Rallin knew he would have to touch base with the FBI office in LA, a form of checking in, but he thought that he would only have to talk to the chief and he would be able to keep it from being widespread. It might just work.

Tannion went on to tell Rallin about what he had in mind for the next few days. Rallin could see the trouble in it and he told him.

"Mercido will still have a contract out on you. You might have stopped the first one, but there's enough money in it that there will be more."

"Maybe not. Vlad tells me that the guy in New York was the best there was in LA. Word on the street has it that he died in the attempt, and that might make people lose interest."

"Still, you need to keep your head down. People here are bound to recognize you again, especially if you head into places where you used to hang out. Didn't you tell me you thought the last hit was because someone recognized you in one of your old haunts?"

"Right, but forewarned is forearmed. I'm keeping to the shadows and I'm Victor French again."

"Won't using the name you used in the past only bring things on quicker?"

"Potenlikov, or rather his wife, saved some of my old fake identification and it was easier to use it than come up with someone new. He and Philips thought it was probably safer than Tannion, but it can't last much longer. You got something else?"

"If you give me a while I could put the FBI guys on it. I could probably come up with a better undercover setup, but if I have to stay in the shadows it might not happen. For now I suggest you stay low."

"That's okay, Mike. I would rather go as French and take my chances at having more people know I'm in town."

"Sure, Jim. I'll stay out of it, but you know I need to check in so someone will know we're here and I'll explain the need for secrecy."

"Thanks, Mike. That's about all I can ask."

"You probably should get some rest and then head out tomorrow."

"Actually, I'm heading out now. As long as I work at night and with the extra gifts I have, nobody needs to be the wiser. I can get by with a minimum amount of sleep, so I'll be fine."

Rallin stuck his hand out and the two men shook hands, and Tannion left the hotel. Rallin was booked into a different hotel, but he had to go to the office before he could get a couple hours of sleep. He had the cab take him to the FBI building. It was after midnight, but there was still a little activity in a building which really couldn't afford to go completely to sleep.

"Now to start the ball rolling on the info Tannion gave me, and I need to see about doing a little police work myself," thought Rallin, as he picked up some of the surveillance equipment they had stored. The truck was available as well. He was able to get in and out without anyone knowing he was there. That is, unless they looked at the sign-out sheet.

51

Tannion knelt down behind a high fence that he was preparing to scale. He wasn't worried about being caught, but he definitely didn't want to be seen either. When he looked over the fence, the house he saw belonged to Victor Mercido. It was time to take a look inside.

He quickly scaled the fence as if it were the short, picket variety. Mercido lived in the high rent district, and the house was big with a seriously large yard that was professionally landscaped, and there were bound to be guards watching it. Tannion moved to his left, keeping the front gate in his view. No guards were in sight, which bothered him no end. Mercido was bound to have the front gate guarded. So where were the guards?

As he moved around to the side of the yard, he found out why there were no guards at the front gate. There was something going on in the backyard. Mercido was throwing a small get-together, and the guards must have been checking out the action. Tannion could see one of them heading back out to the front gate.

"Changing of the guard," he thought. Most likely the one at the gate was unable to get his hands on any of the food out back, so they had arranged to trade spots every so often to share the goodies. Mercido might not even be aware that they left the front gate unmanned for a couple of minutes as they changed.

He found a vantage point at the back of the yard, behind some thick bushes. His eyesight was good enough that he didn't need all the light coming from the party, and it probably gave him an advantage, as he could see in much better than they could see out.

Tannion knew he was going to have to catch Mercido in a situation where he either ordered something to happen that the FBI could prove he caused, or catch him with his hands dirty as he actually did something on his own. That wasn't very likely to happen. What he really needed was a video of Mercido killing someone, or at least being there when someone was killed. The camera equipment was ready, but it didn't look like it was going to happen tonight. There was no sense sticking around to watch a party.

Tannion made his way back to the street the same way he had come. He still had a number of leads that Potenlikov and Philips had provided him with, and the night was still young. As long as he could find enough dirt to hurt Mercido maybe that would be good enough. He really wanted Mercido to spend time in prison and the more he saw, the more he realized that might not happen.

The next stop was in a rather seedy side of Los Angeles where the drug dealers seemed to control the streets. This tip came from Potenlikov and it seemed to be more of a low-end job, but what the hell. That was an area that Potenlikov was comfortable in and so was Tannion.

The room he was looking for was beside a liquor store, which was closed, but when he knocked on the side door a panel slid open, revealing a strong looking, but also very red-faced man. A heavy drinker, Tannion assumed. He wondered what he would find if he shook his hand.

"What?" was all red-face said.

Tannion had been given the password, and as quickly as the door opened, he was in. The smoke hit him immediately, as well as the smell of booze and stale beer. No non-smoking by-law here. The man beside him seemed to reek of cheap cologne, whisky, and cigars. Tannion ignored him and walked inside to see what Potenlikov had given him.

The room was quite large and seemed to be doing a very good business, even at this time of night. It was well past two in the morning, and the poker tables were going strong. There were Blackjack, Texas hold 'em poker, and a couple of games Tannion wasn't familiar with, as well as roulette and craps. He could also see a number of girls wandering around offering their services to an almost all-male crowd. Girls in short skirts were selling drinks and cigarettes. This wasn't the same level as the last gambling hall, but the place was almost full. Tannion assumed it was one that didn't move around and didn't have the same high-end clientele.

There were back rooms for sex, which could also be used for shooting up, as there were several of the clientele who looked to be under the influence of something. It could be booze, as that was readily available, but a look into their eyes said it was more than just cheap liquor.

Tannion wasn't sure what he could do except make some notes alongside the address. After he had looked around for a few minutes to make sure that he hadn't missed anything, he made a mistake. A mistake a few years earlier he wouldn't have made. He decided to head out the same door he had come in and go back to his hotel to get some sleep.

One of the guards at the door noted that Tannion hadn't been there long, and that he hadn't been gambling, drinking, or spending any time with the girls. To him and his boss that meant only one thing; the guy must be a cop. He and a couple of his friends knew what to do with cops.

The guy at the door opened it to let Tannion pass and made a small motion to the head bouncer, who was trailing him. As soon as Tannion was let out the back door, he was grabbed by the two guys the bouncer had motioned to follow him outside. The bouncer came out right behind them, and the three men pulled Tannion further into the alley where the light wasn't as good. Tannion was caught a little by surprise, which he didn't like, but he decided to just go along and see what happened.

The three men who had grabbed him weren't much for talking. As soon as they had him in the alley they started to pound on him. Tannion took the first few hits without retaliating, but that was as far as he was willing to wait to see if they were going to talk. When he realized that wasn't going to happen he took control. The closest man to him didn't even see the punch that took him in the chin and left him across the alley with a broken jaw and jellied brains.

The second and third man went about as easily. The second guy saw what had happened to his friend and tried to take a step away, but Tannion grabbed his arm and swung him into the big bouncer, who had stepped back as soon as the other two had started in on Tannion. As soon as the man Tannion had thrown at the bouncer hit the ground, Tannion hit the bouncer. The guy tried to get up off the ground,

Tannion gave him a couple of head shots, and the fight was over. He left the three men on the street where they landed.

With all three dead on the street, Tannion took a look around to see if there were any witnesses, and seeing that he was alone, he headed out to catch a cab. He thought about going back and making an example of the guy who had let him in the door, but decided against it. The guy knew what Tannion looked like, but he wasn't likely to ever talk to the cops, not in his position.

He made sure to walk several blocks before he caught a cab, as any cabbie would remember picking up someone at that time of the morning. Once he was back in his hotel he locked the door and moved the dresser in front of it. He was going to get some sleep. He wasn't going to be disturbed.

52

Rallin had finally managed to get some sleep in his hotel bed, which wasn't as comfortable as his bed at home. He always had trouble sleeping in a strange bed, and sleeping alone, too. For years, he had been waking up next to Arlene every day and he didn't like to sleep alone. That was the life of a small time cop, but there had been more than a few nights alone since moving to New York.

He was still mulling over everything that Tannion had told him. It was almost too incredible to believe. If it wasn't for the demonstrations, especially on him, he might never have believed it. It seemed too much like something out of a superhero comic or a science fiction book, but he had seen it with his own two eyes. He wished he could tell Arlene about it, but he had promised Tannion he wouldn't tell anyone, and he understood Tannion's fear. Besides, Arlene was in New York and he wouldn't want to say anything over a phone line. Maybe he would later.

Rallin suddenly realized that throughout all the explanations and demonstrations, Tannion had never told him if he had taken a look inside Rallin to see if he were healthy. Arlene had a few problems that he could probably cure, and so did some of their friends. Tannion could probably fix any of their problems, but that might be asking too much.

Early the next morning Rallin made a call to the director, and after a couple of minutes on hold the director's voice came on the line. Rallin informed him of where they were and how the job was going. As far as the director was concerned, Rallin and Tannion were tracking down whoever had put the contract out on Tannion. At least the director seemed to be finally on side and wasn't screaming at him to have Tannion brought in dead or alive.

Rallin asked the director to keep the fact that both he and Tannion were in Los Angeles under his hat for as long as he could. The director understood that if there had been one attempt to kill Tannion, the contract on him hadn't been fulfilled and there'd be others who would try if they knew where he was.

Rallin hung up the phone and headed out of his hotel room to see what he could do to help Tannion. First would be a stop at the FBI building to let the chief know that he and Tannion were in town and what they were there to do.

Rallin walked into the building trying to look as inconspicuous as he could. He'd met several agents who had worked with him to try and catch Philips a while back, and he was hoping to avoid them all. He knocked on the office door and the voice inside called for him to come in.

Rallin hadn't seen the LA bureau chief much since they had first come into LA at the beginning of their chase after Philips, and he hadn't put in much of a showing during the arrests or Philips' surrender. Most of that was handled through the LAPD.

A couple of minutes later, and Rallin had done his duty and was out on the street looking for a taxi. Rallin had asked the chief about an identity for Tannion and the chief said he would do what he could, but he didn't promise anything. The chief understood Rallin's thinking and told him that he would keep it out of the general gossip. Now it was time to get to work. Tannion had given him an address to check out, but first he had the cab do a drive-by. He knew he wasn't going to go in until after dark, but he wanted to see what it looked like in the daylight.

That night Rallin was back at the same address the taxi had driven past that morning, and this time he was driving the truck he had used before. The truck looked like it belonged to a landscaping company, but Rallin knew it would look suspicious if it were sitting on the street too late at night, so he was there as soon as it was dark.

About two hours later Rallin had seen enough. The location was a bust. It was thought to be a warehouse where Mercido would store drugs that had just come across the border. Mercido was known to have a few of these storage areas and a few more where they processed and packaged the drugs.

Rallin parked about a block from the warehouse and settled to wait. He waited and watched for more than two hours to ensure that it was dark enough. In that time there had been no movement and no lights.

It was well after midnight when Rallin got out of the truck and walked the block to the warehouse. He hugged the side of the building to not be seen from inside the warehouse, but there were only a few windows. When he got to the first window he took a look inside, and although it was dark inside there was enough light coming from streetlights through the windows that he could tell it was empty.

Mercido was known to move his locations around and it might just be a down period for this place. Either way, Rallin had nothing. It wasn't the first time he had come up empty, but he had been looking forward to adding to Tannion's list. "Maybe Tannion is doing better," he thought. A quick look in a couple of additional windows confirmed the lack of anything that might be interesting.

Maybe the second location would be more profitable, but it was across town and would have to wait. It was getting close to one in the morning and the trip would take over an hour

"Getting old," thought Rallin. One operation a night and he was done already.

"I bet Tannion does better," he thought again.

53

Tannion had told sleep to come and, as usual, it had. He woke up after only four hours as if he had programmed that into his mind. Four hours was all he would need. It was just after nine in the morning, and it was time to do some day-light reconnaissance, which would require a disguise. After he had a bite to eat in the lobby restaurant, he went out to look for something he could use to hide his identity as best he could.

He didn't want to use the mustache and tourist disguise this time. Rallin said he might be able to get him something, but he had told him to keep the fact that they were in town as secret as he could. So far that had resulted in Tannion not having a cover other than his being Victor French. Maybe he could look just a little different, if nothing else.

He picked up a hat and a pair of sunglasses in a shop down the street from the hotel and he asked the clerk where there might be a costume shop nearby, as he had a costume party to go to. Luckily there was one only a few blocks away and a little later he was looking at different colored wigs. "That should be enough," thought Tannion.

Back at the hotel an hour later Tannion took a look in the mirror and didn't think even Rallin would recognize him. It was time to find Mercido again and see if Tannion could notice a pattern, or anything that would give him something to nail him with.

Tannion knew that Rallin and his men had done the same thing for a few months in an attempt to catch Philips with his hands dirty and had failed, but that might have been because Tannion had warned him. Or, at least, he had warned Potenlikov. Mercido wasn't going to be so lucky. Tannion settled into the front seat of his car and drove to a parking lot he knew was only a couple of blocks from Mercido's office building.

Tannion sat at a table in the restaurant just down and across the street from Mercido's office and thought he might be in for a long wait, but after only half an hour he saw a car pull up to the curb in front of the building. A car that had the look he remembered from his days with Philips. Mercido might be on the move.

Victor Mercido had been in the office since seven that morning and he was waiting for word to get to him. He had several of his people looking for the girls who had killed his men and escaped. A few of them had been picked up off the street in Los Angeles and he was pretty sure they would be stupid enough, or high enough, to go back to where they were working as if nothing had happened. As a result, he wasn't surprised when he got a call telling him they had found one.

She was being held in a house that Mercido used occasionally for this sort of thing. It was in a rundown area where there were more rats than people, and the few squatters who tried to set up camp in the only house that was locked on the street always ran into the type of trouble that kept them moving. Mercido had three of his men living in the house for just that purpose.

By the time Mercido got there, the girl was already tied to a chair in the middle of the living room. The room contained a large television set, an easy chair, and a large sofa, and they were all pushed against the walls, leaving the girl sitting in the middle of the room. There were no pictures on the walls.

The three Mercido men lived there, but they didn't spend any time or energy on the place. They didn't cook, although the gas was hooked up and the electricity was paid for. As far as the city was concerned, a company owned the place and rented it out to the three men who stayed there. They were even on the census roll.

None of Mercido's men had noticed the car that was following them. Tannion had been able to get to his vehicle and follow a few blocks behind Mercido. The big black sedan was an easy mark to follow, and he didn't have to get too close. When they started into the area where the house was located, there was less traffic and Tannion had to hang further back, but with his eyesight and the size of the car ahead of him, he had no problem knowing where it was going.

Tannion saw the black sedan stop in front of a house that looked to be in a little better shape than the surrounding houses. Not by much though. He was still a couple of blocks away, but he was able to see three men get out of the car and walk into the house. He was pretty sure he hadn't been seen, but it was as close as he could get with the car.

A light jog and he was only a couple of houses down from the house Mercido had gone in. He knew that Mercido had been in the car, and it looked like he was one of the three who had gotten out. Tannion could see that he wasn't going to be able to get any closer. The driver was still in the car, and it looked like at least one man was posted outside the house.

After half an hour Tannion saw three men come out of the house and get back into the car. It looked like one of the men was Mercido. They were in a hurry and the car sped off as soon as the door was closed. The man who was stationed outside the house had gone back inside.

He wasn't too sure what he would find, but he knew he had to take a look. He jumped over the next-door neighbor's fence, which almost fell over, and he hugged the side of the house. He peeked in the window, but with the drapes shut he wasn't able to see anything. He decided the direct approach was the best method.

He walked around to the back of the house and knocked on the door. After a few seconds the door opened and the man Tannion had seen working as the lookout earlier was standing there looking at him with a 'what the hell do you want?' look on his face.

Tannion didn't waste any time and hit him with a closed fist to the chin, and he fell like the proverbial sack of potatoes. Tannion caught him just before he hit the ground and propped him against the door, keeping it open in case he needed to make a quick escape.

He stepped into the house and found that he was alone in the kitchen. He had no idea how many men would be in the house, but doubted that the guy who was now out cold in the doorway was the only one. There was only one door into the kitchen and Tannion walked through it, hoping for the surprise factor.

A quick look saw that there were two men and a woman in the room. The woman was obviously dead and the men were on their knees wrapping her up in a blanket. They both looked up at the same time, but Tannion moved like a cat and they were both out before they could stand up.

Tannion took a look at the woman and although she looked familiar, it was hard to tell. Her face had been beaten severely and there looked to be cigarette burns all over her arms. She had been tortured and that gave Tannion the clue he needed as to who she might be.

"I bet she was one of the girls from the warehouse," he thought. "In that case they know that she had help, and they probably got enough of a description to know that it was either me or someone who looked a lot like me. With the dead guys in the house across the street, they would know that it was me for sure. Mercido knows I'm in town."

Tannion left the way he had come. He dumped the guy at the back into the kitchen and closed the door behind him. Before he left he made sure that the three men never woke up. Simpler that way, and they didn't feel a thing.

What they did to the girl and the fact they worked for Mercido ensured they had it coming. Now, assuming Mercido had been warned, what would he do? For that matter, thought Tannion, what was he to do?

54

Victor Mercido started another day in a foul mood, and the little torturing that had the chance of helping ended up only making it worse. The girl hung on for a surprisingly long time, but there was no doubt she would tell him what he wanted to hear. He made sure he was the last person she would tell it to, as well. She didn't die well.

So there had been a man at the warehouse, and by the description, and the way two of Mercido's men were killed, there was no doubt it was Tannion. She could only tell him that it was a big white man and he moved fast and hit hard. He was gone before the shooting was done. That was all that Mercido needed to hear. Now anger was the main emotion Mercido was feeling, but there was a large component of fear as well. Tannion was in town.

As soon as Mercido was back in the office and had downed a stiff drink, he picked up the phone and made the only call he could think of. The voice on the other end took a while to get there, as he had to go through a couple of assistants, but Victor Mercido's name carried a lot of weight in this town. Maybe not as much as the guy on the other end of the line, but still enough to have him answer.

"Victor. It's good to hear from you. What can I do for you?" said the voice on the phone.

"Jackson. Thanks for taking my call." Not too many people would dare call Jackson T. Philips by his first name, and as Mercido was from the old school, he was one of the few who could get away with it. Mercido didn't actually think about whether he could call him Jackson or not, he just did it. It was just his arrogant way. Even if Philips knew that Mercido would call him by his first name as he had in the past, the hair rose on the back of his neck.

"I have a problem, and I think you might be the only person who can help," Mercido said.

"Anything, Victor. Just tell me what you need," Philips answered, although his body language didn't match the voice on the phone. Philips knew they didn't match, which was why he conducted all of his important meetings face-to-face. He needed to see a person's reaction to any situation to truly know where anyone stood, and it was much more difficult to lie with body language.

"It's Tannion. I'm fairly sure he's back in town, and he's hit one of my operations. What do you know about it?" Mercido's voice rose just enough to make it sound a little too much like a demand, and Philips wasn't pleased with the tone, but he answered the question.

"Are you sure, Vic?" Philips asked, purposely using the shortened version of Mercido's name, knowing full well that Mercido hated it.

Mercido went on as if he hadn't noticed the lack of respect the use of the nickname meant. "Yeah, I'm sure. He's killed my men, and stolen some hookers from a warehouse. What do you know about that?"

Mercido was almost at top volume, and Philips wasn't interested in going any further.

"Listen, Victor. You put a hit on Tannion and you failed. Matter of fact, you've put several contracts on him and they all failed, and now I understand that the last one was your best man. As far as I'm concerned maybe you deserve Tannion."

"Now hear me on this, Philips. He was your man and I'm telling you to get him off my back."

That was as far as Philips was willing to be pushed. "You don't ever tell me a fucking thing, Mercido. I hope you've made a will. Tannion will probably kill you. Make sure that you never call me again." Philips banged the receiver down, leaving Mercido holding a dead phone on the other end.

Philips picked the phone back up and made a call. As soon as the voice came on the other end, Philips started talking without a simple hello. "Diggs. I need you to start tailing a guy by the name of Jim Tannion. I don't know where he is yet, but I'll let you know when I do."

"That's okay, Mr. Philips. We know where we can pick him up. What do you want to do with him for now?"

Philips was surprised, but he was pleased that Diggs was already on top of what he was being asked to do. "Don't know how he did it, but this guy might be worth moving up depending on what happens in the next few days," thought Philips.

"Just keep an eye on him. I need to know his every move. He knows too much, but he might still be on our side, so don't do anything. Don't take any chances. With his skills, I'm not so sure there would be anything you could do. Just make sure that he doesn't pick up on your tail. That would cause both of us a lot of trouble."

"No problem, Mr. Philips." The man on the other end of the phone didn't like to hear that he and three of his boys couldn't handle one guy. He had been in Los Angeles when Tannion had snitched, and got lucky to not have been picked up when the feds hit his boss. Tannion was just another snitch who had cost him a job at the time.

He was lucky to catch on with Philips after his boss got jail time and Philips took over. Working for Philips was the obvious move, but that didn't automatically make him a Philips man.

For now he would do what Philips wanted him to do, but the future might be different. He had bigger dreams than following some guy around for someone else, even if the guy paying him was as big as Philips.

55

Arthur Diggs, Artie to his friends, was feeling pretty smug. He was sure that he had surprised the hell out of Philips when he told him that he knew where Tannion was. He suspected that Philips probably thought that Diggs would remember Tannion from a few years back, but there was a lot more to it than that. He liked the idea that he had surprised Philips.

As soon as Diggs got the first phone call from Philips a couple of days earlier, he had put together his four-man team. The three men he picked would work with him, but he knew they weren't the brightest guys. They could do the job, and they knew how to follow orders, even if they couldn't do much thinking on their own if what they were told to do wasn't clear. Diggs knew they would follow his orders if nothing else.

Diggs set the team up, but he was thinking why. He could only come up with one reason why Philips would ask him to set up a team for later, and that was Potenlikov. Diggs and Potenlikov had been at each other's throats in the past, and if it was Philips doing the asking, and as he was not going through Potenlikov, then it probably meant that it was Potenlikov that Philips was after. It seemed to make sense. He hoped that Philips would want the big Russian killed. Diggs would do that himself.

After he set up the team, he decided to keep the three men next to their phones and on call while he did a little recon. If Philips wanted him to kill Potenlikov then he had better make sure he knew more about his routines. It was time for him to watch Potenlikov's every move.

A few hours later Diggs watched as Potenlikov backed out of his parking spot and headed downtown. Diggs found a comfortable distance behind and followed. A few minutes later Potenlikov stopped and Diggs saw a man he thought he should recognize get in the passenger side. It was just a little too far away and too dark for Diggs to be sure who the passenger was, but he looked familiar. Potenlikov drove for a few minutes, then pulled into what looked to be an almost deserted parking lot and got out of the car.

Diggs waited a little over a block away, but with a clear line of sight. The high-powered binoculars made Potenlikov appear as if he were in the car next to Diggs. The man with Potenlikov got out of the passenger side and came around to meet Potenlikov, and when they came together they shook hands. They talked for less than five minutes, and then both men got into separate cars and drove away. Looking through the binoculars, Diggs recognized the man meeting with Potenlikov as soon as he stepped out of the car.

"Shit, that's Jim Tannion," he said to himself. Diggs had seen Tannion a few times in Los Angeles, but he mostly remembered him from seeing Tannion give evidence against Diggs' boss and some of their friends. Diggs had spent some time in the courtroom watching the trial, and knew that he would never forget what Tannion looked like.

Diggs had heard all about the contract Mercido had put on Tannion's head and the fact that Damon Bellows had apparently gotten himself killed trying to kill Tannion. Now Tannion was in Los Angeles. Suddenly Potenlikov was forgotten, and Diggs found himself following Jim Tannion.

Tannion went to the Western Arms Hotel, parked his car in the lot, and went inside. Diggs parked across the street and walked in a few yards behind Tannion. Diggs entered the hotel just as Tannion was entering the elevator. He watched him go in, and as he was the only one in the car, Diggs could tell that he had stopped at the seventh floor.

"So, Jim Tannion is holed up in the Western Arms Hotel, and I might be the only one who knows it," Diggs said to no one in particular. Philips might want him to follow Potenlikov around, but Diggs had bigger fish to fry. At least until Philips actually gave him his orders Diggs knew what he was going to have to do.

Diggs had worked for one of the guys Tannion had helped put behind bars a few years back. As well, Tannion had named a couple of guys that Diggs considered to be friends at the time, but that really didn't bother Diggs much. He had been getting started at the time and when he hooked up with Philips he thought it was a break. He went from working for a guy who wasn't the biggest or brightest fish in the pond to one who was. Upward mobility was all he would call it and he had Tannion to thank for that. Except that Potenlikov didn't seem to like Diggs. Now maybe Tannion would help that mobility again, and it looked like Potenlikov could be in shit too.

A couple of days later when the order finally did come and Diggs was told to follow Tannion around, he knew exactly where he could pick him up. He called his three men and set up camp in the lobby of the Western Arms Hotel to wait for Tannion to show.

Diggs had been thinking about what he could do with one hundred thousand dollars. He could probably find Tannion, take his shot, and then walk away with Mercido's cash. Problem was he was pretty sure that Philips would have him killed soon after. Tannion had worked for Philips, and Diggs knew that Tannion and Potenlikov had become friends. Still, he sure could use the money.

When he had gotten the call from Philips all his thinking changed. If Philips wanted Tannion followed and maybe taken out, then that made it all the more possible to hit Tannion without pissing Philips off, and to hell with Potenlikov. If Philips wasn't considering Tannion to be a friend any longer, then maybe Diggs could make the hit, collect the cash, keep his job, and not have to worry about Philips having him killed.

Diggs made a call to a friend of his who worked inside Victor Mercido's operation. He needed to be sure that Tannion's contract was still on. He was told that Mercido was madder than hell and there was no way he would talk to Diggs. Diggs told him he didn't need to talk to Mercido, but he needed to know if the contract on Tannion was active.

Diggs couldn't be happier with the reply he got. His friend told him that the reason Mercido was so mad was because he was pretty sure it was Tannion who had killed a couple of his men and released a bunch of girls the other night. Not only was the contract still on Tannion's head, but the value had gone up to half a million dollars.

For half a million dollars Diggs would have killed his own mother. He wasn't worried about Philips or Potenlikov anymore, if there ever had been anything to worry about. With that kind of money he could leave town, set up his own shop, and be his own boss. He might even go legit.

Another call to the hotel and he knew that Tannion hadn't shown up yet. It was time for Diggs to take control. A little later and he was sitting by the side door to the Western Arms Hotel in a spot that wasn't too conspicuous, but also where he could still watch the elevator and stairs.

He couldn't see the front door, but that didn't bother him. Any spot where he could sit and see the door made it look like he was either waiting for someone to come in or that he was watching the door. He knew anyone coming in would either be taking the stairs or the elevator, and as Tannion was on the seventh floor, he would probably use the elevator.

He had been sitting for almost two hours before Tannion finally walked in the door. By the time Diggs saw him, he had pushed the elevator button and was waiting. Tannion was dressed in what Diggs would call a tacky outfit, which might have made him look like a tourist, and he had a wig on, but Diggs was pretty sure it was Tannion. When the elevator stopped at the seventh floor he was sure. Now he just needed to wait until Tannion came out.

Diggs called one of his men, and had him sit and wait for Tannion to come down. If Tannion had seen Diggs sitting at the hotel earlier he didn't want him to see him again later. He knew he had to be careful.

He had found an old picture of Tannion from his days in court and had given each of his men a copy. Tannion hadn't changed much so they should be able to recognize him. He might have put on a few pounds, but other than that he looked pretty much the same as he had almost six years earlier. He warned the guy about the possibility of a wig and told him what Tannion might be wearing and hoped for the best.

Diggs went to the café down the block and had a little to eat, and then went to his car across the street and down from the hotel. His man had been told that his only job was to watch for Tannion and to call him when he came down. Then it was all up to Diggs.

Diggs' men might complain when he cashed in the half million and didn't cut them in for a piece of it, but he was the one taking all the risks and all they were doing was following Philips' orders. That's what they were paid to do, after all. Maybe he would have to give them a couple thousand to keep them happy.

Diggs thought it might be a while before Tannion moved again and he was right, but he wasn't expecting it to be as many hours as it was. It was just starting to get dark when his phone rang. Tannion was on the move, and it looked like he had decided against the disguise. Diggs' man told him what Tannion was wearing, and Diggs knew he had changed.

Tannion caught a taxi and headed for the hotel Rallin was staying in. They needed to compare notes to see where they were at with Mercido. Tannion knew he didn't have much. The LAPD should have had enough time to hit the gambling hall and Rallin might have some word from that, plus he might have found something at the other address he was going to check out.

The taxi took about twenty minutes to get Tannion to Rallin's hotel and when he walked into the hotel lobby he didn't see the car pull up to the curb. Diggs wasn't jumping into anything. He had heard how good Bellows was, and if Tannion had hit him first that meant that Tannion was even better. Diggs needed to have a foolproof plan. He couldn't just start shooting on the street. He also needed to get away with murder so his plan needed to be good.

Diggs knew that he was good with a gun and pretty good with a knife, but he had to be sure. If what had happened to Bellows was true, then his plan had to be even better than Bellows'. He pulled out his cell phone and made a call to the man he had left at the Western Arms Hotel. He told him to head home as he was done for the night. Diggs didn't want anyone to see him when he got there.

Diggs went back to his car and headed back to the Western Arms Hotel. He had made up his mind as to what his plan was. Now he just had to set it up.

56

Tannion knocked on Rallin's hotel room door and wasn't surprised to see Rallin sliding his gun back into his holster as he let him in. Rallin's room had a double bed, a small table, and two chairs. They both sat down.

Tannion knew he was second chair and he waited for Rallin to go first. Rallin didn't always see the pecking order, especially if he were at the top, but he went first as he had information he wanted Tannion to know about.

"I just heard from the locals. Last night they hit that gambling establishment you gave them. They went in with a lot of muscle and it paid off big time. They didn't have to fire a shot and they confiscated a lot of gaming material and arrested all the people working at the joint, but even better than that, they arrested a number of the johns who were enjoying themselves upstairs, and one of them was Marco Ruscallo."

"Who's Marco Ruscallo?"

"He's a guy the LAPD have been trying to catch up to for a couple of years. He had an outstanding warrant for murder. His wife was found dead and he was the only suspect, and when he went underground, everything pointed to him being guilty. His fingerprints were on the murder weapon, so they think they have an open and shut case."

"An added bonus then," Tannion said. "What did they think of the rest of the place?"

"I talked to the captain and they were especially pleased with the tip. Not only did they catch Ruscallo, but they arrested a number of people who are known to have gang ties, including being connected to Victor Mercido. They know that it's his joint, but other than a couple of guys who worked for Mercido in the past, they haven't got enough to go after him, but they are calling it a major bust. The building was rented, and if the company on the lease belongs to Mercido that might be a shot. It'll take a lot of looking through dummy companies to get there, but still, they couldn't be happier."

"That's good to hear," Tannion said. "What about the address we got from Potenlikov. Did you get lucky there too?"

"No. That was a major bust. The place was empty and it looked like they hadn't been using it for a long time. It might have been used in the past, but not now."

"Damn. That's too bad. I was hoping to get as much as we could against Mercido, and even if it was all circumstantial maybe we could still find a judge who would let us set up a phone tap or something."

"I don't think we're close to that yet. Did you come up with anything else?" Rallin asked.

Tannion hesitated for a few seconds. He wasn't sure that he should mention the fact that he had killed three men in a house where they were preparing to dispose of a woman's body. As much as he wanted to keep silent, he and Rallin had gone too far for that.

"I followed Mercido to a house in the valley and it didn't end so well." Tannion went on to tell Rallin what he had seen and what happened inside the house.

"Are you sure it was Mercido you saw at the house?"

"I followed him from his office and they never stopped, and I know what he looks like, so yeah, I'm sure."

"Okay. I didn't mean to say you didn't know what you were doing. I'm just trying to think of a way we can use the place to put some pressure on Mercido."

"He probably owns the place, but there would be enough shell companies between him and the house to ensure that we could never touch him. He's smart if nothing else."

"Right," Rallin replied. "But there are four dead people out there that the police should be aware of." Rallin picked up the phone and made a call. After he was connected he asked Tannion for the address to the house they were discussing and he passed it along. The call only took a couple of minutes. "Okay. That might have started the ball rolling."

"As long as Mercido hasn't already had the place cleaned we might have something, but there was more, Mike. The dead girl looked familiar. I think she was one of the girls I helped escape from one of Mercido's warehouses. She'd been beaten and tortured. I'm sure she would have told them anything they wanted to hear, so I suspect she told them of a guy matching my description who helped them in the warehouse. With the two dead guys in the building across the street, we can be pretty sure that Mercido knows I'm in town. If he didn't already, it wouldn't be a big leap for him to make."

"That's not going to make things easier. You need to lie low for a while to see where this is going," Rallin told him.

"I'm not sure I can do that," Tannion said.

"At least go back to your hotel and stay put for a while until we see what happens. I'll talk to the captain again and see if they can do anything as a result of what they find in this house."

"What are you going to be able to tell them, Mike? I don't think they need to know what my part was."

"No. You heard me tell them to go and take a look. As you said, Mercido might have already been there and cleaned up the mess, but if he hasn't, maybe we'll get lucky. I can expect a call anyway. They'll want to know what I know and then I'm not so sure what I can tell them. I'll keep you out of it, though. You would end up back in prison quick if they found that out."

"I'll have to trust you, Mike. There's not much else I can do, and it's starting to look like things are popping anyway, so we might just be able to catch Mercido doing something he shouldn't. If we and the locals keep putting pressure on him, something might happen. Now he knows I'm in town, maybe it's time to come out in the open and see if he tries something."

"Not so fast, Jim. That's pretty risky, even for a guy like you. Let's give the captain some time to take a look and then we can go from there. You head back to your hotel and I'll give you a call when I hear something. Then we should be able to come up with a plan."

Tannion knew it was a good idea to go back to his hotel and that was what he told Rallin he was going to do, but he wasn't so sure he would stay there very long. Maybe a call to Potenlikov would help.

57

The cab ride back to his hotel took a few minutes. Tannion looked around the lobby to see if there was anyone who might be watching for him, but it was quiet, with only one older gentleman in the corner reading a newspaper, and it didn't look like he had even glanced up.

"No need to get paranoid," he said to himself. "No matter what Rallin thinks."

The elevator let him out on the seventh floor and he walked down the hall to his room. The key card worked on the first slide, and he pushed the door open. There was a little light coming from the window and he flipped the light switch on as he closed the door.

As Tannion turned and faced the room, the bullet took him high in the chest, which should have been a direct hit to his heart. The bullet hit one of Tannion's reinforced ribs at a bit of an angle and was deflected up, where it ripped a large hole out of the top of his right shoulder, breaking his collarbone on the way out. Blood hit the ceiling as well as the door and wall behind him.

The wave of pain immediately struck Tannion, but the reinforced rib had done its job and had given Tannion the second he needed. He quickly stopped all the bleeding, muted the pain receptors, and started the healing process, all while he took his first step to the left. The second bullet hit him high in the right leg.

Tannion didn't even feel any pain from the second shot. He felt the hit as a tug and knew that the gunman was good. He was probably a professional. The second shot was low, as he was expecting Tannion to be going down, and hadn't waited more than a second between shots. As Tannion was still standing, the shot hit him in the leg instead of being another body shot.

Tannion knew that the shooter had made one mistake in aiming where he expected Tannion to be, rather than following him. He hoped that there would be a second mistake. Turning the light on had probably blinded the shooter for a second and given Tannion the time he needed.

Tannion's second step took him further to his left, and the second mistake happened. The shooter must have panicked when he saw that Tannion was still on his feet and still moving, and the next shot missed entirely. Tannion felt the breeze as it went past his head. Close, but still a clean miss.

Tannion's third step had taken him within an arm's reach of the shooter, and he grabbed the gun from the shooter with his right hand, and grabbed the guy's wrist with his left. A jerk and a twist, and the shooter hit the wall of the hotel room with a heavy thud. Tannion kept hold of him and pulled him to his feet, and was ready to hit him again. Tannion's punch would have killed him for sure, but this time he held back. Maybe this was a way to get Mercido.

Tannion grabbed the shooter, carried him to a chair, and sat him down hard. The shooter was woozy from hitting the wall so hard, and he was almost unconscious.

Tannion grabbed the towel the maid had left on the bed and used it to wipe the blood off his face. Some of it had gotten into his eyes. It took Tannion a few seconds to grab a tie from his luggage, and he used it to securely bind the shooter to the chair. Tannion didn't want to knock him out, as he wanted him to be awake enough to answer questions. Sitting on the chair, the gunman shook his head, clearing the cobwebs.

"What the fuck? How? That's not possible, I shot you," the gunman muttered, shaking his head. Tannion grabbed him under his chin and tilted his head up so that their eyes met. Diggs looked into eyes that spelled his death, and he suddenly wished he hadn't decided to break into Tannion's room to try to kill him.

"You're lucky that I didn't kill you, and I still might," Tannion told him. "Make too much noise and that will do it, and if you don't tell me what I need to know, that will do it too."

"Fuck you," Diggs cried out, in a show of defiance. Defiance he wasn't feeling.

Tannion grabbed him by his arms and with ease, he picked Diggs and the chair off the floor and then slammed him down again.

"That could just have easily been through the window," he told Diggs.

"Okay, okay. I'll tell you what you want," Diggs pleaded. Tannion could see fear and astonishment in his eyes.

"That was too easy," thought Tannion. "This guy is either not the professional I thought he was, or he's scared shitless of me."

He took a few seconds to take his shirt off and go into the bathroom and clean the blood off. He took a few moments to wipe some of his blood off the wall, door, and ceiling. As he was putting on a clean shirt he went back to his prisoner.

"I know who you work for. How much is the price on my head?"

"Half million," Diggs answered.

"Shit. That's a big contract." Tannion had heard it was one hundred thousand dollars, and hadn't heard about the jump to a half million.

"Yeah, it's big. It wasn't personal. It was only for the money. You got to know that," Diggs pleaded. "If you let me go I can help you. I know things, and I know that you're working for the FBI and I know things that can help."

"That's what I wanted to hear," Tannion told him. "Maybe you'll get to live a little longer. I need to know things about Mercido, and I'll also need to have you testify in court. I might be able to get you a deal. If you testify against Mercido you might not be charged with attempted murder. I might even be persuaded to let you live."

Tannion noted the look on the gunman's face as Tannion told him about what he wanted. Diggs still had fear in his eyes, but now the astonishment had turned to puzzlement.

Diggs started talking. "No. No. Not Mercido. I know stuff about Jackson Philips and his pal Potenlikov."

Tannion heard him, but couldn't be sure. He shut Diggs up as he grabbed him by the throat. "Who do you work for?" he asked.

Diggs struggled to say the word. "Philips."

Tannion turned the chair around and found the gunman's wallet in his back pocket. He opened it up and took out the driver's license. He held it in his right hand, and pulled out his cell phone and dialed it with his left.

"Vlad, it's Jim Tannion. I have a guy here by the name of Arthur Diggs. Does he work for you?"

"Yeah, Jim, but what the hell is he doing with you?"

"Thanks, Vlad," and Tannion hung up the phone, not bothering to answer Potenlikov's question. With a light touch Tannion told Diggs' body to sleep and knew he would be out for hours.

He untied Diggs from the chair, threw him on the bed, and made sure that he was well tied up. Tannion locked the door, and as he stepped into the hall he hung the 'do not disturb' sign on the handle. Tannion didn't get angry very often, but his eyes were on fire and his lips were tight across his teeth. If anyone had been in the hallway, they would have feared for their lives.

58

When Tannion entered the downtown office building he went directly to the bank of elevators. He pushed the up button and had to wait a few seconds for the first elevator to arrive and for the doors to open. As he stepped into the elevator, he noticed that the man behind the desk had picked up the phone and was urgently making a call. He seemed to be willing someone on the other end to pick up the phone.

Tannion didn't care who knew he was coming. It wasn't going to change anything. When the elevator doors opened on the thirty-eighth floor there were three men waiting for him. They didn't have smiles on their faces, but they didn't look like they were going to stop him either. At least they didn't have their guns out. Tannion remembered that Mr. Philips had told them to let him in whenever he showed up, with or without an appointment, and he definitely didn't have an appointment.

Tannion reached for the first man and as soon as he touched him, he was out cold. Tannion was pissed, but he was in control. These guys didn't need to pay for what Philips had done. The second and third men saw the first guy go down and they jumped at Tannion. In a heartbeat they both joined their friend on the floor. He didn't need them to be walking in on what he was going to do.

Tannion threw the office door open and walked in. Jackson T. Philips was sitting behind the desk and Vladimir Potenlikov was sitting across from him. As Tannion barged in both men stood up. Potenlikov called out Tannion's name, but Tannion didn't hear him. He barely saw him.

With a step, Tannion took hold of the corner of Philips' desk and threw it aside as if it were made of balsa wood. The problem for Potenlikov was that it wasn't made of balsa wood, and it hit him hard and threw him against the window. Luckily the window held and Potenlikov crumbled on the floor between the window and the desk.

Another step and Tannion took hold of Philips. Philips was by no means a small man, but Tannion made him look and feel small. Tannion grabbed him by the neck with his right hand and took hold of his jacket with his left and smashed him hard against the back wall. Philips' feet were dangling a few inches off the ground.

Potenlikov was struggling to get up from behind the desk. The wind had been knocked out of him and he was dazed. When he saw what Tannion was doing to Philips he gathered himself together quite quickly. Suddenly Philips' rule of no guns in his office didn't seem like a good idea any more.

Potenlikov came around the end of the desk and rushed over to Tannion. He grabbed Tannion's right arm just below the wrist in order to take it off Philips' neck. Philips hadn't been able to say a word and was turning red. Tannion let go of Philips just long enough to backhand Potenlikov hard enough that he slammed against the desk where he had just come from.

This time Potenlikov was ready and he wasn't hurt badly, but he felt what Tannion had done and realized just how strong he was. Potenlikov was no stranger to brute strength, but he remembered his first meeting with Tannion and how his head had ended up with plaster dust on it from an eight-foot high ceiling. He wouldn't underestimate Tannion's strength again.

Potenlikov threw himself at Tannion, hitting him like a football player, making a tackle around the waist. Tannion was engrossed with holding Philips and the hit knocked him off balance, and he lost his hold on Philips. Potenlikov landed on top of him like a load of bricks, which Tannion barely felt. With a surge Tannion thrust his arms out, letting go of Philips, and Potenlikov was back against the desk again.

This time Tannion stood up and took stock. His rage had evaporated when Potenlikov hit him. He held up his hand to stop Potenlikov from coming at him again, as he could see that was what Potenlikov was going to do.

"Hold on, Vlad. I don't want to hurt you."

"What are you doing, French? What's come over you?" asked the beaten and bewildered Russian.

Philips had gotten up and had moved to put Potenlikov between himself and Tannion and he had a little of his composure back. "French. What the hell are you doing? We're your friends. Why are you doing this?"

Tannion finally came to a standstill. "Okay. You start talking and it had better satisfy me." He wasn't ready to let them off that easy.

"Who the hell is Arthur Diggs and why was he sent to kill me?"

Potenlikov looked at his boss, and it was Philips who answered Tannion's question. "I didn't order Diggs to kill you. I wouldn't do that, French."

This time it was Potenlikov who spoke up, and he directed his question towards Philips. "So why was Diggs there and why did he try to kill French?"

Tannion heard the question and was waiting for Philips to give them both an answer. Philips looked first at Potenlikov and then at Tannion, and let out a small sigh and spoke. "I don't know," he lied. "No way did I tell him to kill you, or anyone," he told Tannion. Philips knew better than to say anything more.

"Well, he sure as hell tried to kill me. He's tied up in my hotel room right now."

Philips reached down and picked up the phone that was lying on the floor. After checking to see that it still worked, he hit a button. He asked Tannion what hotel and what room number, and after Tannion told him, he told the person on the other end to pick up Diggs.

Now they were going to get to the bottom of what was going on. Tannion took out his cell phone and made a call too. "Might as well get everyone involved," he thought.

59

Mike Rallin got to the office building at almost the same time as three of Philips' men, who were carrying a fourth. Rallin came in through the front doors and the other men came in from a side door that was used for deliveries. They took separate elevators, but they all came to the thirty-eighth floor. Rallin got there a couple of minutes ahead of the rest.

Three men met Rallin at the elevator when he stepped out at the thirty-eighth floor, as Tannion had told him to do. At first glance he thought they were going to be trouble, but they escorted him into the only office door available. All three looked a little rumpled. There were already three people in the office. Rallin wasn't surprised to see Jackson Philips and Vlad Potenlikov in the room with Tannion, and certainly didn't need any introductions.

The conversation got going almost immediately, but was stopped only a minute later by a knock at the door and the entry of four men. One of them was being more or less carried. He was dropped in the middle of the room and with a word from Philips, the three men left the room.

Philips was the first to speak. "Diggs. Stand up."

Artie Diggs wasn't able to stand. He had been untied and wasn't hurt, but he couldn't find his feet. Tannion went over to Diggs and through a touch disguised as a light slap, Diggs got some of his strength back and was able to stand up. Tannion could see the fear in his eyes, as if he expected to die in that room.

Philips continued. "You know Vlad, and you've met French. This is Special Agent Mike Rallin of the FBI," he noted, as he pointed at Rallin.

Diggs spoke up, and he looked at and spoke to Tannion directly, almost as if he had forgotten that they had already talked back in the hotel room.

"I shot you. I shot you twice. You should be dead." Diggs stammered a few more words, but Philips cut him off, not really listening to what he had said.

"What were you doing trying to kill Tannion? That's not what I told you to do."

Tannion heard the words Philips said to Diggs and something registered. Philips seemed to realize that he might have said too much.

Tannion asked, "What do you mean that was not what you told him to do? What did you tell him to do?"

"Easy, French," Potenlikov answered, but he had heard the slip as well.

"No, Vlad," Tannion answered, and turned back to Philips. "What did you tell him to do? Tannion asked again.

"He was only supposed to follow you and report back."

"Why the hell did you do that?" This time it was Potenlikov asking the question.

Philips was backtracking. "We talked about this, Vlad. We couldn't be sure which side French was on. He's working for the FBI. I needed to be sure."

"I told you we could trust him. He already got us out of one FBI situation and you know him. French has always been on our side."

"Only if we do things his way, Vlad. He was clear on that point. I needed to be certain," Philips told them.

Tannion cut in. He had been listening to both sides of the conversation and thought he understood where they both stood. "Hold on. Whether either of you trust me or not doesn't really matter right now. This guy tried to kill me. That's what we have to deal with. Mercido has a contract on my head and either he gets me or I get him."

Rallin had been a good listening bystander up until this point. "Wait, Jim. We're not just going in and getting Mercido. We're going to do this by FBI rules, remember."

"Not anymore, Mike. This has gone as far as I'm willing to take it."

"You'll violate your parole and end up back in jail," Rallin told him.

"I'll take my chances," Tannion answered.

"Wait," Philips jumped in. "I might have a solution. I'll talk to Mercido like I did a few years ago and tell him to back off. I think he'll listen to me."

Philips didn't like the feeling that he wasn't in control and Tannion had made that happen, and Philips wanted to get that control back. He saw his chance. Tannion needed more.

"Not good enough, Mr. Philips. I need to talk to him."

"Okay, we'll all go together. I'm very sure that he wouldn't dare do anything as long as I'm there. I could bring a world of hurt down on him and he knows it. All four of us will go."

"What about Diggs?" Potenlikov asked.

To answer his question Philips picked up the phone. A couple of minutes later and the three men were back in the room. "The guys will take care of Diggs."

"You can't kill him," Rallin said very forcefully.

"No. We don't do that anymore. We work the Philips way. They will take him back to his place, and pack his stuff and put him on a bus to somewhere. If he shows up again in LA, then it might not go as easy." This last piece was said directly to Diggs, and Tannion could see by the look of fear replaced by hope that he wouldn't be back.

"A car will be in front in ten minutes to pick us up," Philips told them.

Diggs and the three men left the room. A couple of minutes later Tannion followed Rallin, Potenlikov, and Philips out of the room. "Now we're finally getting somewhere," he thought.

60

When the four men got to the lobby, Philips had a word with the man behind the desk. A couple of minutes later a limo was waiting, double-parked outside the door. All four men piled into the back in an apparent pecking order. Philips first, then Rallin, followed by Tannion and Potenlikov. Tannion and Rallin sat facing backwards, with Philips and Potenlikov taking the facing seat.

The driver drove off without a word from anyone. Philips leaned into the middle and said. "It's only a few blocks. It will only take a couple of minutes."

True to his word, in four or five minutes the limo pulled up in front of the building they all knew was where Mercido had his office. Philips told the driver to wait, and they got out and entered the building.

The building was similar to the one Philips had his office in, with one major exception. Mercido didn't appear to be in control of the building the way Philips was with his. Philips saw them look and answered the unasked question..

"Mercido only rents his space here. He could own the building, but he chooses not to. He thinks it makes him look more like a businessman doing what they all do. Not something I ever cared for," Philips told them.

Tannion noted that Philips seemed to be really in the zone. He was doing the leading, but on top of that he was providing information without being asked. Tannion thought it might have something to do with Philips feeling bad for not trusting Tannion. It also might have been the bad feelings he had for Mercido. Whatever it was, it got them past the front door and into the elevator.

The elevator door opened up on the top floor. Mercido might not own the building, but he made sure he had the best offices. When the elevator opened, two men stood up behind a small desk in the corner. As soon as they saw the four men get off the elevator one of them knocked on the door behind him, and the other came around the desk and pulled a gun out of its shoulder holster.

Philips continued to lead. "Put the gun down and tell Victor that Jackson Philips is here to see him." The guy who had his head in the doorway relayed the message, and then, obviously hearing something from inside that couldn't be heard from outside, opened the door. Tannion was able to hear though, and he heard Mercido tell his man to let Philips in, but he got the impression from the tone of voice that Mercido was only expecting Philips.

Philips walked in first, followed by Rallin and then Potenlikov, with Tannion bringing up the rear. As soon as Rallin came through the door Mercido let out a bellow.

"Who the hell is this, Philips?"

The bellow got even worse when he saw Potenlikov, and when Tannion came in the noise stopped completely, but only for a second. Then the bellowing was directed at Philips.

"What the fuck do you mean bringing him in here? Get him out of here and take Potenlikov, and whoever the hell this is," pointing at Rallin, "and get the fuck out of my office."

Mercido's bad mood rubbed off on Philips. Philips took a step towards Mercido and with his finger pointing at Mercido's chest he said, "Shut up and sit down Mercido. I'll do all the talking."

Two of Mercido's men were in the room. They had stood up when the door opened, and had taken their guns out as soon as Mercido bellowed. They moved forward when Philips did. Mercido saw them and had the good sense to wave them away. They put their guns back in their holsters, but didn't move.

Mercido was mad, but he wasn't stupid. He had already ruffled Philips' feathers earlier and he knew better than to do it again. He suddenly sat down, but Tannion was having nothing to do with it. As soon as Mercido looked to be backing down, Tannion went into action.

Three quick steps and Tannion was around the desk. He grabbed Mercido by the neck, pulling him out of his chair and pinning him up against the back wall.

"Tell your men to sit down, or I'll kill you right here."

Philips, Rallin, and Potenlikov were taken by surprise as well, but to their credit they moved on the two gunmen and took their guns away before they could pull them out again. Potenlikov went over to the door to make sure no one came in.

Tannion looked Mercido in the eye from only inches away. "You want me dead, so kill me."

Tannion waited a couple of seconds and continued. "As you can see, I'm not easy to kill, so instead, I suggest that you cancel the contract before we leave this room and I will let you live."

With that Tannion literally threw Mercido into his chair and went around to the other side of the desk. Philips stepped forward.

"If he doesn't kill you, Victor, I will. Make a call right now and tell your men the contract is off."

Mercido picked up the phone and made a call to someone. It didn't matter to Tannion who he called. Mercido said the words he was told to say, and all the men in the room heard them. As far as Philips and Potenlikov were concerned the contract had been lifted and that was all that was required.

Mercido had a murderous look in his eye, but he finished the call and put the phone back in its cradle. "Okay, it's done, now get the hell out of here. All of you."

Mercido tried to save a little face in front of his men. Philips was having nothing of it.

"If I hear of anyone trying to kill Tannion, or any of his friends, I'll be back, Vic. The next time you won't survive."

The four men left the room and took the elevator to the lobby, and entered the limo that was still parked in front of the office tower. Philips offered to drop Rallin and Tannion off at their respective hotels, but Rallin told him to drop them both off at Tannion's hotel. A few minutes later and they said their goodbyes to the men in the limo, and it drove away. Tannion told them that he would be in touch.

Rallin and Tannion went to Tannion's room and sat down. Rallin started. "I don't think there's much more that can be done here. We can hit the few areas you've gathered data on like we have in New York. We'll get some drugs off the street and maybe catch a few low-level punks, but it won't get back up to Mercido."

"I'll leave that up to you, Mike. I'm done here. I'm going to head back to New York."

"You're giving up on Mercido that fast? What happened to your need for revenge? I thought you wanted this guy."

"Don't worry, Mike. I got what I wanted."

Rallin had the insight Tannion thought he might. If Rallin was anything, it wasn't stupid. "What did you do? You touched him, right, and you did something to him, didn't you?"

"You could say that, Mike."

"But you did do something."

"Let's just say he has a couple of weeks to live. I think that's something."

61

Jim Tannion shook Mike Rallin's hand. He realized that he hadn't taken a deep look at Rallin for a long time, and he did the check. He also knew that for the first time he could take a look, and if he found something wrong, he could fix it, no matter what was known or what was wrong. Even if Rallin knew he had cancer, Tannion could fix it and walk away. It was a good feeling.

Arlene Rallin was beside Mike, and Tannion shook her hand, too. He checked her health, and there were a couple of things that he could fix and he made sure he did. Tannion thought that she probably knew about him as well. Rallin hadn't told Tannion that he had told his secret to his wife, but from the little Tannion knew about Arlene Rallin, and the relationship she had with her husband, he thought it was quite likely she would know even if Tannion had asked Rallin to keep it to himself. Tannion was okay with that, too.

Tannion wasn't good with goodbyes, but he knew this was one that had to be done. After all that had happened he knew that he would have no end of problems staying on with the FBI. With Rallin knowing his secret it was always going to come up, even if Rallin said it wouldn't.

After Tannion flew back to New York, Rallin had stayed in Los Angeles and orchestrated a number of hits on Mercido's operation. As he had told Tannion, they took a lot of drugs off the street, and picked up a few of Mercido's men, but there was never a direct link to Mercido. It hurt him, but in the few days it took to wind down the operation it didn't really matter to Mercido.

Pancreatic cancer can be very painful. The cancer was in its final stage, and had moved beyond the pancreas, into the liver and lymph nodes, and among other internal organs, and it moved fast. Sixteen days after the visit Tannion paid to Mercido's office, Mercido was dead. Tannion told Rallin two weeks, but it wasn't an exact science. Sixteen days served the purpose.

When Rallin got back to New York, Tannion was ready and he handed him his resignation. He even gave his two-week notice, but Rallin told him to clean out his office. It was better for all of them that way. Rallin was disappointed, but wasn't very surprised.

Tannion had one last meeting and that was with his parole officer. Frank Sarvo met Tannion in the same restaurant they had always met at. He even sat in the same booth. Tannion shook Sarvo's hand, and he could tell that the cancer had finally progressed. Tannion thought he would probably be better off not doing anything, but he decided what the hell, and put a cure into action. He wouldn't be in New York that much longer anyway. Maybe Sarvo didn't even know about it.

Tannion was going home. Not exactly home, but closer to home. He was heading for Kansas City. Sarvo had set up a meeting with Tannion's new parole officer for when he got there, and said he should be set.

Tannion would be able to visit his mother on occasion and make sure that she was healthy. Kansas City was big enough to need someone with Tannion's skills. Maybe even with a criminal record. He needed to get a real job and to get his head straight. His gift was more of a curse at times, but when he thought of Mike Rallin and especially Arlene Rallin, it was truly a gift.

Rallin had asked Tannion to keep in touch, and as much as Tannion wasn't sure that was a good idea, he knew that he would. Not having any friends for years hadn't felt good, and having Mike Rallin as a friend did. He might even get to know Arlene well enough to call her a friend, too.

Kansas City wasn't that far away, and he could always catch a flight back to New York. If he ever got back to New York, he would take in a show and see Mike and Arlene.

"I'll make sure I do," Tannion told them, and as he did, he knew that he meant it.

Tannion thought about Arlene Rallin again. "I bet he told her. If he hasn't already, I bet he will now." And Tannion was still okay with that.

If you enjoyed *Tannion Stepping Out* read on to see what happens next:

Tannion Donning Gray

Coming Soon

Read on for a preview of *Tannion Donning Gray*

1

The big house usually conjures up images of a cold place where there are large, tattooed men behind steel bars most of the day, or maybe out in an open area surrounded by high, wire fences. Then the camera pans through a bathhouse scene where the lone new guy is having his first shower in prison. He suddenly finds himself in the company of four or five very large men who proceed to soften him up a little. Maybe there was a little sex involved, and the scene ends with the new guy lying on the floor with the shower pouring hot water onto him as he struggles to understand and believe what had just happened to him.

Whether that scenario is only seen in the movies or not might eventually be determined, but for now Tannion found himself locked in a small cell with the sounds of sleeping and restless men all around him. This was quite different from the holding cell in Los Angeles where he was first imprisoned. It wasn't even anything like the place he was held in New York City during his trial. This was the big house. This was a federal prison. This could be it. This could be where the fun could begin.

He had made the decision in Los Angeles, even before his trial in New York. Tannion wanted to sit in one of these cells, not under an assumed name in a cell in some cushy, resort-type jail like his lawyer wanted. Tannion wanted to be in a maximum security federal penitentiary, and he wasn't about to change his name again. He had done that once and he still had ended up behind bars.

He wanted to be where the types of guys he had spent the past few years looking for were. He wanted to rub shoulders with the rapists, the murderers, the kidnappers, and the thieves. They were all here. People he couldn't find out on the streets no matter how hard he looked, even if he worked for a guy like Philips. Here they were, all waiting for him and they didn't know it.

Tannion hadn't always been this way. The lightning strike that started it all seemed to be light years away, and being inside the prison walls made it seem like a different life; one that wasn't even his.

It was the lightning strike that had given him the skills that had worked so well for him in the past, but had also determined that he would end up lying on his back looking up at the bottom of the bunk above him. A bunk that he was a little surprised was empty.

For now, he was glad that he didn't have a roommate. Maybe eventually he would like to have someone to talk to, but at least not yet. For now he just wanted to savor the moment by himself.

The warden had met with him on the first day he had arrived. He had read the report on Tannion and had seen the news from Los Angeles and then in New York. He had a preconceived idea of what this guy would be like long before he walked in the door. Here would be some low-life snitch who happened to get lucky when he turned against his fellow crooks in order to get off easy. At least in New York they know when a criminal belonged in jail.

The warden, however, was perplexed. Why would a guy like Tannion, who had done what he had done in Los Angeles, end up in his prison, and for that matter, why would he be using his own name? It didn't ring true, but he would find out as soon as he got him in the chair. The warden was good at his job.

When Tannion walked into the warden's office the first thought that went through the warden's mind was that Tannion was bigger than he remembered him from the news, and he looked a little younger as well. Tannion also had a big smile on his face, and had his hand extended to shake the warden's hand, which he gave him.

Tannion took a quick look inside and found a healthy man. He knew that if he wanted to he could make sure that the warden didn't stay that way, but he had no reason to do anything like that. Tannion saw himself as one of the good guys, and the warden was one as well. That meant they should be friends and not enemies.

"Good morning, sir," Tannion started.

The warden could tell in just those three words that this man was no uneducated snitch. He might just prove to be a very interesting inmate. The warden started to say what he had intended to say, but now he wasn't so sure it was necessary or even appropriate, but it needed to be said.

"I know all about what you did in New York that got you here, Tannion, but I also know what happened in Los Angeles," he said, as he reached down and picked up a report to indicate what he meant.

"I expected you would, sir."

"What I don't understand is why you are here? You should be in some upstate resort under an assumed name. That's what I had expected, but here you are. Why are you in my prison, Tannion?"

Tannion looked the warden in the eye and told him the lie that he had worked out in his head for just that question.

"I understand what you mean, warden. Maybe I could have gotten a better deal, but what happened in New York was my fault, and although I'm not a martyr, I deserve to be here. I spent my time in Los Angeles under an alias and it didn't matter. The FBI caught up to me anyway. If someone is coming after me they will find me no matter what name I take. This way I hope to see them coming."

"I'm sure they'll come, and when they do, you'll be leaving in a body bag. You know that, don't you?" the warden asked him.

"I don't think so. I'm not easy to kill. If they come they had better be very careful or very good."

The warden hesitated before he said, "I don't want this in my house, Tannion." The warden was trying to make a point and it wasn't lost on Tannion.

"I know, warden, but it will be beyond my control. If they come, and we're both sure that they will, I'll need to defend myself. You couldn't expect me to do anything else, could you?"

"No. I would expect you to defend yourself, but I would rather it didn't come to that," the warden told him.

"I understand, sir."

"What I want is for you to let me know the moment that you suspect that something is going to happen and we'll try to protect you as best we can."

"I appreciate that, warden, but my experience in the outside world tells me that when it does happen it will happen fast, and there won't be any warning or any time for me to ask for help. Things will just happen, and someone will end up hurt or maybe dead."

"If I find a dead body and it looks like you were involved, it had better look like self-defense, or I'll be all over your ass," the warden said.

"That's all I can ask, warden. One thing I can tell you is that I will never have any type of a weapon. You can shake down my cell anytime you like, but I promise you that if there is a weapon at the scene and a dead body that's not mine, the weapon belonged to him. Will that look enough like self-defense?"

"It might, but I won't know until it happens. For now, all I can tell you is to watch your back and I'll tell the guards to keep a watchful eye out. If something does happen, I might just give you the benefit of the doubt, but if it does happen, I might not be the one calling the shots. I am the law in here, but the legal system always has a say."

Tannion knew that someone would eventually come for him. Having turned state's evidence in the largest organized crime bust in Los Angeles history had made him a lot of enemies. Things might be turned upside down in LA at the moment, but there were people out there who either got off easy or without any time behind bars, and they would find him. It was only a matter of time.

The warden sent him back to his cell, but he did get in the last word.

"Tannion. I don't want to ever hear that you started anything. Do you understand me?"

"I understand, warden."

"Good luck," were his final words, and Tannion thought that the warden might have even meant it.

"Not that bad a guy," he thought. "But he's still the warden and the law. Not a force to be taken lightly."

When the cell was locked for the night and Tannion was alone inside, there was a feeling of loss as he knew he couldn't get past the bars, but there was also a feeling of security as well, as others couldn't get past them either.

The feeling wasn't much different than when he was in the holding cells in LA County where he had awaited trial, but somehow here the secure feeling was still there, but the loss of freedom was much stronger.

There had always been a chance that the trial would go his way before, but from here, Tannion knew his options were limited. The excitement he was feeling earlier abated only a little.

Wayne Elsner is the author of the *Tannion Series*, the *Talanhold Trilogy*, and *Time Tells All*. *Tannion Stepping Out* is the second book in the *Tannion* series and the second book Wayne has published. Watch for more of Wayne's books coming soon.

Wayne is a retired geologist who spends a large part of his time travelling the world with his wife. They are working their way up to one hundred countries visited, and have no intention of slowing down.

Visit his website at **www.wayneelsner.com** for more information, or follow him on Twitter @wayneelsner.